TREASURE OF BABYLON

(An Avalon Adventure)

Rob Jones

ISBN: 9798686716858

Other Titles by Rob Jones

The Joe Hawke Series
The Vault of Poseidon (Joe Hawke #1)
Thunder God (Joe Hawke #2)
The Tomb of Eternity (Joe Hawke #3)
The Curse of Medusa (Joe Hawke #4)
Valhalla Gold (Joe Hawke #5)
The Aztec Prophecy (Joe Hawke #6)
The Secret of Atlantis (Joe Hawke #7)
The Lost City (Joe Hawke #8)
The Sword of Fire (Joe Hawke #9)
The King's Tomb (Joe Hawke #10)
Land of the Gods (Joe Hawke #11)
The Orpheus Legacy (Joe Hawke #12)
Hell's Inferno (Joe Hawke #13)
Day of the Dead (Joe Hawke #14)
Coming Soon: Shadow of the Apocalypse (Joe Hawke #15)

The Hunter Files
The Atlantis Covenant (Hunter Files #1)
The Revelation Relic (Hunter Files #2)
Coming Soon: The Titanic Mystery (Hunter Files #3)

The Avalon Adventure Series
The Hunt for Shambhala (Avalon Adventure #1)
Treasure of Babylon (Avalon Adventure #2)
The Doomsday Cipher (Avalon Adventure #3)

The Operator
*A standalone action-thriller for fans of Jack Reacher
and Jason Bourne*

The Cairo Sloane Series
Plagues of the Seven Angels (Cairo Sloane #1)

The Raiders Series
The Raiders (The Raiders #1)

The Harry Bane Thriller Series
The Armageddon Protocol (A Harry Bane Thriller #1)

The DCI Jacob Mystery Series
The Fifth Grave (A DCI Jacob Mystery)
Angel of Death (A DCI Jacob Mystery)

Website: www.robjonesnovels.com
Facebook: www.facebook.com/RobJonesNovels/
Twitter: @AuthorRobJones
Email: robjonesnovels@gmail.com

TREASURE OF BABYLON

PROLOGUE

January 330 BC, Persian Empire

The young cavalry officer pulled his body down low against the charging stallion's neck and dodged the speeding arrow by a hair's breadth. It flashed past him and buried itself in the hindquarters of a Persian's horse a few yards behind him. The animal roared with pain and threw the rider from its back before slamming a hoof through his skull and instantly killing him.

Bastian swivelled back up into his saddle and ordered his stallion forward into the fray. The horse was a powerful Thessalian named Arion, and now he gave its neck a quick stroke of reassurance before searching for the king. The Battle of the Persian Gate raged all around him, and he didn't want to miss his chance to show his leader how bravely he could fight.

But where was Alexander the Great? He scanned the field and saw the king. He was on the rise of the foothills to the north, desperately searching for the wagons full of treasure. He heard a war cry and swivelled again to see a cataphract – a heavily armored rider and horse – charging toward him, the stallion's magnificent bronze scale armor reflecting the weak winter sun as it broke through some of the snow clouds.

1

Bastian never flinched, but squeezed Arion's barrel with his legs, ordering the powerful animal to increase speed and thunder toward the screaming enemy.

He galloped toward the Persian with his sword high above his head, bringing it slashing down through the icy air and slicing a terrible gouge in the enemy's throat. The soldier clutched at his neck before collapsing to the ground. Blood pumped from the torn artery and sprayed out over the white snow around him.

Bastian scanned the field of slaughter, seeing where next he could put his sword to the best use. Spying a desperate skirmish of dismounted cavalrymen lower down the northern slope, he commanded Arion to charge once again, riding through the bloody chaos at the heart of the battle until he reached his brethren.

But he never got there. Riding into a narrow channel on his way up to the other side of the valley, a Persian in iron scale armor leaped from a jumble of rocks above him and dragged him from the horse's back. The two men crashed to the ground and tumbled through the snowy dirt, desperately grabbing at each other's necks to kill the other man.

Bastian got the upper hand and landed a solid punch in the soldier's face, cracking his head back on the rocks and giving him a few valuable seconds to scramble to his feet.

He drew his weapon and watched the man crawl up off his knees. He glanced for his horse, but Arion was gone, charging off the battlefield through the gathering snowstorm. The man in plate armor was approaching fast, his sword drawn and held aloft, ready for a lethal strike. Bastion dodged the Persian's lunge and hooked his feet out from under him, sending the man crashing onto his back in the frozen scree.

He seized the moment, snatching up his sword and moving swiftly over to the fallen man. The screams of the slain rose around him as he lifted the heavy blade and prepared to kill the man. He felt no remorse. He felt no guilt. He never wavered. He was here to the bidding of his king, and that meant destroying the enemy.

But the enemy had his own ideas, and the man rolled away from Bastian's sword as it sliced through the cold air and struck the rocky ground beneath him with a metallic clunk.

Bastian pulled his sword back as the man got to his feet and readied his weapon once again. He stared into the Persian's eyes and saw a desperate confusion of hatred and fear looking back at him. He was a younger man than Bastian, and more powerful, but his experience was only a fraction of the Macedonian warrior's, and he showed it when he lunged clumsily forward.

Bastian easily parried the lunge and sent the Persian's weapon slicing through the air to his right. Pulling his elbow back, he drove the pommel of his blade into the man's face, smashing his cheekbone and making him howl in pain. Before another second had passed, the Macedonian cavalry officer brought his dagger from his belt and slashed it at the man. The blade skidded along the tiny iron plates which covered the Persian's back until it reached the base of his helmet and struck the metal rim before finding the man's neck.

Bastian drove the blade in hard, severing the Persian's spine and killing him instantly. As the warrior's body slumped to the ground, he clambered up onto the rocks from where the man had launched his attack and surveyed the battlefield for his faithful horse. The skirmish he had seen was over – his brothers had won and were now walking toward him and sheathing their weapons.

Glancing down the valley to the east, he saw they had been victorious, and much of the enemy was now either or dead or fleeing. Alexander's strategy had been successful. While Bastian and his soldiers had driven straight down the valley from the settlement of Yasuj in the west, Alexander the Great had ridden north, crossed the valley west of the enemy and launched a surprise attack from the south. It was a stunning double envelopment, a pincer movement from hell, and now victory was theirs.

He returned his gaze to the men walking over to him. One of them was holding Arion's bridle casually in a bloody hand.

"Your horse, sir,"

"I'm glad to see him again," Bastian said, stroking the horse's neck.

He climbed back into the saddle and cantered east toward his victorious king and commander. Rejoining the other officers gathered behind the king and his generals, he recalled his first day among these elite warriors. The day he had been accepted into Alexander the Great's Companion Cavalry, his chest swelled with pride until he thought it might burst. Only this victory today made him prouder.

"A worthy victory, sire," Antipater said.

Alexander said nothing, but gave a regal nod. He was still counting dead on the battlefield far below. As Bastian drew closer and brought his horse to a stop, the king turned to him, and rode his horse, Bucephalus slowly over until he was beside the young warrior.

"You!" barked the bloodied king.

Bastian could hardly believe King Alexander was addressing him personally. "Yes, sire."

"A party of Persians is fleeing to the east. You are to go with General Antipater and slay them all. Bring back to me what they are trying to hide."

"Yes, sire – at once."

Followed by two soldiers from the ranks, Bastion cantered his horse over to Antipater and they galloped along the south bank of the river until they had caught up with the fleeing Persians.

The broken enemy saw them and responded at once. The elite guard formed a ring around the wagons, but others fled into the foothills.

"After the stragglers!" Antipater commanded.

"Yes, sir," Bastian said.

The young warrior rode after the men with a handful of fellow cavalry officers flanking him. They followed the men's trail until they found them trapped at the base of an unclimbable cliff. They were cornered and desperate. Bastian prepared to put them to the sword when the men threw down their weapons and wicker shields and surrendered. The Macedonian warrior considered slaying them anyway, but decided against it.

"Take the weapons!" he ordered. "Then bind their hands behind their backs and bring them back to the general. They're slaves now."

As his men obeyed his orders, he turned his horse and galloped back into the valley where he found Antipater and the other men. They had been victorious, and the elite guard were now nothing more than heaps of corpses. He was more interested to see the look on his general's face as he stumbled backwards from one of the covered wagons and almost fell over.

"My God!" he said, pointing at the wagon.

Bastian dismounted from Arion and stepped closer to the ageing warlord. "What is it, General?"

Antipater pointed a trembling arm into the back of the cart. He was a man of great education and experience but he looked like a confused child. "I don't know. It started to glow when I approached it."

Bastian drew his sword. "Glow?"

"And shake the ground like some kind of earthquake."

The young cavalry officer was well aware of the general's great reputation in battle, but with this talk of glowing chests that could make the ground shake he wondered if the old man might be losing his mind.

"Are you certain, general?"

"Yes!" the old man snapped, and pointed at a young soldier. "You! Get over there and pull the cover of the wagon."

The soldier approached the cart and Bastian was shocked to see the light his general had described emanating from under the cover section at the rear. As the young man drew closer to the cart the ground started to shake beneath his feet. "It's as you say, sir," Bastian said. "The chest in the wagon has the power to create earthquakes and shine brighter than the sun."

The young Macedonian officer watched in horror as a burst of bright sparks enveloped the soldier and grew so intense he thought he might have to look away. He shielded his eyes and then he saw something that scared his soul for the rest of his life.

The fire swallowed the soldier in a bright flash.

The soldier was gone, and both Bastian and his general knew why the Persians had been riding so far away from the wagon. Anyone who approached it was consumed by its fire.

"We must take this to the king," Antipater said. "It may have a use in battle."

Bastian had his doubts. "This is not for man to play with, sir," he said. "Whatever it may be, it has the power of the gods themselves."

Antipater growled, "We take it to the king!"

Riding twenty paces either side of the wagon, Antipater ordered the men to lead the horses on. They obeyed and started to walk, pulling the thirty-foot harness straps taught and then turning the cart's old wheels back to the west.

Bastian kept a good distance from the wagons as they made their way back to the great king. It was a short journey, winding through a dry riverbed, but no one spoke as they returned with their spoils to their leader. They had all seen the fire, but no one knew what was inside the wagon. No one knew what the Persians had been trying to hide in it. No one knew why their enemy had tried to flee, but they all knew that whatever it was, it had the power to consume a man in fire and turn him to dust.

It had the power of the gods.

1

London, Present Day

"A walnut veneer drinks cabinet?"

"It's what the lady ordered."

Mitch Decker watched the men as they carefully carried the antique wooden cabinet up the steps and disappeared inside his beloved vintage Grumman Albatross float plane. They were standing inside an aviation hangar in London City Airport's Private Jet Centre, and the wind was blowing the rain in through the open doors.

The former US Marine took his hat off and rubbed a hand over his tired face. "But *walnut veneer?* This is just a cargo plane, not a luxury hotel with wings!"

A man with a beanie pulled down to his eyebrows popped his head out the door and looked down at Decker. "Take it up with the lady, mate."

"I intend to, believe me."

As he spoke, another man stepped into view. He was wearing blue overalls and carrying a couple of silk scatter cushions. "Excuse me, guv."

"Oh, sure," Decker gave the man a double take. "Wait a minute – silk cushions?"

"For the leather couch, guvnor," the man said cheerily, and hopped up inside the aircraft.

Decker's jaw dropped. "For the leather… Just hang on a damned minute!"

"Is there a problem, Captain Decker?"

Decker turned to see Selena Moore a few steps behind him. She was standing with her hands on her hips and slowly raised her eyebrows to invite a response from the former pilot. "Well?"

"Is there a problem?" Decker said. "Yes, there's a problem!"

"And would you care to articulate it?"

"Would I care to articulate it?"

"Are you suffering from echolalia?"

"Am I what?"

"You keep repeating whatever you hear. I just wondered, and please don't bother the workmen."

Decker took a step toward her and shoved his hands in his pockets. He knew what she was doing. "I know what game you're playing."

"And what game would that be?" Now she was smiling.

"You're trying to distract me."

"Distract you, Mr Decker? Whatever from?"

He twisted his lips and gave a knowing nod as he looked at her smile. She was beautiful. "Distract me from the fact you're turning my plane into one of London's most luxurious locations."

She gave a dismissive wave of her hand. "Don't be so silly. I said it needed a woman's touch and you agreed."

"A woman's touch, sure," he said, pushing the brim of his hat up his forehead an inch or two. "Not King Midas's touch."

A man walked past with a plasma screen and Selena shuffled in front of him to block Decker's view. "Do stop exaggerating, Mr Decker."

The former US Marine shook his head in disbelief, but turned to her with the ghost of a smile on his lips. "I thought we agreed you were going to call me Mitch?"

9

"That's what I said, isn't it?"

"No."

"Must have slipped my mind, *Mitch*."

The fitters stepped out of the aircraft and the man with the beanie walked up to them. "Right you are, then. We're all done."

"Oh, good!" Selena said. She turned to Decker and held him by the arm. "Shall we go in?"

"To see the damage you mean?"

She slapped his shoulder. "I mean so we can see what a woman's touch can bring to a filthy, greasy old cargo plane."

He gave her a look and gestured toward the open door. "After you, *Lena*."

Since he'd landed in London and parked her up, the interior of the Avalon had been transformed beyond recognition. When he'd left the aircraft, he'd said goodbye to the plane he bought years earlier to be a cargo plane – a mostly empty space in the rear cabin where he could strap down the cargo boxes and not a frill in sight. Now, he felt like he was stepping into the penthouse at the Mark Hotel.

"What do you think?" she said proudly.

"I think the only thing missing is Madison Avenue."

"What do you mean?"

"Come *on*," he said, sweeping a broad hand over the sparkling scene. Leather couches with silk scatter cushions... a plasma screen... and the drinks cabinet is straight out of Gatsby."

"Oh, *thank* you!"

"That wasn't a *compliment*..."

"You do like it, don't you?"

"I like grease, oil, mess. Does this look like something I might like?"

"You're part of a team now, Mitch. You're the official pilot of the London Archaeological Museum's Research and Excavation Department."

"Isn't that basically just you?"

She turned to avoid his glare and stared out one of the starboard windows. "Well... I wouldn't put it quite like that, but... wait a minute."

"What is it?"

"That looks like Oliver Fleming."

"As in your boss, Oliver?"

"Yes."

Decker frowned and joined her at the next window along. She was right. The man hurrying along through the rain on the apron outside was Oliver Fleming, the Director of the LMA. As he stepped into the dry hangar he didn't even stop to sweep the rain from his hair. He just rushed toward the Avalon with a big, red face.

Selena and Decker exchanged a worried glance. "What the hell is he doing here?" the American asked.

"I don't like this," Selena said. "He looks worried. Ollie never looks worried."

When he was a few yards from the plane, Decker and Selena came out and joined him under the plane's starboard wing.

"Ollie – what is it?"

"Thank God I found you," he said.

"What's going on?" Decker said.

Oliver Fleming was not the slimmest of men, and the short run from the airport over to the hangars had taken him to the limit of his physical endurance. Now, he was leaning over and supporting himself with his hands on his knees as he fought to bring his breathing under control.

"I tried to call but you didn't answer."

"Phone's at the office. What is it, Ollie?"

11

"It's your... father, Lena."

Selena stared at Decker with terror in her eyes. She tried to speak but no words came.

Decker pulled Oliver up so they were face to face. "What about her father, Ollie?"

"He's..."

Selena blew out a breath. "Ollie!"

"He's gone missing."

2

Decker watched the young professor of archaeology take a step back and raise two trembling hands to her face. She looked like she'd been hit in the chest with an ice pick. He turned to Oliver. "What do you mean, missing?"

The museum's rotund director had now gotten his short breath under control and the blood had started to drain from his round cheeks. "I got a call an hour ago from the police in Jerusalem. They said he never turned up for a meeting with his Israeli counterpart in the dig. When they looked into it they went to his hotel room and found everything wrecked, and no sign of your father."

Decker looked at Selena and knew she was thinking the same thing.

"What was he doing in Jerusalem?"

He sighed again, and now buried his head in his hands. When he looked up at them, his eyes were as red as the rest of his face. He looked like he was ageing right in front of them. "Your father found something."

"He found something?"

Another sad nod. "In the dig in the Middle East. He found a manuscript, rolled up tight and preserved inside a jar."

"Go on."

"The jar was hidden in the back of a cave in the Judean Desert on the West Bank. That must be why they took him." A pained smile crossed his lips. "But they won't find what they're looking for though."

"And why is that?"

"Because Atticus posted it to me by recorded delivery the day before yesterday – jar and all. He's a wily old bird, your father."

"So you've seen this manuscript?"

"Oh yes, and I could hardly believe my eyes. I thought it was de Vaux and Harding all over again and when I opened the jar I knew at once that we were right. He'd discovered yet more fragments of the Dead Sea Scrolls."

Sclena started to fume. When Decker saw the hands coming up to her hips he knew to take a step back and get ready to put his fingers in his ears. "Just why the hell wasn't I told about any of this, Ollie?"

"Well…"

"My own father is on a dig to find missing Dead Sea Scrolls and I hear nothing about it until someone kidnaps him?"

"I *am* sorry, Lena, but your father specifically wanted to keep you out of it for precisely this reason. He was worried you might get hurt. This is dangerous territory we're on."

"Dangerous territory?" she said.

"You're doing that repeating thing," said Decker, trying to calm her down. It didn't work, so he took another step back.

"My father's gone missing, Mitch."

"I'm sorry, I was just…"

She turned back to Ollie before the American had a chance to apologize. "What do you mean dangerous territory? The Dead Sea Scrolls aren't exactly at the top of every gangster's wish list as far as historical artefacts go."

"No," Ollie muttered, looking down at his polished shoes. "No, they are not."

14

"So why did you say dangerous territory?" Decker said.

Selena had gathered herself together after the shock of Oliver's news, and now she was back to her old self. "All right, out with it, Ollie. Dad wasn't looking for Dead Sea Scrolls was he?"

"No."

"What was he looking for?"

Oliver scratched his head as an expression of awkward embarrassment crept over his face. "Your father has been searching for the Ark of the Covenant."

Decker felt like someone had punched him in the gut – and by the look on Selena's face, so did she. His first mission with Selena Moore and the rest of her team had involved flying into Tibet and discovering the lost kingdom of Shambhala. That had seemed like high fantasy to him, even when he was actually standing in the place, but this was in an altogether different league. The lost Ark of the Covenant was probably the most sacred and sought after historical relic in history, and finding out Atticus Moore was hot on its trail was definitely one way to get the blood flowing faster.

But Selena looked less impressed. "You mean to say that my father has solid, archaeological research leading to the location of the Ark of the Covenant?"

"More or less."

"More or... Ollie!"

"Then yes, but as you can imagine, nothing in this field is straight-forward."

Decker lowered his voice and looked at his boots. "With you guys it never is."

Neither of the archaeologists heard him, and Selena was still looking daggers at her boss. "I can't believe any of this is happening. How long has he been missing?"

15

"Just a few hours, according to the local police."

"He could be anywhere."

Decker took her by the shoulders. "We'll find him."

Distractedly, she changed the subject. "Where is this jar and manuscript?"

"In the cab."

Selena's jaw fell slack, and she was rendered speechless. "You mean a Black Cab?"

"Why, yes. It's how I got here. He's waiting for me at the front of the airport."

Selena turned on the spot and gripped her head in her hands. "Oh my God."

Decker leaned closer to Selena and furrowed his brow. "Wait, is Ollie what you guys call a berk?"

"Yes he bloody is!" she snapped. "We have to take this to Charlie. He has people in the security services who'll be able to help... and it might be a good idea to go and get that cab, don't you think, Ollie?"

"Capital idea, Lena. Capital."

"And you guys spell berk with an 'e', right not a 'u'?"

"Yes," Selena said briskly. It's short for Berkshire Hunt."

"I don't get it."

"Cockney rhyming slang."

Decker looked almost offended. "You don't say?"

Selena put her finger up to his lips to shush him. "Let's just get that jar, shall we?"

*

Oliver Fleming indicated the ancient jar on the back seat with smug pride. He had seemed genuinely offended that anyone would doubt the integrity of a London Black Cab driver, and promptly introduced the man at the wheel as Colin.

Colin gave a cheery wave. "Where to?"

"Thames House," Selena said. "And don't hang about, either."

"Thames House, eh?" Colin said. "Got a date with James Bond?"

The scowl on her face redirected Colin's attention to the road as he drove them out of the airport and turned west to the City of London.

Selena snatched the jar from Oliver's porky hands and started to inspect it. On its own it was a spectacular find due to its near-perfect condition, but the real treasure was rolled up and hidden inside.

As the cab weaved its way across the north of the Isle of Dogs, she carefully pulled the manuscript out of the jar and unfurled its yellowed, crumbling pages. "This is beautiful."

"Isn't it?" Ollie chimed in. "It's written in a very archaic form of Hebrew."

"Undoubtedly," she said, already mesmerised by the ancient, faded letters.

"What does it say?" Decker asked.

"It's a poem," Ollie said.

"It's much more than that," said Selena, her lips barely moving. "The first part is an ode, but the second makes a sly reference to the Ark's location."

"Do you really think so?" Oliver said. "I think it's pure allegory."

"Unlikely," she continued. "This reference to the Angel of God isn't allegorical in my opinion. It's a reference to an idol, a golden statue. When it says the Angel of God will lead the way to the Ark it's referring to an actual statue."

17

Oliver looked almost crestfallen. "A real angel showing the way is so much more beautiful, don't you think?"

Selena did not, and going by what he said next, neither did Mitch Decker.

"So this manuscript is basically telling us to look for a clue inside a golden statue called the Angel of God?"

Selena nodded as she curled the old paper back up and slid it back in the jar. "It's very explicit. It tells us that beneath the Golgotha is a golden statue called the Angel of God, and this statue will lead us to the Ark."

"Golgotha?"

"It's a hill in Jerusalem," Colin said, turning a broad smile on them. "Where Jesus was crucified."

"Yes, thank you, Colin," Selena said. "Eyes on the road please."

"Of course, the crucifixion was centuries after all of this," Oliver said.

Approaching Blackfriars Bridge, Decker felt the hairs on the back of his neck go up as he watched the bright red dot tracing along the shoulder of Colin's jacket and then up to the side of his head. In the comfort and safety of the Black Cab, it took two or three seconds for him to work out what was going on, but then the red light disappeared from sight, and he knew at once that could mean only one thing.

It was a laser sight from a sniper rifle and it was now on its target – someone was trying to kill the cabbie and crash the cab, presumably so they could take out the rest of the passengers.

"Get down!" he yelled, but it was too late.

Colin turned and stared at him, unknowing and confused. He shook his head and started to speak when it happened.

And it happened faster than lightning.

Colin's head exploded across the inside of the windshield and his dead body slumped down behind the wheel. The sound of the gunshot followed a fraction of a second later, and Selena screamed.

Decker looked up to see the cab powering out from beneath the bridge and swerving wildly toward the low brick wall dividing the road from the River Thames. He knew at this speed the cab would make short work of the wall and they would be flying out over the river in a matter of seconds, but the security partition meant there was no way to reach the front part of the cab and seize control.

Oliver pointed a trembling hand at the road ahead. "We're going to crash into the river!"

3

Like hell we are, Decker thought, and opened the rear door on his side. He knew it was crazy, but he had about ten seconds until they smashed through that wall and piled into the Thames, so he had to act fast.

"What are you doing?" Selena said.

"Saving our asses."

"What?"

"I've got to get to the driver's seat!"

"Are you insane?" Selena cried out. "This is my town, so I'm doing the driving!"

"You can't be serious?"

"Why ever not?"

"Because I saw you try and park once," he handed her his gun. There was a small arsenal in the Avalon, checked into customs but he did his best to carry one when he could. It was a lot easier than most people thought it would be. "Besides, someone has to stay behind and shoot the bad guys."

"Ask yourself this question, Mitch: is my parking better than my shooting?"

"You want to climb out here while the cab's still moving?"

Selena twisted her lips. "Fine. You drive."

Holding onto the passenger grip inside the back, he leaned outside the car and opened Colin's door.

A second shot rang out and a bullet pinged off the cab roof a few inches from his face. "Dammit! They're still on our tails!"

He spun around and saw them now – two men in a black Audi directly behind them. One was leaning out of the front passenger window with a pistol in a two hand grip.

"Hurry up!" Selena cried out.

Other drivers honked their horns and pedestrians filmed him on their phones, slack-jawed with disbelief as he pulled the dead man out of the cab and jumped behind the wheel. With a second to spare he wrenched the steering wheel to the right and swerved the cab away from the wall.

A screech of burning rubber left a criss-cross of black marks on the asphalt as he brought the cab back under control and stamped on the gas. Readjusting the mirror to fit a man of his height, he saw the Audi was even closer now, and the gunman aiming to make another shot.

Decker swerved right and tried to lose them in the maze of smaller streets north of the Thames. He turned west and raced along the Strand. The plan was to get to Trafalgar Square and head south to Millbank and the safety of the MI5 headquarters, but then things took another turn for the worse.

"There's more up ahead!" he yelled back to Selena and Ollie.

The replied in unison. "What?"

"There!" he pointed over the steering wheel. "Another car, a Mercedes. There's a dude hanging out of the passenger side with a gun. I take it that's not normal in London?"

"Well," Oliver said. "Not the Strand, anyway."

"They're firing!" Selena cried out.

Decker swung the wheel hard to the left and skidded into the next available side street only to see another Black Cab racing directly toward him.

He honked the horn. "Get over, you idiot! You're on the wrong side of the road!"

Oliver peered through the greasy partition. "It's you on the wrong side, old boy. This is the entrance to the Savoy. Only road in the country where we drive on the right."

Decker was perplexed. "Huh?"

"Do pull over before we crash."

Decker took Oliver's word for it and swung onto the wrong side of the road to a barrage of swearing from the cab driver now on his left.

"It's an old tradition," Oliver said, hanging on for his life. "Dating back to when people used to come in for the theater here and get out of horse-drawn carriages on the other side. The theater was here long before the hotel, you see."

Decker shook his head. "This country just gets crazier and crazier."

"I'll take that as a compliment considering you come from a country where cheese comes in a spray can," Oliver said.

Decker wasn't listening. "The road's running out!"

"It's a turning circle."

"It's too small!"

"Nonsense, the Black Cab is specifically designed to make the turn without doing a three-point turn. These things have a better turning circle than a mini."

Decker hit the brakes and spun around the circle. Driving on the wrong side in England meant the right side for him and for a few seconds he was back at home again, but then he saw both the Audi and the Merc heading down the entrance road. Gunmen in both vehicles leaned out of their cars and opened fire on the Black Cab. Their bullets ripped into the cab's grille and burst the radiator, sending a cloud of steam into the air as other rounds went wide and exploded in the neon sign above the Savoy Theater's entrance.

Speeding around the tiny roundabout, the wheels squealed like trapped piglets as he made the tight turn with inches to spare, and then he increased speed again to power out of the turn. "We need to return fire!"

Selena lowered the window and pushed her head and arm outside. Raising the gun into position, she fired at the approaching cars. The bullets struck the hood and windshield of the Audi and sent it smashing into the box hedge running along west side of the street, but the Merc was still racing toward them.

Selena fired again, her bullets puncturing the smooth gunmetal gray door of the Merc as it sailed past toward the turning circle. The driver responded by swerving wildly and hitting the gas, but the gunman fired again, this time striking one of the rear tires on their cab. It exploded and propelled a cloud of shredded black rubber into the air. One chunk landed with a dull thud on road and Decker immediately felt the vehicle swerving wildly.

"Can you control it?" Oliver asked.

"Sure." He swerved back out onto the Strand. "But we're running out of time. We have to get to MI5 before these guys catch up with us again. With a tire out like this we're sitting ducks." Checking the rear view mirror he saw the Merc powering out of the Savoy's entrance and charging after them along the Strand. "They *really* want this jar, Ollie."

"I should think they do," the old man said.

"But they're not going to get it," Selena said coolly. She leaned back out the car and fired on the Merc one more time. Her first bullet tore into the front left tire and sent the German saloon skidding wildly toward the island in the center of the road. Decker watched the Merc through the cab's rear-view mirror. Sparks and smoke were spewing out of the wheel arch as the wheel's rim carved into the asphalt at high-speed. It smashed head-first into a large cast-iron street light. The hood crumpled like aluminum foil and the car came to a violent stop.

The driver's airbag deployed and saved his life, but the gunman who had been hanging out of the window was propelled through the air like a rag doll and landed with a sickening smack on the windshield of a delivery van driving east on the other side of the road. The glass shattered as he struck it and the van driver hit the brakes, sending the gunman's dead body sliding off the front of the vehicle and crashing down on the asphalt.

"Where did you learn to shoot like that?" Ollie asked, shocked.

"Riley's been coaching me."

"That boy has his uses, all right."

Decker blew out a breath and pulled the Black Cab into a side street. "We'll change the tire and then drive down to meet Charlie at MI5. Something tells me we haven't seen the last of these guys."

4

Deep inside the headquarters of the British internal secret service, Decker, Selena and Oliver were sitting in an outer office by the time Riley arrived. He had been staying with a woman he knew in west London and planning on a week in Ireland, but it looked like that was off the cards now. The Australian walked straight up to Selena and took her by the shoulders, locking eyes on her. "Are you all right?"

"A bit shaken, but we're fine," she said. "They tried to kill us though, for sure."

"And they had two cars," Decker said. "Whoever they are, they mean business."

Selena sighed, impatiently drummed her fingers on her knees and glanced at her wristwatch. "Where the bloody hell is Charlie?"

"He'll be here," Riley said. "Knowing former spooks has its uses and helping to grease the wheels on a case like Atticus going missing is one of them."

Decker agreed. He had first met the laid-back Charlie Valentine in Bangkok during the Shambhala mission. The former MI5 spy had sauntered across the airport with a loose-fitting Hawaiian shirt half-unbuttoned and a straw hat perched on the back of his head. James Bond, he was not, but he could use his contacts at Thames House to help find Atticus quicker than anyone in the world.

When their friend finally arrived, they were all relieved to see he had turned up *sans* straw hat and unbuttoned shirt. Instead he was showing some respect for his former colleagues by way of a charcoal gray Armani suit and a dashing, bespoke Passaggio cravat.

Riley shook his head and rolled his eyes. "On your way to a roulette table somewhere, Charles?"

"No harm in dressing for the occasion. You should try it for once and give your Bogan-chic look a rest."

"Get fu—."

"Armani?" Selena said. "A bit déclassé for you, isn't it?"

He smiled but said nothing.

"How's the gunshot wound from Tibet?" she asked.

Now Charlie winced and played it up and lifted his shirt to reveal a long scar. "Like any other war wound."

"Bugger off, you fool."

Riley stared at the scar in awe. "Why do you get all the cool wounds?"

A woman in a black suit opened the other door. "Mr Sumner will see you now."

"At last," Selena said. "Maybe they'll talk to us now you're here."

"You never know your luck," Charlie said.

They stepped into Paul Sumner's large, corner office with a view of Lambeth Bridge crossing the Thames. The building had been the headquarters for MI5 since 1994 but Sumner's career predated the move by many years.

The man himself was on the phone when they walked in, and for a few moments he listened calmly to his third terror emergency of the day as the rain lashed on the windows. Without ceremony, he clicked the phone down and acknowledged their presence in his office. "You've put on weight, Charlie."

"Thanks, Paul."

"Sit down all of you. You're making me feel nervous."

They took their seats as Sumner crossed the office, spoke a few words in private to his PA and then closed the door. He stepped behind his desk and sat in his chair. "It's been a long time, Charlie."

"It has."

"Busy?"

"This and that."

"You mean like accidentally stumbling on the Kingdom of Shambhala?"

Charlie shrugged his shoulders.

"You're a lucky man," Sumner said.

"You make your own luck," Decker said with a smile.

Sumner gave him a confused look, but then smiled. "I suppose you do, yes." His face grew serious. "Charlie here told me all about your mission. We have a lot to thank you for, Captain Decker. Without you, Shambhala would have been lost to the ages."

"Forget about it," Decker said. "And it's Mitch."

"Can I offer you all some Earl Grey tea?"

"Sounds wonderful," Oliver said, looking around the office.

"I'm sorry but we have no biscuits."

"I'll get over it," Decker said drily. He turned to Selena. "What about you?"

Selena ignored him, and Sumner said, "I hear the LMA is having some trouble with Shambhala?"

Oliver nodded glumly. "Afraid so, yes. It's to be expected, though. No one in the Tibet administration will talk to us, so we're dealing direct with the Chinese Government in Beijing, and that's like swimming through treacle."

Decker's furrowed his brow. "Huh?"

"Molasses," Selena said.

"Gotcha."

"My superiors in the SIS are of course monitoring the situation closely," Sumner said. His tone had changed from cordial to business. "The discovery of Shambhala has made waves around the entire world, and everyone wants a piece of it, but that's not why you're here."

Selena sipped her tea. "Quite."

Sumner took a deep breath and relaxed in his chair. "After you called me, Charlie, I made a few tentative enquiries."

"Any luck?"

The MI5 officer pulled a manila folder from the top drawer of his desk. He opened it and pulled out several photographs. "Do either of you recognize this man?"

Sumner showed them a capture from a CCTV camera on the north bank of the Thames. It was a picture of a man in a hoodie descending into the underground.

Selena gasped. "He's the gunman from the first car!"

"His name is Kai Bloch," Sumner said quietly. "After you called Charlie and he got into contact with me, we were able to use CCTV to follow the driver from the Mercedes that crashed in the Strand. After the accident he headed straight for the Tube."

Selena gasped. "He looks like a ghost."

"He *will* be a ghost if I get my hands on the bastard," said Riley.

"He's a former Austrian commando and expert sniper. We think he entered the United Kingdom yesterday on a flight from Hamburg. We've got agents looking for him all over London but I won't hold my breath. Bloch is absolutely at the top of his game and one of the sharpest blades in the business. He could be anywhere now. Anywhere and everywhere."

After a long silence, Oliver Fleming said, "We think he was taken because he was trying to find the lost Ark of the Covenant."

"Woah!" Riley said. "That's hot."

"Wait," said Charlie. "Don't you die if you look inside that thing?"

"If you've received your knowledge of the Ark from Indiana Jones instead, yes," Selena said. "But there's no such warning in the Bible. The Philistines had the Ark in their possession for a long time and there's no evidence any of them died from handling it or looking inside it."

"In that case we should send Riley," Decker said.

"Very funny, mate."

Sumner gave a shallow nod and used his steepled fingers as an improvised chin-rest. He was the picture of calm.

"You don't seem very shocked," Decker said.

"That's because I already knew."

"You knew?" Oliver said.

"Of course. You don't think a man with Atticus Moore's profile can start a serious search for the lost Ark of the Covenant without attracting the attention of the security services, do you? The man's going to be knighted in the New Year's honors."

"I suppose not," Oliver said.

"And it's not just us who's been tracking him either. CIA, French and German secret Services, Mossad – they're all over this like white on rice."

Decker wasn't surprised to hear it. Up until an hour ago he had no idea the Ark of the Covenant existed, but Atticus was no fool. If he was seriously pursuing it then it had to be real, and if it was real, there were a lot of people in the world who would want such a precious artefact.

"How much do you know?" Selena asked.

"More than even you do, Mr Fleming," Sumner said flatly.

"No surprises there," Oliver said. "Atticus tells me bugger all."

Sumner said, "Your museum, the London Museum of Archaeology has been working with a man named David Herzog from the Rockefeller Museum in Jerusalem for a while now. You're in a co-funded project to locate artefacts from beneath the Church of the Holy Sepulchre, on the hill at Golgotha. In fact, Herzog is awaiting final approval to open the new chamber as we speak."

"All sounds a bit cloak and dagger," Oliver said.

"It's the way the world works," said Charlie.

"Your world maybe, but not mine."

Charlie left it there. "What's the latest, Paul?"

Sumner nodded. "One of my best assets is in Israel right now. His name is Golan and he's been monitoring your father for weeks. This morning he sent me some Top Secret information regarding the Church of the Holy Sepulchre."

Charlie looked drawn. "Christ, Paul."

"Exactly," Sumner said with the trace of a smile. "The information was passed to him via another asset named Moshe Golan whom he runs inside the Mossad, and it's Top Secret for a reason." He paused a beat. "Herzog has located a chamber beneath the church in question, and he was of the opinion that the Ark is inside it."

"But it's not," Selena said. "Thanks to Dad and this Coptic jar, we know that the Ark was taken from the church and the only way to find it is using the clue left in this manuscript by the priest. You have to have read this manuscript to know about the Angel of God and what it looks like."

Riley smiled. "So even when the bastards get into the chamber they still don't know what this Angel of God looks like?"

"David Herzog is not a bastard," Oliver said. "He's a fine archaeologist."

Decker brushed the stubble on his chin with the back of his fingers. "But he still doesn't know what to look for when he breaks into the chamber under the church."

"I don't think so," Oliver said. "Atticus told me neither of them were able to translate it, which is one of the reasons he posted it to us back at the LMA."

"We'll have to hurry, though," Riley said. "It won't take them long to work out what they're looking for."

Oliver frowned. "Depends on the size of the inventory."

"Can we trust this Herzog?" Charlie asked.

Oliver shrugged. "Atticus seemed to think so, but it's others we need to afraid of."

"Exactly, you're not the only people in this hunt," Sumner said.

Selena frowned. "This is all good and well, Mr Sumner, but are you able to help me locate my father?"

Sumner's demeanor changed. His face turned downward into a frown and he linked his fingers and rested his hands on the desk. "Sadly, we know very little. Your father was kidnapped by unknown agents a little after nine in the morning today, local time."

"That means you knew about it before I did!" Oliver said.

Sumner gave a shrug of modesty. "MI5."

"Unknown agents?" Charlie said. "That doesn't sound very encouraging."

"We're working on it, Charles," Sumner said calmly. "You know how these thing work. It's not a Mission Impossible movie out there, but real life. We have to ask questions, bribe foreign agents, get subpoenas to look through CCTV footage... the list goes on. We're doing the best we can, but we have a whole world of misery to keep in check."

"And I'm going to do the best I can too," Selena said, rising confidently from her chair.

"What are you doing?" Oliver asked.

"We're flying to Jerusalem, aren't we Mitch?"

Decker craned his neck up and saw her glaring at him. He got to his feet and pushed his hat back on his head. "Looks that way."

5

Old City of Jerusalem, Israel

Selena watched through the Albatross's porthole window as the Avalon skirted along the coast of Israel. They had broken the journey at Zagreb, and then flown over the Greek islands as the dawn broke. Now, the eastern Mediterranean was sparkling a brilliant turquoise color in the sunshine and just below the portside wing she could make out cars and trucks driving along the streets of the city's Old North.

Before she had left him back in London, Oliver Fleming had told her not to be angry with her father for leaving her out of the loop and now she could see why, but it still stung that he hadn't told her about his work with Herzog and the quest for the Ark. She had agonized over the matter for most of the flight, but now as she drew nearer to the place where her father had been kidnapped, she knew she had to forgive him and focus on bringing him home safely.

She yawned and stretched her arms. Riley was snoozing in one of the bunks at the rear and up front in the cockpit, Decker was reducing the power to the radial engines and banking hard to the left to line up with Ben Gurion Airport. The former marine hadn't passed further comment on the changes she had made to his plane, which ranged from clearing out all the old junk he'd lovingly referred to as cargo, all the way to installing more comfortable seats and refitting the bunks.

A disagreeable whining sound coming from outside the aircraft indicated he had selected the flaps for landing, and moments later a heavy clunk from beneath her feet meant the gear was lowering into place.

The excitement she felt at the start of a mission was tempered by Oliver's news of her father's mysterious departure from Israel. Her meeting with Paul Sumner at Thames House hadn't exactly filled her with confidence either. It turned out that her father hadn't only been lying to her about his quest for the Ark, but that he was being monitored by several security services and that no one knew where he was.

Charlie stepped out of the cockpit and wandered back to her. "Catch up on your research?"

She sighed and tossed her iPad down onto the seat beside her. "I guess."

He smiled and sat beside her. "You don't sound too sure."

"I've been researching the Ark of the Covenant all my life, Charlie. I don't see what difference an extra few hours is going to make now."

"Your life's mission?"

"One of them," she said sadly. "That's why I'm so upset Dad kept me in the dark about his research into it."

Charlie had changed into his "adventure clothes" and now perched his straw hat on top of his head and stretched his arms, yawning loudly. "At least you now know you stand a good chance of actually discovering it for real. Not many archaeologists or hunters of ancient religious relics can say that."

She bit her lip and turned to face him. "Do you really think so?"

"Uh-huh."

"He still lied to me."

He nodded and leaned back in his seat. "And you can ask him why when we rescue him."

"*If* we rescue him, Charlie. I'm so worried about him. He's not world-wise."

"We'll find him," Charlie said.

She gave a heavy sigh. "I suppose there's one advantage to flying in this old floatplane," she muttered. "At least there's no jet lag."

Charlie was now buckling himself into the seat in preparation for the landing. "You need jets for jet lag, but how many archaeology teams have their own aircraft?"

"Yeah, I suppose." She didn't sound too convinced and scowled as Decker hit the rudder to correct for crosswind, sending everyone lurching to the right. "If you say so."

*

After clearing customs, they were met at arrivals by Moshe Golan just as Paul Sumner had promised. He and Charlie slapped each other's backs and chewed the fat as they walked outside and climbed into the MI6 agent's BMW. Golan was a short, lean man with a shaved head and bronzed skin. He wore a white shirt and blue jeans and the sun flashed on his metal wristwatch as he opened the trunk and loaded their bags inside.

"Welcome to Israel," he said as he slammed the trunk shut and walked around to the driver's door. "Paul briefed me on everything."

They climbed in and Golan fired up the engine. As he pulled out of the car park and headed toward the city, Selena's eyes danced over the flat agricultural fields to the east of the airport. Jerusalem was less than an hour away, but any thought of taking a few seconds to enjoy her new surroundings were dashed when Golan said, "No, they're definitely following us."

She leaned forward in her seat. "I'm sorry?"

"I was hoping I was just being paranoid but they're definitely a tail."

Decker glanced at Selena and rolled his eyes. "Why is it that wherever you go, there's always someone tailing you?"

"What are you blathering about? For all we know they're after you."

"Oh yeah, right," his voice was dripping with sarcasm. "Maybe it's that new recruit from Parris Island whose ass I kicked at poker one night."

Riley opened his eyes and looked at Decker. "You play poker?"

"Sure – you?"

Before the Australian could answer, Selena said, "Now you're just being silly. As usual."

"Come on!"

She raised her eyebrows and made a big show of turning away from him. "Parris Island?"

"Marine Corps Recruit Depot."

"Mm-hmm."

"True story."

Golan checked the mirror and watched as the VW kept its distance but stayed within sight of them.

"And just what the hell is that supposed to mean?" Decker said.

"What?"

"That stupid noise you just made."

"It was an expression of disinterest."

Decker smiled and shook his head. "You really are something, lady. I give up a thriving business... what's so funny?"

36

"Nothing at all, please continue."

He crossed his arms and closed his eyes. "I don't want to."

"How's our tail?" Riley asked.

Golan said, "I'm keeping an eye on him."

Outside, the countryside was changing as they drew closer to Jerusalem. The olive-covered hillsides were behind them now, replaced with high rise buildings and industrial factories. They cruised past Latrun, Abu Ghosh and Mevaseret Zion before Golan turned the car south and headed into Jerusalem.

"What about now?" Decker asked. "Our friends still there?"

"That's the funny thing," Golan said. "They're still following us but they're keeping well back and making no attempt to close in on us."

"Could be anyone" Charlie said.

They pulled up outside the hotel and as Golan was helping them with their bags, they all noticed the black VW cruise straight past them and disappear into the traffic on Gershon Agron Street. The MI6 man gave a shrug and pulled the last case to the sidewalk. "Probably just a coincidence, but I'll follow them anyway. I'll meet you here later tonight."

They watched Golan pull back out onto the hot street and then went inside the hotel to check in. Walking over to the elevators, Selena stopped in her tracks. "Dammit."

"What is it?" Decker asked.

"Left my glasses on the front desk. I'll catch you up."

She picked up her glasses off the front desk and headed back to the elevators. Stepping inside, she hit the button for her floor and the doors started to close. She breathed a sigh of relief and in the privacy of the elevator she took out her hair clip and pulled her hair loose, enjoying the feeling of it as it tumbled down over her shoulders. "Peace, at last."

With only a few inches to go until they were closed, a man slipped past the closing doors and hit the button for the top floor. He was wearing a charcoal gray suit and gave her a neutral smile. His right hand gripped a leather-bound Bible.

"Good morning," he said, turning away from her.

"Good morning."

The elevator started to ascend toward her floor.

"How was your flight, Professor Moore?"

Selena felt her skin crawl when she heard the man use her name, and it got ten times worse when he leaned forward and pushed the button to stop the elevator halfway up the shaft.

"Who are you?"

"There's no need to be afraid," he said. "I'm not here to hurt you."

Without even realizing it, she had taken a step back and now her back was pushed up against the cold steel wall of the elevator. "I asked you a question."

"My name is Stefan Kurz," he said casually. He held out a hand to shake, but she ignored it. "I work for an organization in Austria called the Church of the Sacred Light. Perhaps you have heard of us?"

"You tried to kill me this morning in London, am I right?"

He frowned. "I think you are confusing us with someone else. We are a church, and not in the business of trying to kill people."

"Isn't today just full of coincidences..." she muttered.

"What?"

"If you're not here to hurt me, then what do you want?"

"Our proposition is simple, Professor Moore. We want you to work for us."

Selena couldn't believe what she was hearing. "It's very flattering, but I'm already employed by the LMA."

"We know that, Professor. You work for Atticus Moore."

Selena was starting to feel uncomfortable again. "You seem to have done your research."

"Of course, our work is the work of the Lord, Professor Moore. Everything we do is done with the utmost care and diligence. For me it is a calling, a mission, not merely a job."

"I see," she said, and leaned forward to restart the elevator. "That's very reassuring, but I'm not looking for a change of employment."

The doors opened and she stepped out. Kurz followed her into the hall, but Decker was wandering down toward a vending machine beside the elevator shaft. "Wanted a Coke. Who's your new buddy?"

"This is Mr Kurz," Selena said. "He wants me to work for him."

Decker stepped forward and gave her a look to check she was okay. "I'm guessing she told you to get lost."

"She did."

Decker's polite smile turned to a frown. "So it was *you* who followed us from the Airport?"

Kurz shrugged. "Not me personally, but another member of the SCL, yes. They were instructed simply to follow you and report your location to me. You were never in any danger."

"Phew," Decker said sarcastically. "Thank God for that."

Kurz's eyes narrowed almost imperceptibly. "I'm sure he accepts your gratitude."

"It's a no, Mr Kurz," Selena said. "Now, if you'll excuse me, I have things to do."

Kurz raised his voice. "But we all know what is to be found beneath the Church of the Holy Sepulchre. I think you will find the Sacred Light has very deep pockets. If you were to help us we could fund not only this dig but many others in the future."

"Tell me," Selena said. "How are you aware of the new chamber beneath the church? I thought this was totally confidential, with only the team from the Rockefeller Archaeological Museum and the Israeli Government knowing?"

"But you also know."

"The LMA has worked in close conjunction with the Rockefeller Museum for months on this project, Mr Kurz. My question to you remains."

Kurz smiled and took a step back. "We have our contacts just as you have yours, Professor Moore. If a chamber is located and dug out beneath the church, the Sacred Church of Light will know about it before the last shovel is laid to rest."

Selena fixed her eyes on him. "I'm sorry, but I'm really not interested in working for your church. My interest in this is purely archaeological."

"Don't be too hasty. I have been instructed to offer you a large sum of money if you agree to the terms of our contract."

"I'm sorry, Mr Kurz, but…"

"One million dollars if you find the Angel of God for us."

Decker gave a low whistle and turned around on the spot. "That's a lot of aviation fuel, Lena."

Kurz's eyes flicked from the American back to Selena Moore. "And a lot more besides that."

"How do you know about the Angel of God?"

"As I say, we have our ways."

"It's still a no, Mr Kurz. I work for my father and the LMA, and my archaeological findings are their own reward."

Decker glared at Selena and took her by the elbow. "Excuse us a second, Herr Kurz, but we need to talk."

Kurz gave a shallow bow of his head and smiled broadly. "Of course."

Decker wheeled Selena away from the Austrian until they were out of earshot. "Are you crazy?"

"If you mean mad, then I most certainly am not. I am in fact totally compos mentis."

"No you're not! You're nuts!"

"Nuts?"

"Did you hear what that guy just said? He wants to pay you a million bucks to dig up some old relic!"

A long, weary sigh. "I thought I already made it clear that I work for the LMA? Besides, the Angel of God is hardly any old relic. If we're right it could lead us to the Ark of the Covenant." She leaned closer into him and lowered her voice. "And you want to hand something like that over to the first religious whacko that gets his wallet out?"

"Well…"

"I know you're just trying to help."

Decker took the hint and wondered over to Kurz. "It's a no," he repeated. "And that's final."

"One million dollars?"

Decker shrugged and glanced at the Bible. "He that loveth silver shall not be satisfied with silver, right?"

Kurz looked at him oddly, bid them farewell and stepped back into the elevator. They both watched his eerie smile as the doors closed on him and then walked back to their room. "Well, *that* was weird," Decker said as he cracked open his Coke.

"What was weird?" Riley said.

"Some guy from a religious organization just asked Lena if she wanted to work for them," Decker said. "But when I quoted the Bible he didn't seem to know what I was talking about."

"You quoted the bible?" Charlie said.

"Sure, Ecclesiastes 5:10. I went to Sunday School... like I said, weird."

"Not as weird as this," Charlie said, waving his phone at them. "That was Paul back in London. Herzog opened the chamber an hour ago. They're in."

"Which means we've got to get going," Decker said.

Selena was still shaken up from the sinister meeting with Stefan Kurz and was grateful things were finally moving along. "Let's go then," she said. "If we can get to the Angel of God before anyone else we stand a chance of finding Dad."

"And the Ark," Riley said.

"Oh yeah," said Selena. "And the Ark."

6

Located in Jerusalem's Christian Quarter, the Church of the Holy Sepulchre was consecrated in 335AD. Also known as the Church of the Resurrection, the church is on the same site as both the crucifixion and resurrection of Christ. Hadrian, the Roman emperor had a Venusian temple built on the site to cover the location of Christ's burial, but this was replaced with the Church of the Holy Sepulchre two centuries later.

Selena and the rest of her team stepped out of their taxi, emerged into the bright sunshine and met Dr David Herzog. He was standing outside the main entrance with a number of police officers and shook their hands with a solemn frown on his face. "It's good to meet you at last. I'm so sorry about your father. We thought we were safe, but we were wrong." He looked down at the jar in Selena's hands. "At least he managed to get the jar to safety."

"Yes."

"I apologize for the police but you understand why they must be present at a site like this."

Selena looked over the Old City and down the hill to the east. There, sparkling in the bright sun was the golden roof of the Dome of the Rock, dominating the Temple Mount. A holy site for Christians, Jews and Muslims for centuries, it was surrounded by the ancient Herodian walls, baking in the heat of the day.

Herzog turned to Selena. "Your father and I managed to work out the location of the chamber was beneath the Holy Sepulchre here, but that was all we got before we were forced to flee, and Atticus sent the jar to you for safe-keeping. At first we thought it might be located in the Well of Souls."

"As in Indiana Jones?" Riley asked. "Cool."

"No, not as in Indiana Jones," Herzog said with a deepening frown. "As in the Dome of the rock over there." He pointed to the golden roof flashing in the sun over to the east. "We were both worried about the political sensitivities involved in trying to get such an excavation approved."

Selena nodded. She knew exactly what he meant. She had been to the Dome of the Rock a few years ago and seen the place for herself. It was beautiful, with an astonishing display of mosaics and Arabic holy inscriptions covering much of the octagonal arcade and then there was the incredible Foundation Stone. Known as the Well of Spirits in Islam, or the Holy of Holies in Christianity and Judaism, the Well of Souls was beneath the Foundation Stone, but no archaeological dig had ever been approved there.

"Just as well," she said at last. She slipped her sunglasses on and looked back over her shoulder at Herzog. "Don't you think?"

"Indeed. I take it you now know a little more about what we are looking for?"

Selena nodded. "I think we're looking for a golden statue called the Angel of God."

Herzog gasped. "You mean *the* Angel of God?"

"I do, Dr Herzog. Have you found such a statue in the dig yet?"

"Not yet, but we must hurry."

Herzog led them inside the church and after speaking with an official for a few seconds they walked over to a heavy wooden door. The Israeli archaeologist unlocked it and swung it open to reveal a small antechamber, lit by the low amber light of a paraffin lamp. It was cramped and when Riley walked in he banged his head on the ceiling. He cursed and got several disapproving looks in response, but Selena's attention was captivated by the sight of a missing marble slab in the floor and a tunnel stretching away beneath it, stretching into the darkness.

"This is the new chamber?" Selena asked quietly.

Herzog nodded. "This is it."

Decker looked at his watch. "Then shall we go inside?"

Herzog gave an anxious nod and stepped down the makeshift ladder his team had put in place to descend into the chamber beneath the church.

Decker and Selena followed him inside the newly excavated chamber deep beneath the church. As they descended ever further into the labyrinth of tunnels, Selena found herself wishing her father could be here to witness what they were seeing.

This church was built on Golgotha – the site of Calvary Hill – where Jesus Christ was crucified and buried and where Christian tradition said the resurrection happened. It now looked like it was also the site of more holy significance – the hiding place of the Angel of God which would lead them to the lost Ark of the Covenant.

And her father was missing it all.

Herzog, who was leading the way, spoke without turning his head. "When the jar led us to this location, we started digging as soon as we got the necessary permissions, but when your father disappeared I stopped at once and contacted Oliver Fleming. We only reached the final chamber today, but in the short time since we started looking, we have uncovered several important artefacts in some of the antechambers."

"Such as?" Selena called forward.

45

"You'll see for yourself, Professor Moore." Now he stopped in his tracks, turned to face them and lowered his voice to a confidential whisper. "I think this could be the greatest discovery in the history of the world."

Decker raised a sceptical eyebrow, but the look on Selena's face told him she was caught – hook, line and sinker.

"Come!" Herzog said. "We are nearly there."

They followed the Israeli archaeologist along another long tunnel until it opened out into a large chamber with a low ceiling. Two men were hauling some drilling equipment along a narrow path against the far wall, and in the center of the site a handful of people were carefully brushing dust and gravel away from something buried in a small fenced-off section.

"This is amazing," Selena said, staring wide-eyed at the ancient chamber.

"Isn't it?" Herzog said.

Decker whistled. "And until yesterday this was undiscovered?"

"Totally," said the Israeli. "Until Atticus found the jar we had no idea this place existed. This particular chamber was opened only a few hours ago."

"So, we truly are the first," Selena said.

Herzog gave an exuberant nod. "We are the first to set foot in here since it was sealed shut thousands of years ago during the lifetime of Moses himself."

"Professor Herzog!"

It was one of the young women working in the trench.

"What is it, Shira?"

"I don't know – it looks like some sort of handle."

Herzog narrowed his eyes and moved swiftly over to the trench. "A handle?"

"Well… yes, professor."

"Let me see."

He climbed down into the shallow trench and gasped. "It *is* a handle – you've unearthed some kind of trap door." He turned to Selena and the others. "This is new even to me!"

Decker stepped forward and looked at the dusty, old door embedded in the floor of the chamber. "Looks like we're in business."

"You said you hadn't found the Angel of God yet," Charlie said. "Maybe that's because it's down under that trap door?"

"This is undoubtedly the final chamber, yes! It's made of some kind of metal," Herzog said. "And it's far too heavy to be opened by one man."

Decker moved forward and studied the door for a few moments. "If we get some rope around that handle we can get a team together. Should pop right open with a bunch of us pulling on it."

"Danny!" Herzog said to one of the young men. "Go and fetch some rope."

The young man left the cave and returned a few short moments later with a length of chain. "Sorry – the police gave it to me outside. It's all I could find."

Decker took the chain from the young student and threaded one end of it beneath the handle. He looped it around into a knot and after testing it was secure he scanned the chamber for something else.

"What are you looking for, Captain Decker?" Herzog said.

"We're going to need some cloth to wrap around our end of the chain."

"Over there," Herzog said. "Fetch the tarpaulin and bring it to me."

Danny pulled the tarpaulin over and after wrapping it around the other end of the chain they started to pull as hard as they could.

"Heave!" Decker yelled.

They pulled together and the door lifted a few inches before slamming back down in a cloud of dust.

Decker turned to Danny. "Danny, when we lift the door again, I want you to wedge it open with a rock or something. Then we can crow-bar it out of the way."

Danny followed his instructions and the next time they heaved the door open an inch or so, he wedged the handle of a shovel beneath it. They released the rope and the door dropped back down again, but this time the handle ensured a small gap remained.

"Crow-bar," Decker said.

Shira handed him one, and after wedging it down inside the gap he told the others to pull on the door one more time. Working together, they were able to pull the trap door fully open and then right over on its back, where it crashed into the floor with a heavy, mournful thud. When the dust had settled, the small team gathered around the door and peered down inside the new hole they had created.

"Oh my," Selena said with a gasp. "This is unbelievable."

7

"Flashlight," Herzog said, snapping his fingers at Danny who passed him one immediately. The Israeli professor shone the beam down into the darkness and they all saw a deep cavern stretching out beneath them. The floor was littered with chests, boxes and statues and on the second pass of the beam, Herzog's flashlight illuminated a pile of what could only be some kind of precious stones.

"Diamonds?"

"Perhaps."

"We need to get in there!"

"We're too high up to drop down inside," Decker said. "A fall from this height would be fatal."

"We need a longer ladder!" Herzog yelled. "Get me a ladder – at least six meters."

Danny ran from the chamber in search of a full-length ladder, but Decker had another idea. "Give me the loose end of the chain. It's heavy enough to take my weight."

"Take your weight?" Selena said. "Are you insane?"

Herzog was confused. "What is he talking about?"

"I can use the chain to shimmy down inside the chamber while we wait for the ladder."

"But I must be the first to enter," Herzog said, obviously offended by the mere suggestion. "I have spent my life searching for this."

Decker shrugged his shoulders, picked up the loose end of the chain and dropped it down inside the chamber. When it had reached its full length it snapped to a stop a few feet above the cavern's floor. The door it was secured to didn't move an inch. Decker gestured inside the hole. "Professor?"

49

Herzog gripped the sides of the hole with his hands and peered down inside the gloom. When he returned to face Decker and Selena, his face had paled slightly. "All right, perhaps you go first while we wait for Danny to return with the ladder."

Decker went first, gripping the chain with his hands and hooking it around his feet as he lowered himself slowly into the chamber. It took just a few seconds before his boots were touching down on the dusty floor, and then he tugged the chain and called up.

"That's one small step for a man, but one giant leap for this team."

Riley laughed and climbed down the chain. "I'm right behind you, big guy."

Charlie was next and then Selena at the rear. When she hit the bottom of the chamber she gasped with amazement. "This place is unlike anything I've ever seen before," she said, tracing her hands over the smooth edges of a golden statue.

Centuries of uninterrupted dust and cobwebs covered the surface of every treasure chest. The solemn faces of the Greek statues stared back at them with impassive, blank eyes of cold marble. A sound – something scuttling away in one of the darkest corners, and the smell of damp neglect grew heavier as they moved further into the chamber.

"I cannot believe we are actually beneath the Holy Sepulchre!" Herzog said as he touched down in the chamber. His voice was hoarse, trembling with anticipation and uncertainty. Tears welled in his eyes, but he blinked them away. "This is the greatest moment of my entire life."

"Not just of your life, Professor Herzog," Selena said. "This place could very well turn out to be the most important archaeological study in Western culture."

They started their search for the Angel of God. The description in the manuscript was sparse, chronicling it as made of gold, and small enough for one man to carry.

"So, we're looking for something with wings, right?" Riley called out from a far corner.

"Maybe, maybe not," Selena said. "Angels aren't usually described as having wings in the Bible. Mostly they're described as appearing as normal human beings, but both cherubim and seraphim have wings and they're described as being angels, so…"

"So, maybe – maybe not," Charlie said with a laugh.

"What about this?" Decker said, pulling a small statue of a woman praying from a chest. He blew the dust off it and saw it was made of ceramic and not gold. "Nope."

"This?" Charlie said, holding up a golden statue of Christ.

"Think about it, Charlie," Selena said. "Christ was born thousands of years after the Ark went missing."

"Gotcha."

The search went on, with Herzog and Charlie working one side of the room, and Selena and Riley on the other. Decker was working alone on the northern edge of the chamber when he stumbled over something that made his hairs stand on end. "Over here! I think I have it!"

The others joined him and both Selena and Herzog knew at once they had it as the American carefully lifted a golden statue of a seraphim from a pile of dusty rubble in the corner. He gently brushed centuries of dust away to reveal a perfect, golden work of religious art.

"The Angel of God!" Selena said.

Herzog muttered, "Undoubtedly."

51

"Smaller than I thought," Charlie said.

"Is that what your last girlfriend said, mate – or are you describing the statue?"

"Funny."

Selena couldn't take her eyes off the statue as Decker handed it to her. It wasn't as heavy as she had anticipated, and while this surprised her at first, she quickly worked out why, and her heart quickened even more with another wave of excitement. If a golden statue of this size weighed as little as this then it couldn't be solid, and that meant only one thing.

Decker pushed his hat an inch up his forehead and scratched his forehead with a bemused look on his face. "So, that's the real thing, huh?"

Selena looked at him and sighed. With the statue still cradled in her arms like a baby, she stood on her tiptoes and leaned forward to kiss him on the cheek.

"What was that for?" he asked, fighting the blush away.

"For everything," she said. "For saving my life so many times, for flying out to save my father and for helping me find this. Thanks, Mitch."

Decker furrowed his brow and scratched an imaginary itch behind his ear. "No problem, I guess. You're welcome, or something like that."

She rolled her eyes. *Men.*

Returning her gaze to the golden statue in her arms, she was once again struck by the object's intense, mesmerizing beauty. Smooth lines sloped down from the heavenly creature's narrow shoulders, and the serene indifference on its face was beyond description.

"It's undoubtedly a seraph," she said. The word was an ancient Hebrew name for *the burning one*, a reference to the light which emanated from them when they descended from heaven.

"Forgive my ignorance," Charlie said, "but just what is a seraph, exactly?"

"It's a celestial being in the traditions of both Christianity and Judaism and there are several mentions of them in the Old Testament."

"It *is* pretty amazing," Riley said. "And the wings are awesome."

"As winged creatures, tradition holds that they're supposed to fly above the Throne of God in the Seventh Heaven. They're closely associated with legends about apotheosis, too."

Charlie sighed. "In English, if you please."

"Apotheosis is a Greek word referring to the process of becoming divine, it's usually used to describe when a mortal has been elevated to godlike status."

She felt a desperate wave of regret rush over her as she thought about her father. Old Atticus lived for this sort of thing, and it was only thanks to his research that they were even here in the first place, and yet he wasn't here to enjoy the moment with them. Worse, he was missing, presumed kidnapped by an unknown agency that had snatched him from a foreign hotel room. He could be anywhere, she thought bleakly.

Kurz had denied taking him, but could she believe a man like Stefan Kurz? There was something about him that had left her with a very bad feeling after their impromptu meeting in the elevator earlier today, and she didn't like it.

Then again, if he had snatched Atticus to gain some leverage over her, he hadn't seemed in much of a hurry to use it, and that made her think that maybe someone else was behind the disappearance after all.

Visions of her father tied and gagged in some hellhole rose up like shadows at the foot of her bed, and she fought to shake them from her mind. The darkest thought of all was the possibility that he might be dead. She couldn't even go there, and instantly dismissed the thought from her mind.

He couldn't be dead, could he? The hotel room was trashed but he was missing. If it had been a robbery that had gone wrong, they would have found his body in the room. The fact he was missing was a good thing, and no one would have taken him just to kill him in another location. No, whoever had taken him had done it for a reason, and that must mean they needed him. She felt in her heart that he was still alive.

She was rudely shaken from the thoughts of her father by a deep explosion that rocked the ground they were standing on.

"What the hell was that?" Herzog yelled out, covering his head instinctively with his arms.

"Sounded like a thermite grenade," Decker said.

"A thermite grenade?" Selena yelled. "And what the hell is one of those?"

"It's trouble... big trouble."

Now they heard the sounds of people screaming and then Danny's voice as he called out to warn them of the threat, but then they heard the chatter of submachine guns. No one heard Danny's voice again.

"Danny!" Shira called out.

"We've got to get out of here," Decker said.

8

"We're under attack?" Herzog said. "This is unthinkable! There are police everywhere. This is the a holy site!"

"It's not unthinkable," Decker said calmly. "It's happening right now, professor."

"Who is it?"

"We were approached earlier today by a group calling itself the Church of the Sacred Light. They wanted to hire us to work for them, but we declined their offer. I don't believe in the kind of coincidence it would take for this attack on us to be by a second group – not in the space of a few hours, anyway. If you ask me, the smart money's on this being the handiwork of the Kurz and the Church."

"But who are they?" Herzog said.

"We're not sure," Selena said. "Quick research pointed to them being a kind of ultra-religious sect, a cult almost, on the fringes of Christianity."

"But I have my doubts about that," Decker said.

The sound of more gunfire and yells echoed down the tunnel from the entrance up on the surface. "Sounds like they're getting closer," Herzog said. "They must be massacring our police!"

Selena's mind raced as she heard the sound of men screaming high above them up in the Church of the Holy Sepulchre. It sounded like a bloodbath, and she had no doubt that Kurz must be involved in some way – who else even knew about what they were doing here? "All they want is the Angel of God," Selena said. "We can't let them have it. Is there another way out of here?"

Then she saw a familiar face standing over them up in the chamber above the tomb and she knew at once Decker had been right to doubt Stefan Kurz's sincerity. The Austrian was looking down at her with a grin in his face, but the smart suit had been replaced by a black roll-neck and combat fatigues and instead of the Bible his two hands now gripped a chunky submachine gun.

"So the Bible was just a prop after all?" she called up.

"Ah, Professor Moore," Kurz called down. "I see you are like the proverbial rat in a trap, down in this dark little hole."

"What do you want, Kurz?" Decker called up, stalling for time. Herzog was still rummaging around in the back of the cavern desperately searching for a way out.

"You know what I want, *Captain*. The Angel of God."

"And what makes you think we found it?" Selena called up.

Kurz laughed and barked some orders in German. "I'm sure a woman of your abilities could not fail to find such a glorious relic in a place such as this – especially with the famous David Herzog to help her." He grinned and stared into her eyes. "You think I didn't know Professor Herzog was down in your little rat trap with you?"

"I don't know what you mean…"

"Step into the light with your hands up, Herzog, or the girl's dead."

Decker felt his hands tightening into two fists as he watched Kurz's men drag Shira into view. Several meters above them now, and partially obscured by the side of the trap door hole, he saw it was definitely her and she looked scared for her life. "You bastard, Kurz."

"Now, Professor Herzog, and bring the Angel of God with you. You have until the count of three… *Drei…*"

Decker lowered his gaze and after exchanging a look of helplessness with Selena, the two of them watched David Herzog as he stepped calmly out of the shadows in the far corner of the cavern. He was still gripping the golden Angel of God, but gave a defeatist shrug as he drew closer to them. He lowered his voice to a whisper. "I think perhaps there is another way out over there, behind those statues."

Zwei...

"I'm right here!" Herzog yelled out, and stepped into the glare of their flashlights. "Don't harm her, please."

Kurz roughly pushed the girl out of sight again and smiled broadly as his eyes fixed on the statue in Herzog's embrace. "Mein Gott, you really did find it!"

"What now?"

"Tie it to the end of the chain and I will bring it to the surface. When I have it in my hands, I will lower the girl down and you can wait in here until the authorities find you, by which time my men and I will be long gone."

Decker lowered his voice so only Selena and the Israeli could hear. "Yeah right... if we give him the statue there's nothing to stop him dropping one of those thermite grenades down here and burning all of us to death."

Herzog turned to him with two plaintive eyes. "But what else can we do? He has Shira and we know he's happy to murder anyone who gets in his way – think about Danny!"

"I don't kill," Kurz called down. "If I must make a sacrifice, then so be it, but it's not as mindless as murder."

"You tell yourself that, Kurz!" Decker called up. "Anything to help you sleep at night, right?"

A shadow of contempt colored the Austrian's face. "Don't judge me, Captain Decker, I will submit to judgement by God alone! Now, tie the Angel of God to the end of the chain before I am forced to sacrifice yet another in the name of my cause!"

"You can drop the religious act, Kurz!" Decker said.

"I don't know what you mean. The statue, now!"

Herzog desperately scanned the tomb for another escape route and then turned his face up to the light high above. "If you want it, come and get it!"

Kurz laughed. "Surely you can't believe I am stupid enough to lower myself down there and ask you for the Angel? You would kill me before I even reached the floor of the tomb."

"That's your problem!" yelled Herzog.

"I will kill her, Professor!" Kurz shouted.

"Let's switch this around," Herzog called up. "If you hurt her, I will never tell you which one is the Angel! Not ever! You need me!"

Kurz's smug grin turned to a scowl. "Then please allow me to me make a suggestion." He turned to one of his men and spoke in rapid German. The man pulled a metal canister from his belt and handed it to him. Kurz waved it casually in the air and his smile returned. "This is a very powerful thermite grenade, identical to the one that just shook this very church to its foundations. That was when we used one to clear the police and security out of our way at the main entrance."

"I don't like where this is heading," Decker said.

"*You* don't?" Charlie said. "I only just got this tan – I can't die now!"

"I am going to count to ten, and in that time one of you will tie the Angel to the chain and allow me to pull it out of the tomb. If you don't comply, I will pull the pin on this incendiary, wait until the timer is down to two seconds and then drop it into the tomb. You, and everything else down there will be blown into dust."

"It's a very tempting offer," Decker said. "But I think you're bluffing."

"Can you be so sure?"

58

"If you blow the Angel to dust, then you're search is over before it's even started."

"Oh, really?"

"Sure," Decker said calmly. "I recognise that thermite grenade, Kurz. That thing's going to burn at close to four thousand degrees, and yet the melting point of the gold in the Angel statue is only one thousand degrees. You drop that thing down here and you can kiss your statue goodbye and whatever the hell you want that's inside it."

Kurz laughed, louder this time and almost sincere. "You are indeed a worthy adversary." He cocked his gun and pointed it into the hole. Ordering his men to do the same, Decker and the others were soon looking into a firing squad of half a dozen men, each armed with a cutting-edge submachine gun. With nowhere to hide in the tomb, it would be as simple an execution as ever there was. "My new plan is to cut you to shreds with these bullets. Have you, by any chance, a smart answer to this plan?"

Decker sighed and his shoulders slumped. He turned to Selena and the others. "I'm fresh out of ideas. You?"

"You win," Herzog called up. He picked up another golden statue they had found and tied it to the bottom of the chain. "You win, you bastard!"

Decker saw what he was doing, but giving the Austrian the wrong statue could only buy them a few seconds.

Kurz gave another laugh as he pulled the chain up. Everyone was silent as they watched the golden Angel of God slowly ascending – not into heaven but into the arms of Stefan Kurz. The Austrian greedily untied it and studied the object before comparing it to a sketch he had on a piece of paper. "Wir haben die Statue!"

With no ceremony, he pulled the pin on the thermite grenade and counted down until the fuse was almost burned.

"Auf Wiedersehen!" he cried out, and released the powerful incendiary into the tomb.

9

"Get down!" Decker yelled as he grabbed Selena and pulled her to the ground.

The explosion from the thermite grenade ripped through the chamber beneath the Holy Sepulchre, its white-hot flames instantly incinerating anything they touched. Without explanation, David Herzog dived toward the explosion, landing on the floor of the tomb a few inches from the grenade. Grabbing the golden statue on the floor he threw it back to them. "This is the real Angel of God!" he cried out. "Now run! Get the Angel out of here before they realize what we have done!" Still clutching the blast wounds on his head and throat, Herzog crashed down into the pile of relics.

"David!" Selena cried out, catching the statue and fleeing behind the marble statues with Decker. The explosion was savage, lighting the tomb as bright as the sun and radiating a heat she thought would melt her skin, but the row of marble statues at the far end of the tomb provided enough cover and distance to protect them from the worst of the explosion.

Herzog's bravery had won them the true Angel of God, but it had cost the Israeli professor his life. As his shredded body collapsed into the pile of burning treasure chests behind him, he had used his last seconds of life in the best way he could. The experience had left Selena in shock, curled in a ball and clutching the Angel of God to her chest as if it were a life jacket and she were on a burning boat.

"This way," Decker said, springing to action. "I thought I saw a way out behind Aphrodite…"

"What about David?"

"He's dead, Lena," Riley said. "

Decker nodded. "And we're next if we don't get the hell out of here!"

Selena felt a wave of sorrow for David Herzog as his body lay obscured in the flames and smoke at the center of the chamber, but the sensation of Mitch Decker tugging at her elbow was enough to shake her mind back into the moment.

"This way!" he called out over his shoulder. "I think I see what he was talking about up ahead behind those statues."

They staggered through the dust and smoke, stumbling over fragments of exploded artefacts. Shredded wood and bent iron dowels and handles from the treasure chests were strewn all over the floor of the chamber as they made their way across to what they all silently prayed was another exit.

They reached the long line of ancient Greek statues lined up against the far wall. Decker wiped the sweat and soot from his face and blinked in the low light as he desperately scanned the ancient stone faces. In Selena's burned hands she held the Angel of God as if it were her only child. "Which one's Aphrodite, Lena?"

"Here!" she called out.

Decker ran to her and immediately heaved the statue over. It fell to the ground with a heavy thud and revealed a crack in the wall behind where it had stood for so many centuries. "My God! He was right."

Then, through the noise of the flickering flames behind them, they heard the sound of Stefan Kurz yelling in German. "Warten! Das ist die falsche Statue! Sie haben uns betrogen!"

Decker glanced at Selena. "I'm guessing that's not good, right?"

She nodded and blew out a breath. Wiped the sweat from her forehead. "You guess right. Kurz knows Herzog gave him the wrong statue. He says we betrayed him."

"*We* betrayed *him*? God dammit! He promised he'd let us live and then threw a goddam thermite grenade at us!"

"He's a bastard, all right," Riley said.

Charlie passed a hand over his sweating face. "You can say that again."

Selena shrugged her shoulders, but her response was cut short by the sound of Kurz's men throwing rope ladders down into the chamber.

Decker's officer training kicked in. "All right, get into the tunnel and I'll try and pull the statue up to block the entrance and buy us some time."

"It's too late!"

One of Kurz's men was on them, firing through the smoke. Riley charged forward and swung the arm of a broken statue at him, smashing him around the back of the head and knocking him dead in one blow.

"There's plenty more where he came from!" the Australian said. "We need to get out, and now!"

Decker sprinted through the smoke and snatched up the dead man's gun. Checking the magazine to count how many rounds were left, he scrambled over the rubble and skidded to a halt behind one of the chests.

Kurz didn't hesitate to order his men to return fire, but Decker never flinched. "Hurry, get out of here!"

Selena looked on in awe as the American risked his life yet again to save hers – and the Angel of God. Decker had ducked back down behind the chest to avoid a lethal fusillade of semi-automatic fire. She gasped as the bullets shredded the chest's lid and tore chunks off the sides of it, blasting the leather straps off and sending clouds of splinters bursting into the air all around him.

"Stay down, Mitch!"

"You don't say?" he called back over. "And what the hell are you still doing here, Lena! I told you to run!"

"But what about you?"

"I'm right behind you!"

She hesitated for a few seconds and then did as he had said, slipping through the gap in the wall and disappearing like a shadow. Behind her, Decker scrambled a few meters closer to the tunnel and took cover behind one of the fallen statues.

"You have nowhere to run!" Kurz yelled through the smoke. "You are trapped like the rats you are. Hand over the true Angel of God and I will let you live."

Decker kept his mouth shut. He knew Kurz was goading him into giving away his new position. He reached out for a chunk of Apollo's arm and hurled it through the smoke as far as he could. It crashed down in the far corner and Kurz and his men swung their firearms around one-eighty.

They opened fire with a savage ferocity that would have killed him stone dead had he been over there, but the feint worked, and now he slipped over to the tunnel, crouched down in the dirt and heaved the statue up on his shoulder. Taking a breath, he then raised it up sixty or seventy degrees before manoeuvring his way behind it and pulling it up to block the gap. "That should buy us a few minutes."

"Over there!" Kurz yelled. "Behind the Aphrodite statue!"

Kurz ordered his men to fire and the rounds blasted the statue to pieces and struck Selena, ripping through her upper arm. She screamed in pain and immediately dropped the Angel. She hit the dust at the same time as the statue, but by the time she had rolled over and reached out to grab it, it was already in the arms of Stefan Kurz and he was looking down at her with a shit-eating grin on his pock-marked face. He snatched up the statue and aimed his gun at Selena.

"Everyone stand where they are, and raise your hands!"

They obeyed, and Kurz pulled the hammer back on his gun. "Goodbye, Professor Moore."

Charlie was closest and jumped forward, but Kurz powered the stock of his weapon into his face and knocked him out. With the former MI5 man dead to the world, Kurz aimed his gun at Selena once again. She closed her eyes and prepared to die when she heard a heavy grunt and a scuffle. Opening her eyes, she saw Riley Carr diving through the air and colliding with Kurz. Her ex-boyfriend slammed the Austrian into the tomb's floor and the two men rolled and grappled with each other.

Kurz pulled a knife from his belt and slashed it in Riley's face. The blade missed but the end of the handle struck him on the temple and almost knocked him out. He rolled off Kurz and struggled to his feet but the Austrian was already standing and kicked him hard in the ribs, putting him down into the dust again.

With the statue in their possession, Kurz and his men evacuated in the escape tunnel that Decker had planned to use, turning and firing on them to keep them pinned down as they receded into the darkness.

Decker scrambled to his knees and saw Selena was out cold now, and her face had turned ashen white. He ran to her and lifted her head into his lap. A pool of blood was seeping out of her shoulder wound and congealing in the sandy gravel beneath her. Looking across the chamber, he saw Charlie was still out cold too.

Riley ran to her. "Fucking bastards!"

"Get after him, Riley!" Decker yelled, and tossed him the gun. "I'll look after them."

The Australian looked anxiously at his unconscious friends. "You sure?"

"Yes, I'm sure, dammit! The last thing Lena would want is for that son of a bitch to take the Angel!"

"I'm on it," Riley said.

Decker watched the young man sprint into the tunnel after Kurz and his unit, and then turned his attention back to Selena, unconscious and wounded in his arms.

10

Riley Carr ran through the darkness of the tunnel, determined to catch up with the men who had shot Selena and killed David Herzog. Halfway along, he heard a tremendous explosion and instinctively dived for the dirt with seconds to spare. A river of fire streaked inches above his head and blasted smoke and brick dust all over him as the energy from the explosion burned itself out down the tunnel.

He guessed Kurz and his crew had found a way out but needed to make it large enough for them to escape through. With the sound of Kurz screaming in German at his men up ahead, he scrambled to his feet and sprinted to the end where it turned into what looked like another crypt. Light flooded in from a small hole in the ceiling and piles of stone and plaster littered the floor beneath it. This is what they had blown up to make good their escape, and he saw at once that Kurz and his men had stood on an old stone tomb to reach their escape route.

The Australian easily leaped up onto the tomb and pulled himself up through the hole until he was standing on a side street to the east of the church. He scanned the area for any sign of Kurz and his men, looking further east down the hill and shielding his eyes from the flash of the burning sun on the Dome of the Rock's gold leaf.

A quarter of a century ago, the King of Jordan had sold one of his foreign homes to pay for the nearly-two hundred pounds of gold required to cover the roof. It flashed in the burning sun and dazzled the Australian as he squinted in search of the thieves, with no idea where they had gone.

A scream gave him the answer he was looking for. He spun around and saw the men moving away from the Church of the Holy Sepulchre at speed, kicking and punching anyone who got in their way. One man approached them with his hands raised. He was trying to talk, but Kurz fired on him almost point blank and killed him on the spot.

Thousands of people now bolted in every direction, fearing a major terrorist attack at one of the world's holiest sites. Kurz was unmoved by the reaction and increased the terror by firing more rounds into the air. After barking more orders at his men in German, he and his team continued their way toward the maze of backstreets to the west of the Temple Mount.

Riley glanced at the man Kurz had shot as a crowd of well-meaning men and women risked their lives to carry him to safety, but he knew no one could survive a point-blank attack with a Heckler & Koch. "Bastards," he muttered, and took up his pursuit of the tomb raiders.

By the time he reached the street running north-south of the old hill, Kurz had vanished yet again. Police sirens now echoed down ever street as the first responders raced toward the scene of the shooting back at the church. Tourists fleeing the chaos obscured his view in every direction. Leaping onto the roof of a parked Hyundai, he shielded his eyes from the sun again and scanned the area once more for any sign of Kurz.

For a second there were no more clues, but then he saw a man in the street up ahead. He was in uniform, and looked dazed and confused, holding his head in his hands one minute, and then pointing and shouting down the road the next. The Australian followed the man's pointing arm until he saw an Israel Post van swerving in and out of the traffic toward the Temple Mount.

The flicker of a smile crossed his dry lips. "Got the bastards," he muttered. "Now all I need is to get me some fuckin' wheels."

He searched for a vehicle he could use when the delicious smell of tomato and hot cheese drifted past him, followed by the familiar rasping sound of a two-stroke engine. It could mean only one thing, and he turned over his shoulder to see his thoughts confirmed: a young man was riding toward him on a Vespa. Stacked in a small cage on the back were half a dozen pizzas.

"Riley, mate – never look a gift horse in the mouth."

As the Vespa cruised past, the driver cast a curious glance up at the man standing on the roof of the parked Hyundai and wondered what he was doing up there. He didn't have to wait long to find out. As he passed the car, Riley Carr leaped from the roof and crashed down on top of the man.

The Vespa slipped out from beneath them both and wobbled its way over to the kerb where it crashed over on its side and spilled pizzas all over the hot asphalt. The Australian expected a fight, but the man looked at the pistol in his hand and scrambled back like a crab. When he was far enough away he waved his hands in the air and reached into his pocket. "Here! Take my wallet!"

He tossed it through the air and Riley caught it in one hand. "Not a robbery mate – I just need your bike. If it survives I'll park her up and put the keys under the seat. And I don't want your wallet, either."

He tossed the wallet over and ran to the bike. Heaving it up, he kicked the starter and fired the engine up again. He revved it a few times and took off after Kurz in the post van without even looking over his shoulder. "Never look back, mate," he said to himself.

69

Speeding into the traffic, he turned a sharp right and joined the last place where he had seen Kurz. It was no more than an alley, cobblestones on the ground and market stalls on either side. He was amazed the Austrian would even consider trying to drive a van down here and wondered if he had made a mistake when he looked ahead and saw the red rear doors of the postal van shining in the sun.

The alley was so narrow that the sides of the van were striking the walls as it raced through the labyrinth, spitting showers of amber and white sparks into the air – but this was the least of his concerns. Now, the rear doors burst open to reveal one of Kurz's men in the back of the van. He was holding a submachine gun which he now aimed at Riley. A fiendish smile appeared on his face, and then he gave a mocking wink.

"Jesus, Riley!" the Australian said. "You really can be an idiot sometimes."

He was right. The van barely fit down the alley and that meant the Vespa had nowhere to run and hide.

The fusillade began, firing full metal jackets all over him.

He swerved the bike from side to side to avoid the barrage, but the alley was too narrow to make any meaningful evasive manoeuvre and the bullets snaked after him wherever he went. Pushing hard to the right, he plowed the bike straight into one of the market stalls, smashing it over and spraying a jumble of souvenir scarves, taboon bread and Jerusalem bagels up into the air.

Brushing a coating of sesame seeds and za'atar powder off his face, he swerved hard to the left to avoid more bullets. The man in the back was casually sweeping his weapon back and forth at the Australian, almost playing with him as they blew through the alley at breakneck speed.

Engines revved, stall holders dived for cover and now Riley Carr pulled the gun from his waistband and aimed it at the Israeli Post van. "Have some back, you bastards!"

Loosing three rounds, he struck the van with every shot. The first two punctured holes in the licence plate and the third made its mark in the chest of the man with the gun. The impact of the shot knocked him back until Riley lost him in the gloom of the van's interior. The Australian took advantage of the shock unfolding in the back of the van and increased his speed, racing ever closer to Kurz.

Almost close enough to touch, Riley stuffed the gun in his pants and prepared to jump from the bike into the back of the van. The alley was running out and up ahead was a road where they would have the advantage, but just as he was figuring out the best way to get into the van, his eyes opened wide with disbelief.

The other men in the back of the van were hurling their dying colleague at him. He could hardly believe what he was seeing. "Not exactly an act of Christian charity is it now?" he called out.

Their response was to heave the man out of the rear doors directly at him.

He hit the brakes and swerved as the dying man came tumbling out the back of the postal van and hit the ground like a bag of potatoes.

Narrowly avoiding the half-dead man by inches, Riley glanced over his shoulder to see his body tumbling into a food stall where he knocked a pile of piping hot shawarma wraps, pickled turnips and chicken schnitzels all over himself. "Not the way to go, mate."

His satisfaction was cut short when he realized the others were getting away and almost at the end of the alley. He increased speed and put the Vespa on a course for the van ahead of him. The Angel of God was in there, and this was the last chance he had. If he let them get away now they'd be gone forever and so would Selena's chance of ever finding the Ark and her father.

He fired on them once again. Closer now, he hit the tires and shreds of black rubber were sprayed all over the place by centrifugal force. With both rear tires blown out, the van scraped along the cobblestones with a shower of amber and white sparks spitting out from the rimless wheels.

The disaster unfolding at the back had distracted the driver, and now the van smashed into the wall and mounted a series of low, steps. Riley watched with a mix of horror and pleasure as the entire vehicle tipped over on its side and came to a smoking halt at the end of the alley. The men inside were too dazed to noticed that the Angel rolled out the back and came to a stop on the cobblestones.

Riley snatched up the Angel of God and quickly threw it in the back with the greasy takeaway orders. Kurz was crawling toward his gun but Riley kicked him in the stomach and knocked him over onto his back. "That's you fucked, you wanker," he said, and gave them the bird as he turned the Vespa and revved the throttle. Skidding away into the market place in a cloud of burned rubber, he checked the rear-view mirror and saw Stefan Kurz crawling from the wreckage of the van. The Austrian tripped over the bent fender and stumbled into another pile of taboon bread that had fallen when they'd crashed into the stall.

"Couldn't have happened to a nicer man," Riley said.

An unusually calm Stefan Kurz brushed the breads off himself but stuffed his gun in his belt and turned back to the van. Riley thought it strange that Kurz would give up the hunt for the Angel so easily, but then realized that others in his team were still on his tail and fled for the cover of the Western Wall. He wasn't surprised to see Kai Bloch and another man beat a man off his motorbike and give chase, screaming in German as he pushed through the crowd. They wanted the Angel and they weren't going to stop until they got it.

One man standing behind a table full of Siddur Jewish prayer books tried to bring one of the men down. A brief struggle ensued before Bloch spun around and fired on the man, blasting him back and knocking over the table and prayer books.

Riley knew he had to draw Bloch away from the crowd. Scanning the area, he saw the Mughrabi Bridge and headed straight for it. The wooden bridge was new, built in 2004 to connect the Western Wall with the Mughrabi Gate which led into the Temple Mount. Riley Carr was not the most diplomatic member of the team, but even he could guess the sort of publicity the LMA would get if he was caught in a gunfight inside the Temple Mount. "You'll start World War Three or something, you stupid bastard," he muttered to himself.

He climbed up on the roof of the covered bridge and saw a wall at the end of it. The wall was connected to the famous Western Wall, and if he could get on to that he could sprint north along the wall and climb down at the other end in the Old City. He had the Angel, and now all he had to do was lose Bloch and his mate. Slipping into another labyrinth of side streets seemed like the best plan, but there was no way of getting there with Bloch and the other man fanning out to the west of the wall.

Stuffing the Angel inside his trousers with a skyward apology, he jumped up with all his power and just managed to cling onto the edge of the wall. Hauling himself up he started to sprint to the Western Wall. Turning north, he started to make his way along the top of the wall, aware now of the fuss he was creating, but he had no choice. Three heavily armed Austrian mercenaries were intent on killing him and they had all the other escape routes covered.

He was just starting to think he'd made it when it happencd.

The second gunman fired from the south of his position on the wall and the bullet ripped over his leg. It was only a flesh wound but when he dodged to the right to avoid it he lost his balance and tumbled over the edge of the Western Wall, the Angel of God still in his pants.

11

Mitch Decker waited until the paramedics stumbled through the smoke and rubble and found where he was cradling Selena in his arms. "Over here!" he yelled.

The two men were part of the larger team of first responders that had descended on the Church of the Holy Sepulchre after Kurz and his men had started using high explosives and shooting innocent tourists. They knelt beside Selena's unconscious body and got to work. One of them began to check her vital signs while the other opened a heavy metal box full of medical equipment.

The US Marine Corps had given Decker substantial medical training as part of his officer course, and he had done everything he was able to do in the circumstances, but he breathed a sigh of relief when the professionals turned up with all their kit. "She took a heavy blast from one of the grenades, and then she got shot," he explained. "She's been out cold ever since, more or less." He told them when it had happened and what he had done, and then they got to work.

The paramedic responded by immediately checking her airway was clear, and then asked, "What's her name?"

"Selena," he said. "Call her Lena."

The lead paramedic leaned over her and checked her breathing. "Lena? Can you hear me?"

She began to rouse, mumbling incoherently and turning her head gently from side to side. "What... where..?"

"Don't try and talk," the paramedic said, and now he checked her pulse. "She's showing good responses."

Decker passed a hand over his mouth and gave a silent prayer of thanks. Selena turned to him, her eyes now fully open and smiled at him as she squeezed his hand. "Go and get the bastards," she said quietly.

"Are you sure?"

Even now, she managed to give him her best look of weary disdain. "You really trust Riley Carr out there, all on his lonesome?"

Decker gave her a reassuring pat on her shoulder. "I'm sure he's got everything covered."

*

Riley Carr clung to the edge of the Western Wall for all his young life was worth as the Angel of God slipped beneath his belt and slowly made its way down the leg of his pants. Considered by the three main religions to be one of the most holy sites on Earth, the site was always bustling with a mix of excited tourists and pilgrims and today was no different, except for the additional attraction of a former SASR corporal dangling from the wall.

Riley had known some tricky scrapes in his time, but hanging off one of the world's holiest structures with a golden statue of an angel sliding down his trousers was rapidly making its way to the top of his list. Throw in the angry Kai Bloch who was now padding his way along the top of the wall toward him and it could easily take the cake.

He scanned the area for a new escape route. Behind him up the hill was Golgotha, the Hill of Calvary, where they had just come from. The place where Jesus was crucified, and then resurrected – or so they had told him in Sunday School. It was also the place where Riley Carr was about to meet his maker if he didn't find a way out, and fast.

Below him was the vast plaza usually filled with worshippers and tourists, but now it was rapidly emptying. In the distance he heard police sirens. Things were quickly spinning out of control. He looked below into the square, but it was too far below to make safely in a jump.

The Angel slid down further, now passing his knee, and below him he now saw Bloch's associate standing on the cobblestones. As soon as the Angel slipped out the bottom of his pants all he would have to do was catch it and run.

"It's over, corporal!" the man yelled up.

Kai Bloch gave a good laugh. "He's mine now, Lechner."

"Like hell is it over!" Riley called back, struggling to hold his leg up and keep the Angel from falling into Lechner's arms. "And I'm not in the army anymore!"

Lechner laughed but quietened down and watched his associate Bloch as he climbed the inside of the wall.

Riley's hands were slipping on the dry stonework of the ancient wall. He knew he couldn't hold on for much longer – either to the Angel or his own life. If he fell it was a straight fall nearly one hundred feet to a stone courtyard and instant death. He blew out a desperate breath and pushed his leg up close to the stone wall to try and wedge the Angel in place and stop its downward passage to Lechner far below him.

But Lechner was tiring of the chase. He glanced at his watch and sighed, and then called up in English to Bloch. "Hurry up! We have a plane to catch and the police are on their way."

The surly Austrian peered over the top of the wall and looked down at Riley as he struggled hopelessly in the warm Jerusalem breeze, hung out to dry like an old shirt after a day at the beach.

He looked up at his enemy and offered a toothy grin. "I don't suppose there's any way we could talk about this?"

Bloch responded with a smirk and a shake of his head, and then he climbed up into the window space and began to smash his boot down on Riley's right hand.

Riley cried out in agony. Looking far below him, he saw Stefan Kurz had now arrived on the scene.

"Kill him!" Kurz yelled up. "Then we get out of here."

*

Decker and Moshe Golan swerved into the courtyard in an unmarked car and skidded to a halt beside some steps to the north of the plaza. "There!" Decker cried out. "He's hanging off the goddam Western Wall!"

Before Golan had a chance to express his shock, Kurz and his men turned in response to the car's arrival, and immediately drew their weapons and started firing.

"Get down!" Decker yelled.

Golan did more than that. As he ducked his head below the line of the dashboard, he slammed the car into reverse and stamped on the throttle. The car's two litre engine growled in response and the car surged backwards along the narrow lane where they had just come from.

Bullets pinged off the hood and drilled up the windshield, carving a mess of spider web fractures in the safety glass. Kurz ordered another wave and this time the rounds shattered the glass completely and bullets began to penetrate the car, tearing up the roofing felt and eating into the side pillars.

Golan continued to reverse away from the assault, but now the bullets raked into the grille and exploded the radiator, sending a cloud of steam bursting into the hot Israeli air. More rounds now shredded the two front tires, blowing both of them out but Golan was pinned into the alley and had no way to go but straight back.

"This guy never gives up!" he said.

"We've got to go back and help Riley!" Decker yelled.

They burst out the other end of the alley and Golan swerved the car away from the line of fire and hit the brakes. He turned his worn, leathery face to the American. "And what do you suggest we do? We have to wait for reinforcements!"

"He'll be dead by then, and Kurz will have the Angel!"

Golan snatched at the radio receiver and pulled it to his mouth. The coil cord wobbled back and forth in the sunlight, and steam rose up from the trashed hood at the front of the car. "This is Golan! We need backup at in the Temple Mount right now!"

The radio crackled and popped, and a distant voice promised police assistance as soon as possible.

Decker looked at Golan with pleading eyes. "Moshe, half the police are back at the Church of the Holy Sepulchre. We have to do this alone."

Golan knew in his heart the American was right. He said nothing, but reached into the car's gun strongbox between the two seats. He handed him a Jericho 941 semi-automatic pistol used by the Israeli Defense Forces. "When we go back in there, fire like you're shooting at the devil himself!"

Decker checked the mag and Golan slammed his foot down on the throttle and steered back into the alley.

*

Riley Carr screamed in pain as the Austrian's boot came smashing down on his fingers once again. It turned out that Bloch was an artist in the production of pain and was switching the target of his rage from Riley's right hand to his left hand in a brutal assault of alternating agony.

The Australian's screams echoed out across the Western Wall Plaza and dissipated as they rippled out over the Temple Mount; if he thought holding on with both hands was tough, then he had just entered into a whole new world of pain. Somewhere below him, he heard Kurz and his men open fire a second time. They had gone crazy with the automatic weapons a few seconds ago and for half a heartbeat he had thought he was the target and almost let go in fear.

Then he had realised they were shooting at someone else, and now they were doing it again. The target of their assault seemed to be in a vehicle approaching at speed from one of the roads opposite the plaza. Hanging on with his left hand now, as Bloch prepared to smash his right hand, he craned his neck down to the right just in time to see what looked like something from a wrecker's yard burst into the courtyard and drive straight at Kurz and his men.

Decker and Golan fired on Bloch now. He was an easy target on top of the wall and he dived down and flattened himself to get out of the sight.

Knowing that Kurz was distracted, Riley breathed a sigh of relief but it was short-lived. As Bloch got back to his feet and smashed down on his right hand he only just managed to bring his other hand up and grab the ledge in time to stop himself falling to his death.

The Austrian was getting angry and manoeuvring his huge bulk in order to smash both hands at once. Riley felt the Angel slip down to the bottom of his trouser leg now and had an idea. Used to hanging off the ledge with one hand, he leaned down and lifted his leg at the same time to decrease the distance between his hand and the bottom of his pants and then took hold of the Angel. In a flash, he used his considerable muscle strength to swing the heavy gold Angel up and smash it into Bloch's right kneecap.

The Austrian howled in pain and collapsed back onto top of the wall. Riley risked hurling the Angel on the top beside Bloch so he could use both his arms to haul himself back up over the edge, and crashed onto the narrow space at the top of the wall.

Rolling to a stop, he leaped to his feet just in time to see Bloch snatch up the Angel and use it as a weapon, holding it firmly in his meaty hand and waving it in Riley's face as a warning not to come any closer. He began to move back toward the internal stone steps that led down to the interior of the Temple Mount, but the Australian saw he was limping badly and knew how to exploit a weakness.

He lunged forward, ducking to avoid the Angel as Bloch swung it at him in an entirely predictable move. Riley was younger and fitter, with years of Australian SAS Regiment training under his belt, and now they were fighting on an even surface he knew he had the advantage.

"How's it feel fighting mano-a-mano, you old bastard?"

Bloch said nothing, but continued to make his way toward the steps.

"Cat got your tongue?"

Now, the Austrian made another tactical error. Instinctively he turned to check where the top of the steps were. He had to do it to stop himself falling down the staircase, but Riley knew he had to do it too, and now the young corporal made his move.

Powering his leg up and landing it in the man's sternum, he drove Bloch backwards down the steps. He released the Angel and Riley watched as he tumbled and crashed all the way to the bottom. When he hit the ground, he staggered to his feet and aimed his weapon at Riley one more time, but then his radio crackled.

Snatching it from his belt, he nodded and turned to see Israeli police closing in from every direction, their guns raised. Bloch turned into a ghost and slipped into the shadows of the wall before darting into a dingy gateway and disappearing out of sight.

Riley picked up the Angel and watched the policemen give chase. "Good luck with that," he said, and dusted himself down. Getting up off his knees, he turned to walk back along the wall when he saw two armed Israeli soldiers standing on the wall and walking toward him with their guns raised into the aim.

"G'day guys!" he said cheerily. "I was just about to call you."

"Don't move," they said.

And he didn't.

12

Riley Carr cracked open the window and a warm breeze blew into the small hotel room. Decker, Selena, Charlie and Moshe Golan were all gathered in a small semi-circle around the Angel of God which the Yasam officer had placed on the desk at the foot of the bed. Moshe Golan had let Riley out of his prison cell an hour earlier after a call from the British Embassy who had intervened after Charlie called Paul Sumner back in Thames House. Getting the Angel out of police custody had required even more finesse.

Now, they were all together in the quiet room, their attention very much captivated by the strange seraph on the desk. Its smooth golden curves glowed in the gentle sunlight and gave the icon an aura of almost being alive.

"Now we're not being shot at you can really admire the thing," Riley said. "She's prettier than a peach, all right."

Selena silently agreed. While Riley was getting to know the ins and outs of the Israeli justice system, she had been in the Bikur Cholim Hospital having her wounds assessed and treated. Thankfully, the bullet had only grazed her, and her concussion was minor. They had wanted to keep her in for observation, but she had insisted on checking out and getting the team back together after what had been a catastrophic start to the mission.

"What do you think, Lena?" Riley repeated.

Too mesmerised to answer, she was captivated by the icon standing on the wooden desk. A solemn face turned to heaven, its hands clasped together in prayer and stretching around its back in delicate arcs, two intricate wings with the most detailed feathers she had ever seen cast in metal.

"So what do we do now?" Decker asked. He ran his hand through his hair absent-mindedly, as if the act of doing so would spark a solution to his question.

"We wait until Yitzhak Dahan arrives," Golan said. His tone indicated that was the end of the matter, but Decker had a question.

"And who might that be?"

Selena sighed. "He's the Director of the Rockefeller Museum, am I right Mr Golan?"

"You are. It's only proper than he takes over from here. David Herzog was, after all, commissioned to deliver the Angel to the museum here in Jerusalem."

"Wait just a minute, mate," Riley said, turning and walking over to Golan. "I nearly got my clangers blown off chasing this thing down and bringing her back here to the hotel. You think I'm going to just watch as you hand it over to some bloke, just like that?"

Golan drew himself up to his full six-foot frame and squared up to Riley. "I am an officer in the Yasam, Mr Carr, and you are a tourist in this city with zero jurisdiction. If I say we wait and hand the statue over to the director of the Rockefeller, than is exactly what we will do."

"Is it now?"

Decker raised a hand to stop Riley going toe to toe with Golan. "Stand down, soldier. He's only doing his job."

"And I'm only doing mine," Selena said. The three men turned to see she was now holding the statue up in her arms and had turned it upside down to inspect the base in the light.

"What are you doing with that?" Golan said. "Put it down at once."

"I don't know what this is," Selena said, totally ignoring him. "But it's not gold."

"Not gold?" Golan said, shocked. "What are you talking about? Texts about the Angel are famous for their descriptions of the gold's purity. Some say it comes direct from heaven."

"I doubt that very strongly," Selena said. She tapped the base and then pushed her fingertip right through it. A tiny cloud of dust puffed up when she pulled her finger back out again. "Unless there's a plentiful supply of balsa wood in heaven."

"Balsa wood?" Decker said. "Just what the hell is going on?"

"It's too heavy for balsa wood, Lena," Riley said. "I had to carry that little bastard around the back streets so I should know."

Selena continued to pick a hole in the base. "The statue is gold, but the base is balsa wood and there's a narrow cavity inside."

"You must stop right there!" Golan said. "We must wait until Director Dahan is here."

"Oops, too late," she said, and the balsa wood base popped out onto the floor. She held it up to the light and a faint smile appeared on her lips. "There's something inside!"

Decker, Riley and Golan exchanged a concerned look. The Yasam officer was first to break the tense silence. "I don't think this is right. If what you say is true, and the Angel of God was located in a chamber beneath Calvary Hill... then there's a good chance whatever is inside the statue could be a world-changing piece of history. We should wait until there is at least one official from the museum, or even the government before we proceed."

"Don't be such a sook, Moshe," Riley said. "You afraid you're going to end up like those dudes at the end of Raiders of the Lost Ark or something?"

Golan gave him a look. "They were Nazis, so… no."

Selena pulled out a piece of paper from inside the Angel and after setting the icon back on the desk she held it up to the window and gasped. "It has some writing on it but it's tiny."

"So get a magnifying glass on the bastard and see what it says!"

Decker gave the young Australian soldier a disapproving look. "Do you have to swear every time your mouth opens?"

"I abso-fuckin-lutely do not, mate."

Decker laughed and shook his head. "I might sound crazy but I'm glad you're on my side, Riley."

"What does it say?" Golan said, glancing at his watch. "The director should be here already."

Selena rolled her eyes and gave a long, deep sigh of despair. "I can't read Hebrew, but…"

They all leaned in. "What?" Decker asked. "What does it say?"

"I'm guessing this is a takeaway falafel menu, Moshe?"

She handed the paper to Moshe Golan and his face dropped from excitement to sadness. He looked like he'd been crushed by a lead weight. "Yes," he said. "This is just a takeout menu for a local falafel company."

They all turned to Riley.

"Well I didn't fuckin' put it in there!" he protested.

"We guessed that much," Charlie said.

"And it's my hypothesis that they didn't have falafel takeouts in the time of Moses," Selena said, glaring at

Riley. "So when the hell did Kurz have the time to switch it?"

Riley's face lit up like a Christmas tree as he put the pieces together. "Bastard must have done it when he crawled out the trashed van. It crashed into the falafel stand in the market! Son. Of. A. Bitch. I actually admire the bloke."

"For *fuck's* sake," Charlie said.

Golan's phone rang. He raised it to his ear and walked out the room.

Riley shook his head. "I thought it was odd when he never gave chase after I snatched it off him. Thought maybe I'd just knocked the wind out of his sails a bit too hard when I planted my boot in his guts. He never had time to tell the rest of his men that he'd switched it so they must have just kept after me thinking I still had it."

"Either that or they just wanted to kill you," Decker said.

"I know how they bloody feel!" Selena said. "How could you have let this happen, Riley? They could be anywhere now."

Moshe returned from the hall and slipped his phone into his pocket. "Not anywhere, no. That was my boss. We think we know where they might have gone."

After a long pause, Decker said: "If that was your boss, then what did he just tell you?"

"I'm not sure I can say."

Selena sighed. "This is getting ridiculous, Moshe. Why not?"

13

Golan looked in two minds about the situation and gripped in chin in his hand for a few moments as if to support his head while he made such a difficult decision. He shook his head in answer to a question he had silently posed himself, paced up and down the hotel room and then finally blew out a long, stressful sigh. "Yes, it's true that the call I just took was with my boss back at Yasam HQ, and yes, it's true they have run some enquiries and come up with a name."

"So what's the problem?"

"The problem is the name belongs to someone who is located outside of Israel, and that is not within the Yasam's remit. The information must be passed to Mossad, and only then can a decision be taken about deploying Israeli forces."

"But my team are ready to go right now, Mr Golan," Selena said. "And let's not forget that I am representing the London Museum of Archaeology, an institution formally connected with the Rockefeller Museum right here in Jerusalem."

"I understand, but…"

"And let's not forget that it was a joint dig involving both these museums that was just raided by Kurz and his thugs. The items in that dig, including the Angel of God are to be shared between the two institutions for the public good of both nations."

Golan sucked his teeth and started to pace up and down the room once more.

"Jeez, mate, you'll wear a groove in that carpet in a minute."

"It's very complicated," the Israeli said. "A decision like this is above my pay grade."

"The way I see it, it's perfectly simple," Decker put in. "The LMA has some kind of a right to exhibit the statue, if not now then at some point in the future, but now it's been stolen by a bunch of crazies, am I right?"

Riley dropped down onto the bed and stretched out his full six-foot two inch frame. "Bang on target so far, mate."

Golan made do with a sorry nod.

"So far, so good," Decker continued. "So, we have a right to pursue the original contents of the statue and we have the means to do so right now. Any delay could easily mean none of us ever sees what was inside, so waiting for the chain of command to cross over to Mossad and then issue orders seems like a bad plan to me. Our team has a plane, and all the necessary skills to retrieve the Angel of God's secret for the LMA."

"And the Rockefeller," Golan said. He sounded like he was starting to warm to the idea.

"And the Rockefeller, indeed," a look of hope began to flicker in Selena's eyes for the first time since Golan had returned.

"So what do you think, Moshe?" Decker said. A cautious smile broke on his lips. "Want to come with us and find out what your statue was hiding?"

Golan's face grew serious. "And also get my revenge?"

"That too."

The Israeli was silent for a few seconds. In that way of his, he folded into himself and turned away from them. He paced over to the window and they watched as he squeezed his hands, full of stress and uncertainty, and bring them up to rub his neck. Then, his body language seemed to change. He straightened up and grew taller, and his arms dropped down to his sides. He pulled his gun and checked the mag and then slid it back inside the holster. When he turned to face them all the anxiety was gone and now his worn, tanned face hosted an expression of steely determination. "You say you have your own plane?"

Decker and Selena exchanged a smile, but Riley was the first to speak. "Thank fuck for that, mate, and welcome to the mayhem."

"Thanks, I think…"

Decker said, "You said you had a name?"

Golan nodded. "We used CCTV to trace the man called Kurz back to a hotel in the city's west. Once we had that we were able to trace what emails he was sending out of the hotel."

Charlie's eyes lit up. Now Golan was talking his language. "And?"

"They traced the email account to an ISP in Austria. Further investigations revealed that the ISP belongs to a woman, an Austrian national. Here."

He held up a grainy black and white image of a woman with blonde hair. She was tall, and good-looking but the details of her face were obscured by the long range from which the picture had been taken. "Do you recognize her?"

"Not me," Riley said.

Selena shrugged. "Nor me."

"What is this, Moshe?" Charlie said. "What's going on?"

Moshe Golan sucked his teeth and put the photo back in his pocket. They all heard the sound of the clock ticking on the wall. He took a long time before making a reply and didn't seem to mind how much of their time he wasted. "This woman is Dr Ursula Moser. Does her name ring any bells?"

"Wait a minute," Selena said. "Hasn't she got something to do with a church?"

Moshe gave a brief nod. "That's right, she's a theologian who runs the Church of the Sacred Light. She's a serious recluse, rarely venturing outside the confines of her compound in the Austrian Alps. She has spent a considerable part of the last few years concentrating her efforts in various African countries, but as I say, she spends most of her time at their headquarters in the Austrian Alps. Here."

"And the coincidence just keep on coming." Selena said.

Golan looked confused. "I don't understand."

"Earlier today, the man that approached me – Kurz… he told me he was with the church."

"Looks like Moser's pulling his strings," Riley said.

"Right," Golan growled. "And Bloch too. He met her back when she was trying to establish the church in Angola. He was the muscle that kept local warlords out of the picture. Bloch is an operator. He gets things done. Dirty things no one else would touch."

"I don't like coincidences like that," Decker said.

"Me neither, mate," said Riley. "Looks like this Moser hired Kurz and his crew to get the Angel and take us all out."

"Anyone above Moser?" Decker asked.

"Maybe. The Church's biggest donor is heavily veiled behind layers of bureaucracy and what looks a lot like money laundering practices but it looks a lot like it might be coming from Hagen Global Industries."

Selena was ashen.

"Lena, what's the matter?" Decker said.

"I know that name," she said almost in a whisper. "My father knew Tor Hagen many years ago. If I recall correctly, he has something to do with biological science."

Golan nodded. "You're right. Hagen Global Industries is the baby of a Norwegian recluse by the name of Tor Hagen. His specialist field was originally DNA sequencing but now HGI's tentacles stretch all over the world. Wherever there's any cutting-edge science, Tor Hagen has an interest in it, and most often a controlling interest."

"And where do we find this guy?" Charlie said, still struggling with the bottle of mineral water.

"No one knows. He has homes all over the world, but he moves around so much that no one ever really knows where he is, not even the Mossad."

"That's a great start."

"But Moser's our lead," Selena said. "We know she's the one who's been pulling Kurz's strings, so we need to start there."

"Right," Golan said.

"Wait just a minute," Decker said. "Wasn't this Hagen guy on the cover of Time recently?"

"Not recently," Golan corrected, "but yes, Tor Hagen was featured once by Time a few years ago. It was something to do with his research into sequencing crop genomes, but as I say, he is involved in anything to do with science."

Selena looked confused. "I read that article, but the thing that stands out to me now is that when he was asked about religion, he said he was a strict atheist."

Riley was still on the bed, struggling to make the remote work. He looked up for a moment and said, "So what's the problem with that? Lots of people are atheists."

Selena rolled her eyes. "Oh, do keep up, Riley. Moshe just told us Hagen Global Industries is the biggest donor to the Church of the Sacred Light."

"Ah… gotcha."

"Precisely," Decker said, frowning. "Why would a committed scientific atheist be diverting serious levels of financial funding to a pretty far out religious organization?"

Golan shook his head. "You're right, it doesn't make sense – not unless he's just using them to evade tax or launder money, maybe."

"I'm not buying that," Decker said. "There's a specific connection between Moser's church and HGI, and I'm thinking that when we know what it is a lot of this is going to start making sense."

They all agreed. "So what's next?" Riley said.

"First, we need Diana," said Selena. "She's the best hope we have of working out whatever was inside the Angel."

"Where is she?" Charlie said.

"Portugal."

"And you say this Moser is based in Austria?" said Decker.

Golan gave a confident nod. "Of that there is no doubt. The Church of the Sacred Light's headquarters is in the mountains above Innsbruck."

"My parents used to take us skiing there most seasons," Selena said, her face glowing for a moment at the pleasant memory. "I know the city well."

"This isn't a skiing holiday, Professor Moore," Golan said firmly. "We're going there to find the criminals who desecrated the Holy Church and the Temple Mount, murdered innocent people and stole a sacred artefact."

"You hardly need to tell me that, Mr Golan," she said sharply. "I was blasted across the chamber by one of their grenades and nearly killed by them, and I'm presuming one of these people has my father as well."

Golan was suitably chastened. "I'm sorry, but you shall have your revenge."

"I'm not looking for revenge, Moshe," Selena said quietly. "I want the contents of the Angel of God returned to its rightful owners and if we can bring Moser and the others to justice then so much the better for it."

"Of course," Golan said.

"Now," Selena continued confidently. "Mitch, ready the Avalon for a flight to Innsbruck, please. Riley and Charlie go and get some supplies for the flight, and Moshe can make sure things are all clear with the Austrians. In the meantime, I'm going to telephone Diana in Porto and ask her to meet us there at her earliest convenience."

"I see you know how to lead," Golan said.

Selena looked at them all for a moment. "Well, what are you all waiting for? We're flying to Austria within the hour. Chop chop!"

14

Innsbruck, Austrian Alps

"I always wanted to come here," said Riley. "I used to ski in the Australian Alps and that's great, but nothing like this. You were pretty lucky that your parents used to come here, Lena."

"There is nothing like this where I'm from, either," Diana said. She had arrived on a commercial flight an hour earlier and waited for the Avalon with a cup of coffee and an old text book on ancient Hebrew.

They were driving a hired car along the south bank of the River Inn as they headed toward the Grand Hotel. The flight was quiet and uneventful, unless you counted Moshe Golan's complaints about the turbulence. Now, they had reached the oldest part of the city and the streets grew narrower. Old cobblestone squares and clock towers huddled beneath a Persian-blue sky as they cruised past pedestrians and tourists, none of whom had the vaguest idea about what was at stake tonight.

Selena sighed. "God, I hope Dad's all right," she said absent-mindedly.

Decker didn't know what to say. From his position behind the wheel he was able to check the rear view mirror and scan the faces of the others in the car and it looked like they were all thinking along the same lines. They all knew Atticus Moore was involved in this business to some degree, but exactly how was an unknown factor. Reassuring Selena felt like the right thing to do, but it was hard when he had no idea what had happened to her father, and she knew it.

Another half-kilometre passed beneath them, and eventually the former Marine said, "Whatever's going on, we're going to find out."

She sighed, but made no other response.

"No news is good news, right?" Riley said.

Selena tried to smile, and Riley held her hand. "I know Atticus, and I know he's all right."

"I hope you're right," she said at last.

Diana gave her a reassuring smile. "We'll get him back, Lena."

They passed through the small city before leaving it behind and heading further east toward the smaller settlements of Rum, Thaur and Absam. Turning left off the main road they began to ascend up into the foothills of the Alps. Lined on either side by tall, black pine trees, the road quickly narrowed and began to twist and turn as it snaked its way deeper into the Austrian mountains.

Traffic was light, restricted mostly to expensive saloons ferrying tourists from their ski lodges to an evening of sightseeing and coffee-drinking in Innsbruck. Higher now, and the snow was heavier on the ground but the sky was still blue and dry. A setting sun far in the distant west was painting the peaks a bright coral pink and the digital temperature gauge on the instrument panel was showing minus twelve.

Decker turned the heater up and flicked on the radio as he hit the gas and overtook a dawdling Fiat. Glancing at the dashboard clock, he knew he would be dark soon, and turned on the headlights. The drive had been unusually relaxing, and the awesome beauty of the surrounding mountains had made it feel almost like a weekend break, except for the fact that Selena's father was still missing and the Angel of God's ancient secret had been stolen.

"We're almost here," Selena said. Her voice was sharp and cold in the silence of the car. She looked up from the screen of her phone and gave Decker the ghost of a smile. "Just up ahead on the left."

"In that case we'd better pull up here somewhere," he said. "There's no need to let the bastards know we're about to give them a house call, right?"

They all agreed, and Decker slowed the Audi, searching for somewhere they could leave the vehicle without a member of the public seeing it and reporting to the local police as stolen or broken down. Another few hundred meters passed before he noticed a side road twisting off into the twilight in the east. "We'll park her in there."

He indicated right and pulled over into the side of the road. Killing the engine and lights, the cosy, warm atmosphere they had all gotten used to since the airport was gone and replaced with a new cold and the gathering dusk.

"We need to get a move on," Golan said. "We don't want to be blundering about up here in the dark. One false step and you could go down a crevasse or over the side of a ridge."

"Thanks for that image," Diana said.

"There's the first security perimeter," Golan said, scanning the snowfield between the forest and the compound. "That fence running just beyond the trees."

"Let me see," Decker said, and Golan passed him the monocular. He saw a low stone wall around a meter high with another meter of balustrade fencing on top of it. He smiled. "That's not a security perimeter. I broke through tougher than that to steal apples from the neighbor's farm when I was a kid."

"May I?"

Decker passed the monocular to Selena and made another check of the area behind them to make sure they hadn't been tailed by anyone. It still looked clear, with no sign of any human activity except the lonely, winding trail of their own footprints in the snow, snaking back to the clearing in the forest where he had parked the Audi.

Selena readjusted the monocular for comfort and sighed. Her breath plumed in the freezing mountain air. "The main building looks a little better protected though, don't you think? Look at that cliff face."

Riley warmed his hands with his breath and stamped his boots on the ground to get the blood flowing. "Let's have a butcher's, Lena."

He took the monocular and studied the main compound. "She's right, chief."

Decker had a second look. The sprawling compound was nestled into a fold on the western side of the mountain and Selena was right – there was more security in the form of another fence and also on his last count at least half a dozen CCTV cameras. Worse, the whole thing was perched at the top of a flat rock face around twenty meters high.

"To be expected," he said in a calm voice. "And nothing we can't handle, right?"

"What about the cable car on the other side of the mountain?" Diana asked.

Decker shook his head. "Too heavily guarded down at the lower terminus. It's this way or we go home. Everyone cool with that?"

"Absolutely!" Selena said.

"Good," Decker said flatly. "Now you and Diana go back to the car with Charlie. Moshe, go with them."

"What?"

"You heard me. Neither Selena, Diana or Charlie have the sort of military training or experience needed to get into a place like this without giving us away or getting hurt, and I'm not going to risk their lives just so we can find out a bit more about Fräulein Moser."

"I'm not going to sit here and do nothing while you have all the fun!" Golan protested. "I'm on this mission now, just as much as you are!"

"Me too!" Charlie said.

"I never said you were going to do nothing," Decker said. "We need a diversion, and you guys are it." He stopped and studied the architecture of the building for a few more seconds before turning to the Australian. "What do you reckon – twenty minutes?"

"Make it thirty, mate. First the rock face, then there'll be ice on the roof."

"You guys go back to the car and in twenty minutes' time I want you to pull up to the main gate and create some sort of a fuss."

"Fine, then take this," Golan said, and handed Decker his Jericho pistol.

As the darkness gathered around them, Decker and Riley made their way up the slope that led to the bottom of the rock face. The freezing twilight offered just enough light for them to see the path ahead but was dark enough for them to slip into the shadows if one of the guards happened to peer over the edge.

When they reached the face, Mitch Decker looked up at the climb ahead and blew out a deep breath. "Looks a lot tougher from this angle."

Riley nodded. "It's a piece of piss, mate. Trust me."

15

Decker once again craned his neck up at the cliff face and scratched the back of his neck.

"It's at least fifty feet, maybe more."

"I'd say more like sixty," Riley said. "Better get started."

Decker turned to face the young Aussie. "But we don't have any equipment, not even in the car. We'll have to find another way in."

"Another way in? There *is* no other way in, mate! You saw the place – all the other approaches are covered by electric fences and armed guards."

"You can't be serious? I know you're half-crazy but this is insane!"

"It's my way or the high way, mate."

Decker looked up at the cliff face once again and shook his head with disbelief, not at the sheer scale of the job ahead of him, but because he was even considering doing it.

"Ever done soloing before?"

"Huh?"

"Free solo climbing. Climbing up on your own and without any equipment."

"Not really," Decker said. "Some stuff in basic training but not mountain climbing without ropes, if that's what you're talking about."

Riley rubbed his hands together and warmed them with this breath. "It is indeed what I am talking about, me old mate."

"I'm not liking where this is going, Riley." He locked his eyes on him. "Not at *all*."

"Yeah, it's a tough gig but we gotta do it. Normally you'd go up in advance with ropes and clean the route, but we haven't got time for that."

"Or ropes."

Riley chuckled and had already started to study the climb to the top of the cliff. "Or the ropes, no."

A gust of wind buffeted Decker and he stepped in closer to the cliff face to find some cover. "This is crazy."

"Not really – it's not that high. We can free climb twenty meters no worries at all. We'd need chalk powder on a hot day but not in this."

"Chalk powder?"

"Dry the sweat, mate." He clapped Decker on the shoulder and laughed. "We'll be lucky if we can even feel our fingers after ten minutes in this so we'd better hurry up."

"Why not use gloves?"

"No gloves. You need to feel your way up a face like this."

Decker followed the Australian with caution. He was a trained marine, but the days of slogging through muddy ditches and getting shot at were starting to become a distant memory now. He was older, and a little chunkier. Besides, he was a pilot, not a Special Forces operative. Then there were the conditions to consider. The freezing cold temperature had numbed his hands and fingers, plus the wind had started to get up and was cutting across him from the valley to the south. He knew how easy it would be to make a mistake and there was nothing below him but a broken back, and that was if his luck kicked in.

Looking up, the young Australian seemed to have no such concerns. He was actually humming some kind of guitar solo as he located every crack and ledge and effortlessly pulled his tough, lean body up the rock face, meter by meter.

It took the older American a little longer, but he was determined not to be outshone by the younger man.

"You all right back there, grandad?" Riley called down.

"Hey, I've got a lot more experience to carry than you do."

Riley laughed. "I'll remember that one, pops."

"At least I'm old enough to use a razor."

"I have stubble, mate, and it ain't gray like yours."

Decker gave up as he watched Riley climb up over the edge of the rock face. He was out of sight for a second and the American was alone on the cliff. The wind howled and he almost lost his grip. It was safe to say he'd had enough but then Riley's beaming face appeared just above him.

"Crikey – you still down there, mate?"

"I'm almost done."

"Well listen, I'll give you a hand up but just let me go grab a shower while you make the last meter."

"Asshole," Decker muttered under his breath.

Riley grabbed his hand and pulled him over the edge of the rock face.

Decker collapsed on his back in the snow and took a few seconds to get his breath back and slow his heart. "Don't ever ask me to do that again."

"No worries, mate. Maybe we'll ask the next villain we have to attack to put a stair lift in or something."

"You're a real funny guy, Riley."

They got to their feet and started to march across the snow toward the institute. Only seconds had passed when Riley peered into the falling snow and yelled at Decker.

"Get down!"

A man in the snow fired his weapon in the half-light, the noise of the rounds dampened strangely by the snowy mist all around them. Decker and Riley dived for cover behind the trunks of a small clump of pine trees near the edge of the cliff.

Decker fell first, collapsing down into a snowy void like a brick dropped from a bridge. A look of terror crossed the face of the gunman as he went down next, and then the hole sucked Riley down next.

*

Ursula Moser warmed her hands in front of a sumptuous, crackling fire for a moment or two and then turned to face the tanned, chiselled man sitting in the chair beside her. He did not return her gaze, but instead stared at a small metal object she had just given to him. It shone dully in the light of the fire and held his attention in an almost magnetic way.

"Well, Dr Marchand? I presume you're able to deliver on your promise and tell me the meaning of this object and what the code written on it says?"

The French archaeologist ignored her and continued to stare at the object. "And you're certain this was found inside the Angel of God?"

"Very."

"Incredible. I've never seen anything like it, Fraulein Moser. Never in my life! And I am the man who discovered some of the most mysterious missing treasures in history!"

"The high opinion you obviously have of yourself will mean nothing to me unless you are able to tell me what the code says on the side of this key."

"As I said – I have never seen anything like it before. Whatever it is, it's written in some kind of pictogram style. Not my field I'm afraid, but I believe one side of the key could be giving a location, and the other side might be some sort of prayer."

"A prayer?"

He shrugged. "I wish I could be of more help."

"But it's definitely a key?" Moser said.

Marchand nodded, as he held up the tiny piece of metal. It glinted in the soft light of the institute's study. There was a flat area on one end that resembled the bow of a key, and then a well-crafted shank which was snapped off a couple inches away from the head. "I mean, what else could it be?"

"Exactly," Moser said, her voice drifting into the sound of the fire. "It's a key, Dr Marchand – a key that will lead us to the Ark of the Covenant."

"But we need someone who can translate this code. He won't be happy if we fail."

Moser gave him a sharp look. "We're not going to fail, Henri."

"You seem very confident."

"We all have our own agendas," she said coolly. And she was right. Tor Hagen might be searching for the Ark, and she coveted it too, but if she was right, then there was something else hiding with the biblical relic, something that she wanted to rescue even more than the Ark itself.

*

All three men had been swallowed by an enormous crevasse twisting deep inside the glacier. Decker led the way to the bottom, smashing into the icy walls as he tumbled helplessly downward. He scratched at the blue ice in an attempt to slow his fall but it was too smooth and hard. A few seconds later he crashed into a ledge of snow and ice a few meters from the bottom of the crevasse.

The gunman landed on a ledge several meters above Decker, but Riley got the short end of the stick and went straight to the very bottom, cracking his head on the ice and passing out in the darkness below.

Decker took a second to get his bearings. His head was still spinning with the fall and the impact of the abrupt crash landing on the icy ledge. He sat up straight and scrambled back from the side of the narrow ledge until he was as safe as he could get and then he called down to his friend.

"Riley?"

Silence.

He craned his neck up and looked at the gunman. All he could see from his vantage point was the man's arm dangling over the side of the ledge he had landed on. There was no movement so he guessed he'd gotten knocked out by the fall as well.

"Riley, are you okay?"

The icy wind howled over the top of the crevasse high above him.

He punched the ice on the ledge. "Dammit all!"

Decker had read about a man, in Austria of all places, who had tumbled inside a glacier not far from Innsbruck. He'd survived a week in the dark and cold before mountain rescue services found him, and that was without an armed gunman down there trying to kill him.

He heard the sound of Riley moaning down in the darkness below. "Riley!"

"Bugger me with a pitchfork, that *hurt*."

Decker grinned. "Good to have you back, you silly bastard."

"What the hell just happened?"

"You might be concussed so just take it easy. We fell down a crevasse. Looks like another twenty meters to climb if we want to see another sunrise."

"Can't believe I was so stupid."

"We were under fire."

"Talking of which – where's the bastard with the gun."

"Look up." His words echoed in the icy darkness.

Riley stared up into the narrow void and saw the gunman's arm dangling over the ledge. "Is he dead?"

"I hope so, but I don't think so. He probably hit his head on the way down like you and knocked himself out. I guess I was the lucky one this time."

Riley got to his feet and squinted into the darkness at the bottom of the crevasse. "Sometimes if you walk along the bottoms of these places you can just walk right out of them."

Decker's breath clouded in the air in front of his face. "And this time?"

"No such luck. Looks like the only way is up – right past sleeping beauty up there."

"If he wakes up this place is just one giant barrel – and we're the fish."

Riley made no reply, and when Decker leaned over the ledge he saw the Australian was already climbing back up the crevasse. Five meters up, he was holding himself with a three-finger grip wedged into a split in the ice. "I could be on the verandah now, sinking a tube... getting that scotch fillet just right."

Decker laughed, but a glance up at the gunman's limp arm quickly sobered him back up again. "I hear you, man."

The Australian finally made it up to Decker's ledge and crawled up over the edge. His fingers were blue and numb, and blood was starting to coagulate around a hefty graze on the side of head.

"Is that where you hit yourself?"

"No, I just had a really bad itch."

Decker gave him a sardonic look. "Is this the famous Aussie sense of humor?"

"That's rich coming from the land that gave us Amy Schumer."

The American shrugged. "Please accept my apologies."

Far above his position at the bottom of the crevasse, Riley was able to get a better look at how to climb back to safety. His eyes lingered on the dangling arm. "Gotta hope the bastard is dead, I reckon."

"It's still risky."

"We've got to climb right past him, Mitch. There's no other way."

Decker gave a resigned nod and Riley warmed his hands. "All right, let's get this pig in the truck."

"Huh?"

Riley didn't answer, but wedged his fingers into another crack in the ice and pushed himself up until his right boot was on small shelf in the crevasse wall. "Just follow what I do, and don't look down."

"Why do you keep saying that?"

They climbed ten meters up the ice wall and approached the ledge harboring the gunman. He was almost close enough for Riley to reach out and touch when they saw the arm move a few inches.

"Fuck," Riley said.

"What is it?"

"Bastard's not dead, that's for sure."

"Oh, shit."

Decker saw the man's arm twitch and then they both heard him groaning in pain as he slowly regained consciousness. "This isn't good."

"Tell me about it!" Riley said.

The man clambered up from his position until he was sitting with his back against the ice wall. For a few seconds he was still again, and then he leaned forward and peered over the edge of the crevasse. Seeing Riley and Decker within arm's reach, his eyes opened in surprise. He raised his submachine gun and aimed it at them, but Riley was close enough to reach out and grab the weapon's muzzle before he started firing.

The man resisted, wrenching the gun back and trying to turn the barrel into Riley's body as he prepared to rip him in half with some devastating automatic fire. The Australian was a move ahead and powered a left hook into the man's right temple, blasting his head back into the ice wall.

As the man's skull cracked against the blue ice, he squeezed his gun-hand and pulled the trigger back. The muzzle flashed in the darkness of the crevasse and raked a neat line of holes in the ice on the far side. Riley cursed, pushing the gun's barrel back with the back of his right arm while delivering a second hefty whack to the man's jaw, this time knocking him out. As he slumped back down on his ledge, Riley snatched the weapon and heaved himself beside the unconscious gunman.

"Come on, mate," he said. "We're almost outta here."

16

Decker and Riley took a few seconds until they were sure the coast was clear again and emerged from the crevasse. They were almost at the institute's main complex now and sprinted through the half-light until they were at the base of one of the building's walls.

"Up we go, mate," Riley said, and made his hands into a cradle. "I'll give you a leg up, as the vicar said to the verger."

"Can't you take anything seriously?"

"Me? No way, mate! That's the fastest way to the grave. Now get on top of this fuckin' wall."

Decker stepped into Riley's hands and the Australian boosted him up. When he was safely in position he leaned down and gave Riley a hand, pulling him up beside him. It was almost full night now, and their breath formed into thick clouds in front of their faces as they surveyed the building in front of them.

A man walked below them in the courtyard they had just crossed. He had a rifle slung over his shoulder, and they both ducked down to avoid him. He turned and walked back toward a smaller building they guessed was some sort of security office and then began to crouch-walk along the roof-line once again. Both men knew what losing their footing at this height would mean, and the ice encrusted on the apex of the roof made slipping and falling even more likely than usual.

They made their way along the roof-line until they reached the section where the cantilevered extension joined with the main part of the building and some metal steps ran up to the next floor. Somewhere below them in the front courtyard they heard the sound of men talking and laughing.

Lowering themselves down again until their profiles merged with the roof, Decker peered down to his left and saw two more men with rifles over their shoulders as they lit cigarettes. One of them waved the match out and tossed it into a snow-bank at the side of the circular drive and then wandered down toward the main gate.

"Lena's bang on time, mate."

Decker nodded but said nothing.

They made fast progress up the circular, metal steps and were on the next level of the compound within a few short seconds. Dark now, and with the full moon rising above the mountain ridge-line to the east, they knew they were harder to see and this gave them the confidence to move faster.

They reached the top of the steps and found themselves on the top floor of the compound, standing on a balcony that ran the length of the main building on its northern side. The windows were all shut firmly against the bitter cold, but a door at the end of the decking promised better results. Decker could see from the chairs, tables and ashtrays that this was a space used by the inhabitants to come for a break and a smoke, and he had a hunch the door might be in such regular use that it would be unlocked.

He was right, and breathed a sigh of relief. Forcing a window or door could easily trigger an alarm and then everything would come crashing down in a hurry. They stepped inside out of the cold and emerged into what looked like some sort of canteen area.

The Church of the Sacred Light was a secretive institution but he guessed the headquarters building would staff at least a hundred people during business hours, so a canteen made sense. Luckily, the late hour meant there was no one around, but he noticed that the interior lights were on. He walked over to the electric kettle and touched the side of it with the back of his fingers.

"And?" Riley said.

The American nodded. "Still warm, so someone's on the night shift."

"Maybe that cowbag Moser herself – or even Kurz."

Maybe, thought Decker. He almost wished it were true so he could dish out a little thank you for what he had done to Selena beneath the Church of the Holy Sepulchre back in Jerusalem. He noticed on the wall above the kettle a fire-safety plan of the building. Neither man spoke much German, but both could work out what the big red arrow pointing to the canteen meant: SIE SIND HIER.

"You are here," Riley whispered. "Gotta love German efficiency, mate. They've even given us a free map to help us kick their arses."

Decker sighed as the Australian ripped the plan off the wall of the small kitchen area. "They're Austrians."

"Yeah, whatever."

They studied the plan and tried to work out where various rooms were using their high school German. "This way," Decker said at last.

Checking through the glass panel of an internal fire door, Decker pushed it open to reveal a short corridor running parallel to the balcony outside. On the right, a long window ran the length of the corridor giving spectacular views of the Alps beyond, but both men were more interested in the doors on the left. They opened the last door to reveal a flight of stairs, and silently made their way down to the lower level where the offices were located.

111

Hearing someone approach, they ducked into an empty office. Riley peered through the crack in the door. "It's that bastard Lechner! I can take him out now!"

"Sure, and raise the alarm before we even get what we want."

Riley accepted the point, and after Lechner had jogged up the stairs they moved forward into the management section of the institute. "Over there," Decker said, pointing to a heavy oak door at the end of the corridor. They drew nearer. Screwed to the door's upper panel, a shiny brass plate read: DIREKTOR URSULA MOSER.

"Bingo," Riley said.

Decker slowed his breath and pulled Golan's Jericho from his belt. "Here goes nothing."

He knocked on the door and waited for a response, but none came. He exchanged a look with Riley, who shrugged his shoulders. "Mate, what are we fuckin' waiting for? Go in!"

Decker opened the door and the two men stepped inside the office. It was a large, traditional space in stark contrast to the ultra-postmodern design of the building itself. Soft, studded leather seats positioned either side of a crackling fire gave the impression of someone's private drawing room rather than the nerve center of a religious organization. Across the other side of the room was a hardwood desk the size of a small aircraft carrier. It was covered in papers and telephones, and behind it on the wall was a reproduction of Pompeo Batoni's *The Crucifixion.*

Riley stared up at it and gulped. "Wow."

Decker was drawn to the painting too. The 1762 image struck awe into his heart, and the mood was finished off with the solemn clicking of the large antique grandfather clock standing beside a door leading to an anteroom. He scratched his head and took a step closer to the image. "We need to get out of here."

He made his way over to the desk and started rifling through the papers in no particular order.

"What are you looking for?" Riley asked.

He shrugged. "How the hell should I know? Just anything that might help. We know Kurz took whatever was inside the Angel and we know he brought it here, or at least, we know he was supposed to bring here... wait."

"What is it?" Riley asked.

Decker jabbed a thumb at the anteroom door. "I hear faint voices on the other side of this door."

They opened the door, expecting to find Moser and Kurz, but instead they found themselves in another long corridor. "They're down here."

They walked along the corridor until they reached the top of a large spiral staircase and peering over the edge they saw the woman from Golan's photo with another man they didn't recognize. They were standing at the bottom of the stairs and it looked like their conversation was coming to an end.

"That's Moser, all right," Decker said.

Ursula Moser was not what Decker had expected. The photo had shown almost no detail, and when Golan had first mentioned the name he had, perhaps unfairly, visualized an old, squat woman with short hair and a face like a well-worn leather seat. Instead, she was lithe and fit and much younger – maybe even younger than him. Her blonde hair was tied back in a neat, professional pony tail and two arctic-blue eyes hovered above a slim aquiline nose. The portrait was finished off with the most beautiful cherry lips he had ever seen.

Turning to face Riley, he saw she had made roughly the same impact on the young Australian too, and he had to nudge him gently in the ribs to stop him drooling. "Way outta your league, corporal."

"I think she might be one or two above yours too, mate."

"And you say that like you could get her just like that." Decker emphasized his point by gently snapping his fingers.

"I'm not saying I could get her just like that, mate. Just saying that I'm not sure the juice would be worth the squeeze, if you catch my drift."

Decker rolled his eyes. "Wonder who the dude is?"

"Search me but looks like he might be holding what we're looking for, in which case, it's playtime." He started rummaging around in his bag and pulled out a small device that looked like a camera.

"What the hell is that?"

"My little box of tricks."

"And what's inside it?"

"Well, let me introduce you to a Spectra Laser Mic. It can hear through windows or walls, but I'm just praying it didn't get damaged when I took that tumble into the ice cave."

He quickly set it up, slipped on some headphones and directed the invisible beam down at their conversation. "Hang on – I'm getting something. It's from inside the Angel," he whispered. "The bloke's some kind of archaeologist and he's calling it a key."

Now, another man walked into view and joined Moser and the archaeologist.

"There's that bastard, Kurz," said Riley as he tracked the Austrian gunman across the hallway. He approached Moser and the two of them spoke in German for a few moments. For a second, things started to agitated but then Moser raised her voice and that seemed to settle the matter. The unknown man said goodbye and headed for the entrance at the end of the hall, and Moser and Kurz stepped through the door at the base of the stairs and walked into a large room.

"Bugger it sideways," Riley said. "They're out of the mic's beam We have to get closer."

They made their way down the stairs until they reached the hall. Slipping into the room opposite the room Moser and Kurz were in, Riley readjusted the beam.

Kurz moved over to one of the leather chairs by the fire while Moser walked to the drinks cabinet and momentarily slipped out of sight. Riley heard her dropping ice into some glasses and then the sound of splashing liquid. She returned a few seconds later and walked over to Kurz. Handing him one of the glasses, she sat in the chair opposite him and each took a drink. A moment of peace followed, and then she started to speak.

"We getting all this?" Decker said.

Riley nodded. "It's all being recorded, and Diana speaks some German. With luck we'll get something about what this key does."

"Stand up, and raise your hands."

Decker felt his stomach turn. He looked over his shoulder to see Lechner standing in front of a retracting bookcase. Riley had not heard the Austrian because of the headphones, so Decker tapped him on the shoulder.

"What is it, mate?"

Decker jabbed another thumb behind him, and Riley turned his head slowly. "Aw, fuck it. Secret door's not fair, mate."

Lechner cocked his gun. "Shut up and turn that laser off."

"Easy, mate."

"You know what happens now?"

"Don't tell me," Riley said. "You have ways of making me talk?"

"You're going to meet the Direcktor."

17

To say Ursula Moser was surprised when Lechner marched the two invaders into the room was an understatement. Even Kurz looked shocked and rose from his chair by the fire as the prisoners drew closer.

"What the hell is this?" Moser said.

"Found them through there, listening to everything you were saying on this." He threw the Spectra laser onto the floor and it landed with a smashing sound.

Riley winced. "Jesus, mate! That cost an arm and a leg."

"Silence!" Moser said. "And leave us, Lechner."

Lechner gave Moser Golan's Jericho and left the room.

"These are the men I told you about," Kurz said. "Bloch nearly killed the tall one on the Western Wall."

Moser studied the two men as if they were exhibits in an insect house. "So, you are the men who have been causing me so much trouble. You should have accepted our offer of employment back in Jerusalem. If you had, we could be working together to find the Ark, but now you must die, and I will still find what I'm looking for."

"I like a lady who knows her mind," Decker said.

"And I like a man with sophistication, so that rules you out."

Decker was about to reply when Riley dropped to his knees and pulled the rug out from under Kurz. The Austrian commando fell back and cracked his head on the mantelpiece, giving the Australian enough time to grab his gun and train it on Moser.

The Austrian woman reached for the Jericho on the mantelpiece but was too late.

"Hand it over, Fräulein," Riley said. He was holding Kurz's gun firmly in his right hand and aiming it squarely at Moser's head. "You move an inch and you're dead."

She obeyed and released the gun. It thumped down on the rug.

"Now kick it over to my friend."

The Austrian kicked the pistol across the rug toward Decker, who snatched it up and checked the mag. Clicking it back into place, he gave Riley a quick nod and then aimed the gun at Moser.

"What do you want?" she said icily. "Is this some kind of robbery?"

Riley laughed. "You're the thieves, not us."

Moser glanced at Kurz and gave him a look that would have struck fear into even the toughest of men. She ranted at him in German for a few seconds before Decker hushed her down. "That's enough!"

"It seems my colleague here has been stupid enough to bring you into the heart of our organization. This is most regrettable and he will be dealt with later for it."

"Where is it?" Decker said flatly, still training Golan's gun on her.

"Where is what?" Moser said.

"You're stalling for time, and making me angry," Decker said. "You know what I'm talking about, Direktor Moser. Your man here stole something from inside the Angel of God and replaced it with a falafel menu. Very funny, by the way."

Kurz scowled.

"And we want it back."

She gave a cold, hateful smirk. "Ah, now I understand. You require me to give up the contents of the Angel of God – but what I don't understand is why you think I would do that?"

118

"Because I'll shoot you if you don't," Riley said, He fired a shot into the fire and blasted burning wood and sparks all over the rug. Kurz desperately stamped them out with his boot. "You get the next in between the eyes, Moser. Where's the object?"

"Very well." Moser slipped a small metal object from her pocket and held it in the air in front of their faces. It sparkled in the low light of the fire. "Is this what you seek?"

"I reckon so," Riley said, beckoning with the fingers of his free hand. "Hand it over."

She hesitated. "But do you know what this is?"

Decker frowned. "My first guess is a key."

"Doesn't look too much like a key," Riley said. "The small end looks wrong."

"The bit," Decker said.

"Eh?"

"The other end of the key is called the bit. You hold the bow, then you have the shaft or shank, and then the bit is on the end that goes in the lock."

"Jesus, mate," Riley said with a wry smile. "I bet you're a lot fun at the Trivial Pursuit table."

Decker shrugged. "Uncle was a locksmith."

"Ah."

"It *is* a key, I assure you," Moser said, ending the banter. "It is the object Kurz here found inside the Angel of God."

They heard the door open and Decker and Riley turned and saw the archaeologist. He was in the open doorway, holding a lit cigar in one hand and looked bemused to find them standing in the room holding guns.

"Get in here," Riley said.

"Not so fast," said a voice from behind the archaeologist.

119

Decker was shocked to see Selena and Diana enter the room with a blade at Selena's throat. Kai Bloch pushed them deeper into the room and glared at them. "Drop your guns or I'll slit her throat."

"What is this," Riley asked. "Musical guns?"

Decker stared at the combat knife with dread. The second's hesitation was enough for the others to act. Kurz moved like lightning, smashing the gun from Riley's hand while Moser reached out and pulled an ornament on the mantelpiece. It was a lever, and now the bookcase behind her swivelled open to reveal a secret passageway.

"I found them in a car out the front," Bloch said.

Moser looked concerned. "Was she alone?"

Bloch gave a barely perceptible shake of his head. "Nein. There were two men on their way to the gate house. There was a skirmish and they fled into the forest."

"What's going on, Lena?" Decker asked. "What happened?"

Riley looked at Diana. "Yes, what happened, Di?"

"Moshe, Diana and Charlie walked to the gatehouse to cause the diversion, and when they were gone, and I was alone, this creep turned up."

"Dammit," Decker muttered. "I hope they didn't end up in a goddam crevasse."

"Bring her with us. Hagen will be pleased." Moser said. "Goodbye, Mr Decker."

Mitch Decker wasn't amused by Riley's musical guns comment, but that's what it felt like. As he watched Moser, Kurz and the rest of the thugs dragging Selena into the recess behind the bookcase his mind raced with the agony of what to do next. When the bookcase slammed shut, they both heard a loud gunshot.

"Lena!" Riley said, and rushed forward to heave the bookcase open.

Diana gasped. "They shot her!"

Decker knew better. "They just blew the mechanism that opens the case. No way are we getting through that now."

"Where do you think it leads?"

"They're not going out the front. They don't know where Charlie and the others are for one thing. They could have positioned themselves in any number of tactical locations by now – near their cars, the front entrance. No, they can't risk it. If you ask me, the smart money's on the south slope of the mountain."

"You can't mean the cable car?" Riley said.

Decker shrugged. "Sure, why not? It's a direct line all the way down to the lower terminus in the valley and then a short drive into Innsbruck. If they have a car down there somewhere they'll be out of here and at the airport in no time at all."

Riley picked up his bag of tricks. "So what are we waiting for, mate?"

They sprinted through the institute until they reached the south side of the main building. Through a large window wall beneath the observation deck they were able to see the cable car's wheel house. It was a small, isolated building a few hundred meters away from the main complex, accessible via a flat lawn now covered in a foot of snow. They rushed outside and took cover behind a Volvo parked up beside the main building.

"There they go!" Decker said. He pointed to a small group of people making their way between the institute and the wheel house along a covered walkway.

"I see Lena!" Diana said.

"Me too," said Riley. He curled his hand into a fist and gently thumped the window to his right. "Just can't believe the bastards got her, Mitch."

"We'll get her back."

"You're damned right we will. Bring the snow chains for that car!"

As Decker ripped the chains off one of the Volvo's tires, Riley watched as Moser and the others entered the building and slipped out of sight, and then they heard the sound of a heavy-duty electric motor start up.

"We need to get a move on!" Riley said, and the two men began running through the snow. Up ahead, Stefan Kurz was pushing Selena into a cable car. When the rest of them were safely inside, Lechner operated the car from inside the wheel house control room and then dashed over into the gondola before it jerked into action. He slammed the door behind him, and they began their descent into the swirling snow.

18

They reached the wheelhouse and activated a second cable car. From back at Moser's compound it had looked secure enough, but now that it was suspended hundreds of feet above the Austrian Alps they all felt the sense of danger and vulnerability.

"We're never going to catch them up!" Decker said, raising his voice to be heard above the sound of the bullwheel which filled the upper terminus.

"We can do it!" said a desperate Diana.

"Yeah, faint heart never won fair lady, mate," said Riley. "Besides, we can't let an old slagger like Moser beat us!"

Jumping into it and slamming the door shut, it swung gently in the cold mountain air as it made its descent toward the valley below. Looking through the forward window, Decker watched anxiously as the gondola containing Moser and her men trundled ever closer to the ground station.

Decker wasn't exactly certain what a *slagger* was, but it didn't sound good.

"Let's do this!" Riley scanned the gondola's roof for a few seconds and cursed.

"What's wrong?" Decker said.

"Some cars have an access panel in the roof, a kind of hatch, but Moser obviously went for the budget model."

"Roof hatch?"

Riley looked at him like he was crazy. "Sure, a roof hatch. We've got to get outside, mate."

Decker's eyes widened. "Outside? We're at least a thousand feet above the mountain!" He shook his head. "And you say *I'm* crazy. Sheesh."

"It's simple maths, Mitch. Our gondola, and Moser's gondola are both going at top speed and they're five hundred meters ahead of us. They're going to get to the ground station way ahead of us. She's probably already radioed down for a car. By the time we get there they're gone, mate. Them and Lena."

Decker took a deep breath and blew it out to calm his nerves. "So, what are you saying? Like you just said, we're both going at the same speed."

Riley now turned and pointed at Moser's cable car with his finger. "No, I said the two *gondolas* were going at the same speed."

"I don't like where this going, Riley," Diana said.

"*You* don't like it?" Decker said.

"It's where *I'm* going you're not going to like."

"Huh?"

"This is the plan – me and you climb outside, Mitch. You bring the Jericho, get yourself a cozy little place up there so you can give me some cover fire."

"Why not do that from inside?" Diana said.

"Glass is too thick," said Decker, immediately understanding Riley's logic. "We'd waste too many rounds trying to blow it open."

Riley laughed. "Give that man a cigar."

"And you?" Diana said, already wide-eyed with disbelief at Riley.

"Me? I'm going down that cable until I get to Moser's gondola and I'm kicking their arses and getting Lena back."

"Absolutely not," Decker said. "We have a responsibility to get Selena back but not if it means doing something so insanely stupid that it costs us the life of another member of the team."

Riley shook his head. "Relax, it only looks insanely stupid because you're a flyboy, a big girl, a creampuff, a cupcake, a—"

"Hey!"

"I'm Aussie SAS, mate. They make us do shit like this if we want our brekkie in the morning."

Diana took a step back and ran a trembling hand through her raven black hair. "Meu Deus! You actually *want* to do this!"

The Australian gave them both a wide, toothy grin and then slapped each of them heartily on their shoulders. "Who wouldn't?"

"So with no roof hatch, it's out the main door, then?" Decker said.

"Right."

Diana gasped. "But it's a straight drop hundreds of meters to the ground!"

"Gotta earn that brekkie, Di," Riley said, and swung open the gondola door.

A blast of icy air filled the cable car with snow and felt like raven's claws scratching at their skin. With the wind now pushing inside the car, the entire gondola began swinging more violently from right to left as it continued to trundle down the steel monocable above it.

"Hang on!" Riley said. "This baby's starting to fight back!"

Gripping one of the safety rails inside the car, he leaned his head out of the door and searched for the best way to the roof. He shook his head and sighed. "Why has everything got to be so fuckin' hard?"

Decker looked at him. "Huh?"

Riley leaned back inside the gondola. "I said it's a piece of piss, mate. Because of the way it's designed, the top half of the car cambers in toward the roof, plus there's a ledge running along the bottom of the windows and a rim around the roof too, so we should be able to get up there without too much problem."

Decker wasn't convinced, but he knew he had to do it to save Selena. "Let's get on with it."

Riley leaned into his bag and pulled out a small GPS tracker. "You never know when these babies come in useful." He slung the snow-chain over his shoulder and moved over to the door. "Oh, and for fuck's sake – don't look down."

"I'll try and remember."

"And Diana – when we're up there shut the door. That'll stop her blowing all over the place like a drunk driver."

"Got it. Take care!"

Riley warmed his hands and then made the leap into the unknown. Reaching his hand around the side of the car, he gripped the other side of the open door. Holding it as hard as he could in the freezing wind, he swung himself out until he was hanging off the open door. With both his boots now pushed into the shallow inch-deep sill on the bottom of the door's lower window, he tried to lift his right leg up so he could jam the toecap of his right boot under the sill of the upper window.

Decker looked on grimly as the Australian got the position he wanted and started to push up to the upper half of the gondola, when his boot slipped off the rubber sill and he crashed back down again, everyone thought he was a dead man.

"Fuck me dead!" he cried out.

"Meu Deus, Riley!" Diana cried out. "Be careful!"

Riley cursed again and only just managed to find another grip before tumbling off the side of the swinging gondola. Snow and ice blasted his back and numbed his fingers as he tried the same move once again. They were only a third of the way down the mountain but he had a lot do if he was going to stop Moser and Kurz making off with both Selena and the strange key from the inside of the Angel of God.

Pushing his boot up into the upper sill, this time he was able to get a better hold and use the position to push himself up over the upper half of the car and reach the rim running around the roof. Grabbing it with both hands, he hauled himself up over the side of the gondola and reached the relative safety of the roof.

Without wasting a second, he scanned for something to hold onto and found the base of the grip attaching the gondola to the cable. Hooking his boot around it he then stretched over the roof of the car until he was hanging off the side of it. With his upper body now dangling over the side, he lowered his hand down for Decker.

"All right, Mitch! It's a great view up here, mate!"

Decker reached out and copied Riley's earlier moves, only this time he had the benefit of the Australian taking hold of his hand and helping him up onto the roof. When they were both holding onto the fixed grip, Diana threw the lever and they both heard the door shut. The gondola immediately reacted by swinging less in the wind, the same freezing wind that now scratched and tore at them as they sat isolated on the roof of the gondola, hundreds of meters above the razor-sharp rocks below.

Decker checked the weapon. "Eight rounds, Riley."

The men shared a doubtful look. "I'm going up now," Riley said. "It won't take those bastards long to work out what I'm doing, and that's when you get busy with Golan's pea shooter."

Decker nodded. "Good luck."

Riley laughed and started his climb up the grip. "Luck's for losers, Mitch."

The former Australian SAS corporal ran his mouth at top gear and he knew it, but inside he felt the same doubts and fears as everyone else, and he knew what he was attempting to do was one of the craziest things in his life. His main concern was confirmed when he reached the top of the grip and saw the cable close up for the first time. It was braided. This would slow the chain, but he hadn't come this far to give up now.

Who dares wins, right? he thought.

Looping the chain over the gondola cable, he tested its strength by hoisting his body weight up on it and holding himself there for a few seconds. When he was satisfied he could hold his weight, he pushed himself off the grip and started to slide down the cable.

He picked up speed much faster than he had anticipated, and friction created by the snow chain against the braided cable caused a shower of amber sparks to spit out in every direction as he raced down toward Moser's gondola. Glancing down beyond his boots, he saw nothing but white, swirling mist and the occasional glimpse of a jagged granite rock sticking up out of the snow. If the chain broke, he'd have ten seconds to curse his stupidity before smashing to his death on those rocks.

Bloch saw him first, and rapidly drew Kurz's attention to what was happening. Moser was sitting with Selena at the front of the gondola, but now she got up too and walked to the rear window. Slack-jawed with disbelief at what she was seeing, it took her several seconds before she started issuing Kurz and Bloch with orders, and Riley had known all along what those orders would be.

Waving everyone in the gondola to the back of the car, Kurz and Bloch opened fire with their submachine guns on the rear window. The thick safety glass shattered until it was opaque, and then Riley heard the two men hastily trying to smash it out of the frame with the stocks of their weapons.

He raced closer to the car with every second it took them to try and beat the rear window out, but he knew the second they had a clear shot his life was in Decker's hands. Only the American could keep the enemy pinned down at the front of the car and stop them firing on the ultimate sitting duck, and he had to do it without hitting Selena too. When he thought about accidentally killing Selena with a stray bullet, he was almost glad he was the one sliding down the cable.

As he knew it would, the shattered rear window finally popped out of the frame and tumbled out of the gondola. Twisting and turning in the air, the heavy wind picked it up as if it were a piece of paper and blew it into the oblivion below, out of sight forever.

Riley saw Kurz and Bloch raise their weapons and aim at him, but then he heard a single crack and both Austrians dived for cover below the window sill at the back of the gondola. Decker had hit the side of their car, a moving target, with the bullseye targeting of a top-class sniper and forced both men to hit the deck.

Riley was almost there now, the sparks still flying out from the snow chain looped over the braided cable. He was so close he could hear Moser yelling at Kurz to fire on him again but it was too late. Seconds away from the rear of the gondola, Riley raised his legs ninety degrees to his body and flew straight in through the open window, crashing into the floor of the car and tumbling to a halt a few inched from Moser's boots.

The Direktor responded by kicking him in the face, almost knocking him out, but Riley had taken worse and quickly got to his feet. He gave Moser a laser-fast back slap and knocked her to the floor before winking at Selena and passing her the GPS tracker. "Fuck, what are *you* doing here, mate?"

"Riley, you're such a stupid tosser... look out!"

Before he turned, he felt someone grab him from behind. Craning his neck to see what was going on, Kurz and Bloch had grabbed him and were pinning his hands behind his back. He fought hard, but when Lechner joined in it was three on one, and they were all former Special Forces men. With a great effort, they heaved him over to the open window and threw him out of the cable car.

Riley spun around in the freezing air. They were around thirty meters high now, and he could see the roof of the lower terminus in the distance as he fell. A few seconds later he smashed into a deep embankment of snow piled up in the valley. It cushioned his fall, and then he started tumbling down a ravine on the southern slope of the mountain. When he finally came to a stop, he looked down at the lower terminus at the bottom of the valley and saw Moser and the rest stepping out of the cable car and walking over to a large black SUV parked up and idling in the snow.

He staggered to his feet and started to brush the heavy snow from his head and shoulders. "You blew it, mate," he muttered. He felt the anger rise in him as he saw Bloch forcing Selena into the car. "And fuck it all, dammit!" he yelled and kicked a rock halfway across the ravine.

19

Norway

Tor Hagen strolled across the broad hardwood decking outside his study and drank in the breathtaking view of the fjord far below. He opened a gold case and slid out a slim, fresh cigar. Silently cutting the head off the cigar, he placed it between his lips and slipped a gnarled hand inside his blazer's silk pocket.

He drew out a solid gold lighter and preheated the foot of the cigar, and then fired up the tobacco. Back on the table inside was a small bundle of cedar strips, but out here a lighter would suffice, and now he ignited the tip while rotating the cigar.

Drawing on the cigar until the embers were established, he slipped the lighter back in his pocket and breathed out a cloud of the aromatic blue smoke. Another drag on the cigar, and yet more admiration of the view. Snow-capped mountains receded in the bright sunshine, dwarfing the pure, still fjords pooling at their bases. This was truly the land of the gods.

"We're getting closer, Ursula."

Moser coughed, and waved Hagen's cigar smoke out of her face. "We only have the key. Without knowing its meaning we're no closer to the Ark at all."

"But we have more than the key, don't we? We have Atticus and Selena Moore. I am certain that between the two of them they will be able to derive the Ark's location from the key."

"Marchand couldn't."

"Marchand is not Atticus Moore, and neither is he the great man's daughter, either. Trust me when I tell you that."

They were interrupted by the sound of tapping on the sliding glass door behind them, and without turning, Hagen waved a hand to gesture that the person should step outside and join them.

A moment later, Stefan Kurz was standing beside him. He was wearing a black roll-neck with a gun in a shoulder holster, and swept his blonde hair away from his forehead as he approached him. "He's still not talking."

Hagen sighed and narrowed his eyes. The mountain wind howled in the trees surrounding the complex. "Perhaps he needs a little more encouragement. Bring our new guest to the laboratory and we'll see if that loosens his lips."

They took an elevator down to the lower levels of the compound and when Hagen pushed open the lab's doors, he was greeted by the anxious, angry face of Atticus Moore. The old professor was wearing his usual tweed jacket with elbow patches, and a cream shirt, his linen tie loosened at the neck. A pair of brown cords completed the package, and all of it was crowned with thinning white hair, swept back away from a deeply-creased forehead.

"Tor, you bastard."

"How are you, old friend?" Hagen said.

"Don't call me that."

"Why ever not? Are we not old friends?"

"I thought we were, yes, but then you had me beaten up and kidnapped by a human mountain."

"Leif," Hagen said wistfully. "A loyal servant, but not overburdened in the IQ department, I'll admit. I could do better."

"You had me drugged and flown out of Israel. I woke up here to find myself a prisoner, Tor – and you ask if we're old friends."

Hagen gave a nonchalant shrug. "Time moves on, I suppose. Once, we were good friends. I was disappointed when you refused to share your research on the Ark with me. Very disappointed."

Atticus stared at him with disbelieving eyes. "And this is what you do when you don't get your way?"

"I cannot allow anything to get in the way of progress, Atti."

"Don't call me that. Only friends call me that."

"Stefan here has asked you to translate the symbols on the key and you have refused."

"Of course."

"I will ask you one last time, and then I will get nasty."

"You can't sink any lower, surely."

"You would think," Hagen said, and beckoned at someone standing behind the door. A moment later Kai Bloch walked in, and he was holding Selena Moore in his grip. She was gagged and blindfolded, and when Atticus saw his daughter like this, he lunged forward to help her, but Kurz beat him down with the grip of his pistol.

"Not so fast, Atticus," Hagen said.

Atticus wheezed on the cold, polished tiles of the lab. "You bastard, Tor. How *dare* you do this to my daughter? She has nothing to do with this."

"Translate the symbols, Professor Moore. Now."

Atticus stared at his helpless daughter, and knew he was running out of options. "You're bluffing, Tor. You're not a killer."

Hagen nodded and gave a heavy sigh. "I was expecting this... Lechner!"

The Austrian pushed a button and an internal door opened to reveal a monstrous machine that looked like a cross between an anti-aircraft gun and a laser.

"What the hell is this, Tor?"

Hagen beamed with pride. "You are looking at a directed-energy weapon, enabled by a superconducting generator. This one is powerful enough to bring down aircraft, but its power could be made much more devastating with the right materials."

Selena gasped when she heard a terrible howl emanating from a nearby room somewhere else in the lab. "What was that?"

"Nothing that need concern you."

"It sounded like something in pain."

"I told you it was nothing," Hagen snapped. He turned to Lechner. "Advise Dr Korhonen he has a problem in Lab 6."

Lechner gave a nod and left the room.

Hagen said, "But let us return to the weapon. Let me show you what it can do by firing it at your daughter."

"No!"

"Kurz, bring the girl over here and secure her in the firing range."

"Please don't!" Atticus cried out. "You'll kill her!"

"First, a demonstration of its potential, I think." Hagen gripped the firing handles and spun the laser turret around on its base until it was pointing at one his men in the corner. He opened his jaw in disbelief as his eyes settled on the menacing lens of the laser aimed right at him.

Hagen ripped the gag off. "Your father here refuses to help me, even when your life is in the balance."

"Dad?" Selena cried out from behind the blindfold. "What's going on?"

"It's all right, Lena!"

134

"No, it is *not* all right," Hagen said, turning to Atticus. "Translate the symbols or I will start killing!"

Atticus's stricken face contorted with terror. "For God's sake, Tor! Please!"

"That's a *no* then."

Without warning, Hagen fired at the man.

Atticus watched in shock as he just stood there and made no effort to save himself.

"Run, man!" Atticus yelled.

The laser beam crossed the room at the speed of light, and with a gentle turn of the turret, Hagen cut the man in two just above his waist. He fell to the floor in a spray of blood, his arms and legs still twitching as he died right before them.

Everyone screamed in horror at the move Hagen had just made, but the Norwegian was unfazed. "You will agree, I'm sure," he said calmly. "That there are better ways to leave this world." He swivelled the laser around until it was pointing at Selena. "Now, I presume your attitude has adjusted since the last time we spoke, Atticus. Will you help me locate the Ark, or not?"

Atticus Moore visibly slouched as the terrible reality of the situation finally struck him. He blew out a deep breath and sullenly nodded his head. "Yes, Tor, I will help you locate the Ark, but now you let my daughter go and you never threaten her again!"

A heavy silence settled over the laboratory for a few seconds while Hagen studied the old English professor for any sign of deceit or treachery. When he was satisfied that the threat against his daughter had broken him, he deactivated the DEW and gently picked up his cigar from the ashtray beside it. "I knew you would accept my terms in the end, Atticus."

Atticus's face darkened with hatred. "Take that blindfold off my daughter, now."

Hagen snapped his fingers and Lechner obeyed.

"Dad!" Selena cried out. "I'm so glad you're alive. Are you okay?"

"I'm fine," he said, glancing at Hagen with anger in his eyes. "Where's this key, Tor?"

"In my study. We go there now."

20

Selena Moore walked beside her father as Hagen led them through the complex toward his study on the upper levels. It was a strange place – half home and half medical research facility. Walls and floors were white, with clean lines and vaguely smelling of disinfectant, but black and white pictures of the Norwegian wilderness hung on the walls, and she even spotted a vase of roses on a table beside an elevator. Imagining Hagen rattling around such a place on his own in the middle of the Scandinavian winter made her skin crawl, especially when she thought about the mysterious Dr Korhonen.

For a time, the only sound was their footsteps on the shining white tiles as they marched through the labyrinth that was Hagen's home, but then the Norwegian recluse turned to them and spoke.

"You could be part of the new empire," he said. "Both of you. Going forward into such a brave new world I will need intelligent, educated people just like you to work with me on my projects. I have spent thirty years searching for the Ark, and you are both world-renowned in your field – why not join me?"

"I'd rather drown in a swamp," Atticus said, the disgust palpable in his words.

Hagen turned to Selena. "And you? Would you rather drown in a swamp like your ignorant father or help me build a better new world?"

"My father is a brilliant scholar and brave man," she said defiantly. "You are pond slime." She crossed her arms over her chest and took a step toward Atticus. "There is your answer."

Hagen nodded his head, a scowl forming on his creased face. "Very well, then you have made your choice. You will still help me find what I want, and then you will be executed. The level of assistance you offer me will determine the manner and speed of your death. Help me get what I want without hindrance and you will be killed quickly and painlessly, deceive me and I will make sure your deaths last weeks. Perhaps I'll let Dr Korhonen introduce you to some of his experiments in the lower lab."

Selena took a step closer to her father. "You're despicable, Hagen."

"I'm rich and powerful and I always get what I want. I advise you now – both of you – do not anger me any further."

Selena was still struggling to believe that men like Tor Hagen could even exist in the world. He was a lethal mix of narcissism and egomania and the truth was he terrified her even more than Rakesh Madan and his insane pursuit of Shambhala. The fact he had toiled for over thirty years on his project to locate the Ark told her all she needed to know about his drive and determination, but there was much more about the man she wasn't sure she even wanted to know – starting with just what the hell Dr Korhonen was doing in the basement laboratory.

"Come on, Lena," Atticus said at last. "We'd better get on with it and give him what he wants."

Hagen smirked, but didn't hear what Atticus said next when he leaned in closer to his daughter and dropped his voice to a whisper. "We just have to delay things as much as possible and hope to hell Riley and Decker get here before…"

He finished the sentence with a tight squeeze of her hand.

138

"Fine," she said at last. "Let's get on with it. I want this nightmare over as soon as possible. I've already been chased around London, knocked out in Jerusalem and nearly killed on a cable car in the Austrian Alps – I'm not sure what could be worse."

As she finished, another agonized howl echoed up the stairs leading to the basement section of the laboratory. Hagen's response was cold and impassive. He fixed his ice-blue eyes on them and then a dead smile appeared on his face. "Come – we have much to do and I'm sure Dr Korhonen would appreciate a little more privacy."

They followed Tor Hagen along the corridor leading toward his study. Floor to ceiling window-walls lined each side of the corridor and each side offered a breathtaking view of the Norwegian landscape. The older man stopped when his cell phone rang and he took the call. When it ended, he gave them an apologetic smile. "I have some unexpected business to deal with. Lechner here will keep you entertained in the meantime, and then you will be brought to my office where you will translate the key."

Selena shuddered and glanced over Hagen's shoulder. To the left was an endless series of snow-capped mountain ridges receding into a hazy horizon, and to the right was the enormous fjord to the north of the compound. Sparkling turquoise water reflected the sunlight and dazzled her, and then she felt her father's arm as he wrapped it around her shoulders and gave her a reassuring hug.

"We'll be all right, Lena."

"I hope you're right, Dad."

"Of course I'm right."

*

Decker closed his eyes and rubbed his temples. This mission had been a total disaster from the moment they had started on it, but at least Riley had managed to pass the GOS tracker to Selena on the cable car. Without that, they would never have known the exact detail of Hagen's current location.

Outside, the wind was racing across the Norwegian Sea and blasting against the office windows of Politiførstebetjent Jens Olsen. Olsen was the equivalent of a British police inspector or somewhere between an American lieutenant and captain. He walked back into the office and sat opposite Decker and the others. He was fit with a lean face and the faint trace of a ski tan around his slate gray eyes.

"It seems you were telling the truth, Captain Decker."

Decker opened his eyes and looked up at Olsen. "I already told you that."

Olsen looked vaguely apologetic. "You understand why we have to check. When a team of foreign treasure hunters walks into your office and tells you one of their own has been kidnapped in the search for the lost Ark of the Covenant, it's not exactly the sort of thing you just accept."

Decker was sounding wearier by the second. "I guess not, but we're still in a hurry."

"You are not in the Wild West here," Olsen said quietly. "You are in Norway, and in Norway there is a correct way to do things. As foreigners, you must realize you have no jurisdiction to go around harassing and arresting Norwegian citizens."

"We understand that," Charlie said.

"Yeah, we're not fu—... we're not idiots," added Riley.

"More than that, the man you are accusing of this crime is not exactly a normal citizen. Tor Hagen is one of Norway's richest men, world-famous in the international scientific community and is on first name terms with the highest of our society. Just last year he was awarded the Medal for Outstanding Civic Service in Oslo by King Harald himself."

"That may be the case," Decker said patiently, "but we know he's behind the kidnapping because we found the evidence of it ourselves. Right now, up in his little cabin in the mountains, he is holding two of our friends – Professor Selena Moore and her father Atticus against their will."

"That's presuming they're still alive," Charlie said.

"Yes, I understand. You have already told me this – I have made a note of everything you have said."

"So what do you propose to do about it?"

Olsen sighed and crossed his hands behind his head. "All right, all right. I will send an officer up to his little cabin, as you put it." He started chuckling at his words.

"What's so funny?" Diana said.

"Hagen's country retreat is one of the most expensive private properties in the country. It's a vast complex built into the side of the mountain with views stretching right out over one of the most beautiful fjords in Norway. It's not only where he lives for part of the year, but he also has extensive laboratories up there. He calls it *Valhalla*."

Decker shifted uncomfortably in his seat. "Captain Olsen, I wouldn't recommend sending a single officer up there, if that's what you're intending to do. We're almost certain there are a number of heavily armed Austrian mercenaries up there protecting a woman named Ursula Moser. She runs an international church."

"This is a not a big American city and I don't have the resources to send an armed troop up to Valhalla to investigate church leaders and scientists who you claim have kidnapped your friend. Having said that, it is my responsibility as the police chief here to take any accusations very seriously, so I will send two constables up with the sergeant."

"And allow us to accompany them?"

"I can't stop you travelling up to Valhalla with them. Norway is a free country. However, I can insist that you do not interfere with my officers as they carry out their duties and you do not trespass on Hagen's property."

"Sounds like we have us a deal, mate," Riley said.

Golan looked less impressed. "We will do whatever we have to do in order to bring the contents of the Angel of God back to Israel."

Olsen looked doubtfully at them, and then buzzed his assistant. They spoke in Norwegian for a few seconds and then a young woman knocked on the open door. Olsen called her into the office and introduced her.

"This is Politibetjent Karin Larsen," he said.

Karin noticed the look on their faces when Olsen introduced her rank. "It's Sergeant Larsen." She tossed some car keys in the air and caught them with a wink. "Let's get out of here."

They walked to the car park and climbed back into the hired Volvo XC90. Buckling up in their seats, Diana spoke first. "Mitch, heater please!"

Decker fired up the powerful engine and turned the heat up to full. It was around zero degrees outside and the westerly coming off the sea pushed it considerably lower than that. Warming their hands as they watched Karin Larsen and her two constables climb into their police-marked VW Passat, Decker gently pressed the throttle and followed the Norwegian police officers out of the subterranean garage and up into the watery daylight of downtown Stavanger.

They followed Larsen south through the city, passing expensive well-maintained properties and tree-lined park-lands before disappearing inside a long tunnel. They emerged at the other end to find themselves outside of the city and driving through an industrial district. After a brief glimpse of an outer belt of suburbs they turned east and quickly moved into the countryside. Here, the hills either side of the road started to grow into mountains, and the snow increased in speed and volume until Decker was forced to put the windshield wipers on full.

"How far is this place, d'ya reckon?" Riley asked

Decker shook his head. "On these roads, hard to say. But if it wasn't for Larsen up ahead we'd never find it. That's for damned sure."

"Speak for yourself," Golan grumbled.

Charlie grunted, crossed his arms over his chest and closed his eyes. "Wake me up before you go-go, yeah?"

"Sure," Decker said sarcastically. "Have a nice sleep."

21

After an hour and a half of kicking their heels in what was little more than a jail cell, Bloch released Selena and her father, and they stepped out into the corridor to see Tor Hagen once again.

"My apologies, but I had to speak with a local police chief I know." He gave them a faint smile. "But now we go to business."

Selena watched the lithe, dark-suited frame of Tor Hagen as he marched with purpose along the corridor a few meters ahead of them. Sunlight diffused by the tinted glass shone on his silvery hair and now he raised his watch to check the time. "We must hurry." Any thought of attacking him was ended abruptly by the presence of Bloch who was still walking behind them with a gun in his holster.

Selena lowered her voice. "But what if they're not coming, Dad? They snatched me in Innsbruck and there's no way to know Riley or Mitch or any other others even knows where I am."

Atticus Moore gave a heavy sigh and shrugged. "From one scientist to another, I think now might be the time to have a little faith."

"In God?"

He gave her an odd look. "In your friends, my dear."

She smiled and was glad her father was with her. She knew between the two of them they could delay Hagen and work out some way to escape, with or without Decker and the others.

They reached Hagen's office. He opened the door and gestured for Atticus and Selena to go inside, but ordered

144

Bloch to stand outside the door. When he closed the door he took off his suit jacket and hung it over the back of his chair. "I do so wish you would change your mind about helping me. It would be such a waste to have you both killed." He started to pour three brandies. "Will you join me in a drink at least?"

"Can we just get on with it?" Atticus said tersely. "You'll forgive me if I don't share a toast with a man who has threatened the life of my daughter."

Hagen gave another shrug and sipped his brandy. Setting the glass on the desk he opened a large walk-in safe and stepped out a moment later with the key from inside the Angel of God.

"My God," Atticus said. "It's beautiful."

"Isn't it just?" said Selena.

"This is the key Moser's people found inside the Angel of God back in Israel. I want you to translate it. Is that something you can do?"

"I think so," Selena said. "Dad?"

Her father pulled his glasses out of his pocket and held them up between his eyes and the key. He gave a vague nod. "I should think so."

"Veldig bra!" Hagen said. "We are already making progress."

Atticus turned to his old friend. "Tell me, Tor. Why did that man in the lab simply stand and allow you to cut him down with the laser?"

Hagen narrowed his eyes, weighing up how much to tell his old friend. "Because he was created to be like that. Or re-created, you might say."

Selena was confused. "I don't understand."

"Has this got something to do with Dr Korhonen?" Atticus asked.

Hagen nodded. "Mikko and I have been working on genetic therapy for many years now, Atticus. I've come a long way since we were at university together."

Atticus turned a confused face to Hagen. "Genetic therapy? What do you mean, exactly?"

Hagen looked out at the snow over the fjord and sighed. Bloch and Lechner were standing a few meters away with their guns in their holsters. It was all very cordial. "Scientists have been able to create super-strong mice by using gene manipulation to suppress a muscle-growth inhibitor which resides naturally in the body's DNA," he said smugly. "The discovery that this one miniscule inhibitor was responsible for how much muscle strength we have was an enormous step forward for mankind, but it has taken my genius and determination to move things to the next level."

"What do you mean 'the next level'?" Atticus asked cautiously.

"By manipulating a genome regulator called NCoR1, scientists were able to create genetically modified mice with double the strength of normal mice, but that is the current limit of their research." He turned and faced them with the window behind him, his gaunt face now cast into shadow. "But I have gone much further. I have created a genetically modified type of human with five times the strength, speed and agility of a normal man, and more than that, I have created them to be utterly obedient to me, their creator."

"My God." Atticus took a step back toward Selena. "I thought I knew you, Tor. All those years ago when we were at college together, but now I can see I don't know you at all. You're quite mad."

"And where is the line between madness and genius? Is God a genius, or is he mad?"

Atticus's words were weaker, now, and quieter. "You're insane... totally insane."

"No! I successfully combined the genetic modification of both the muscle accelerator and muscle inhibitor, enhancing the first and removing the second altogether. Specifically modifying corepressors, of which I certainly know more about than any person alive, I was able to alter the expression of genes critical to muscle-growth, but also critical neurological functions that regulate things like speed of motor skills. Modifying obedience was even more complex, but the results will strike awe into your hearts."

"My father's right," Selena said, and moved a strand of hair out of her face. "You're totally out of your mind. Can you even hear yourself?"

"And where do these human lab rats come from?" Atticus said.

Hagen's reply came without hesitation. "The homeless, mostly."

Selena gasped, and Atticus shook his head in horror. "Tell me this is a nightmare."

Hagen started to laugh. It was a sinister, gravelly chuckle without the slightest hint of humor. "I can understand the average low-level thinker not understanding the implications of such progress, but I had you and your father pegged several rungs above that. You disappoint me."

"And you disgust me, Tor," Atticus said. "You've reduced human beings to the status of lab rats without the vaguest sign of remorse or guilt."

Hagen turned his back on them and gazed out over the fjord far below the research facility. "Remorse, you say. Why would I feel remorse for moving the field of genetic science forward so far? I have done more to progress research in this area than any man or woman alive! In a few short years I have achieved more than anyone else has across the course of their entire careers, and you talk about guilt."

"You're kidnapping people off the street and modifying their DNA without their permission, Tor," said Atticus. "You're trying to create an army of mindless super-strength thugs for your own warped agenda! What happened to the ethics you used to talk about so much?"

Another cold laugh. "Perhaps a demonstration of my work?"

"Don't make us party to this abomination, Tor!" Atticus said.

"Where's your sense of scientific curiosity, Atticus?"

Hagen called through to his personal assistant. "Please send him in, Berit."

"Yes, sir."

A tense few seconds passed until the door opened. A large, muscle-bound man with cold, impassive eyes padded into the room and stood silently on the rug. "Ah, Arvid. Thank you for joining us."

Arvid said nothing.

"Arvid here is one of my earlier works, but I'm sure you'll be impressed nonetheless."

"For God's sake, Tor!" Atticus snapped. "Put an end to this madness, please!"

Hagen smiled and waved his finger in front of his face. "No, really – I think you're going to be very impressed by what you see."

"I doubt that," Selena said.

"Arvid, raise your right arm."

Arvid obeyed instantly.

"And your left."

He obeyed again.

148

"Lower them."

Aside from the crackling fire, the only sound in the room was Arvid's shirt rustling as he obeyed the order, once again silently and without question.

"Arvid, please pick up the filing cabinet at the end of the room."

Arvid walked to the cabinet, squatted slightly and embraced the large, steel cabinet with his arms. He lifted it into the air and straightened his back, remaining in that position without moving while Hagen turned to Selena and Atticus. "You see, he is utterly loyal and obeys without question. Now, Arvid, put your hand in the fire."

Selena gasped. "I can't believe this is happening."

"And what does Mrs Moser and her church make of this, I wonder?" Atticus said.

"Moser knows what I allow her to know."

Arvid walked to the fire and pushed his hand into the embers. There was no scream, no howl, no attempt to withdraw the hand. The man never flinched as the smell of burning flesh drifted over from the flames.

"Enough, Tor!" Atticus cried out. "You've made your point."

"I think not, but as you wish... Arvid, enough!"

The man pulled the badly burned hand from the fire. His red, sweating face was contorted from the effort it had taken to absorb the pain without flinching.

Hagen stepped to his door and opened it. The cold wind howled into the plush office and blew a little snow onto the rug where it quickly melted in the heat of the fire. "Arvid, step outside onto the balcony."

The young Norwegian again did as he was ordered and stepped outside into the freezing wind. The snow whipped around him and started to accumulate on his head and shoulders.

149

"You've made your point," Atticus said.

Selena was still nauseous and holding her sleeve up to her nose to block the smell of burning flesh. "Yes, enough of these stupid games."

"Arvid, climb over the balcony."

Selena sensed a flicker of hesitation in the young man, but then it was gone again and he was climbing up over the frozen metal bars of the balcony. She watched him fight to stay level in the power of the wind.

A devilish smirk crossed Hagen's face.

"Bring him in at once! End this madness."

"If searching for the Ark is madness, then what does that make you?"

"I want the Ark for archaeology, Tor. It's for the world, for our history. Tell me, why do *you* want the Ark?"

"What makes you think I am not motivated by the same altruism?"

Atticus laughed bitterly. "Don't insult my intelligence, *friend.* Why would anyone who had dedicated their lives to creating this... house of horrors, search for the Ark for the benefit of humanity?"

Hagen caved in faster than Selena thought. It was as if he wanted to tell them the truth.

"You are right, of course. My quest is not altogether altruistic, but whether or not it would benefit humanity – that is up for debate."

"I don't understand."

Hagen sighed. "I believe the Ark is made, at least in part, from what today we would call a Type III superconductor – much more robust and with a significantly higher critical magnetic field."

"My God," Atticus said. "You want to turn the Ark into a weapon."

22

The answer to Riley's question turned out to be a little over sixty kilometers, and the mountainous terrain toward the end of the journey meant nearly two hours had passed by the time Sergeant Larsen indicated to pull into Valhalla's private approach road.

Golan saw it first, craning his neck up to look through the top part of his window. "My God," he said. "It looks like a small city."

Riley whistled. "Who knew there was so much dough-ray-me in science? If I'd have known that in school I'd have joined the nerds instead of beating them up."

They emerged from their car and got used to the cold wind as the police officers checked their weapons. Larsen handed Riley a police rifle and told him it was for emergency use only. He gave her a two-fingered salute and a wink. "Got it."

After promising not to get involved in the enquiry, they watched the police drive to the main entrance, while they climbed a snow bank to the south. After finding a good place to view the compound, they wedged themselves up against the trunk of one of the enormous spruce trees surrounding the property. The former US Marines pilot slipped his trusty monocular from his pocket and scanned the front façade of the sprawling complex.

"Can you see Larsen?" Diana asked.

"Sure can. She's walking to what I'm guessing is the main entrance. Damned place is like a luxury hotel."

As the Norwegian police officers made their way from their car to the front entrance, Decker continued to survey the surrounding landscape. Seeing nothing of interest, he turned the monocular back on Hagen's complex. Larsen and her constables were standing outside the door in the cold, still waiting for someone to answer. Their breath clouded in front of them and drifted up into the air. Decker followed its path until he was looking at the upper levels of Valhalla.

"Must be the private quarters up top," he muttered. "Judging by what's in the rooms." Lowering the eyepiece he swept it along the far north of the building. "And by the looks of things, that's part of his laboratory over there."

Charlie nudged Decker in the ribs. "Wait – someone's opening the door."

Decker moved the monocular to the front entrance. "They're talking to someone now. He's inviting them inside."

"Great," Diana said. "Maybe they'll have some coffee while we're freezing our asses off out here and Lena and her father are still trapped."

"You heard Olsen," Decker said. "There's a correct way to do things in Norway."

Far down beyond the road, a freight train trundled past on it journey south.

The first gunshot took them all by surprise. Decker dropped the monocular into the snow and fumbled to snatch it back up again. Brushing the snow off it he raised it to his eye just in time to see one of the constables staggering backwards out of the main entrance and collapsing on the hood of the police VW.

"Holy crap!" Riley said. "That escalated quickly!"

Larsen and the other constable burst from the entrance and darted for the cover of the VW, each drawing their police-issue pistols as they went.

"Looks like they asked some awkward questions that old Hagen didn't like too much," Charlie said.

"This Hagen is a psychopath," Golan said dolefully.

"We have to help them!" Diana said.

Decker looked at the Australian. "I think this is the kind of emergency Karin Larsen was talking about, Riley."

"On it," he said, pulling the rifle from his back and sliding a round into the chamber.

"I see Kurz," Decker said. "He just came out of the compound."

Decker watched the Austrian take cover behind a parked Jeep and start to fire on Larsen and the surviving constable. The Norwegian police fought back bravely, and the two groups exchanged heavy fire for a few seconds but then a man appeared in an upstairs window with a submachine gun and started pounding the police VW with rounds. Tearing holes in it like it was made of cardboard, Larsen and the younger officer were pinned down.

Riley raised the rifle into the aim and squinted down the sights. "Time to say goodnight, you little bastard!"

One shot.

It struck the gunman in the forehead. He dropped the submachine gun and fell back into the upstairs room.

Aware he was drawing more fire from the Norwegians, and startled at the sound of Riley's shot, Kurz crouched lower behind a Jeep and desperately scanned the area behind the house for any sign of the sniper.

"Bastard's panicked," Decker said. "He's getting on the radio."

"Trying to get some back-up," Charlie said. "Can you take him out, too?"

"Nah, mate. Gave myself away when I plugged that son of a bitch in the window. He's tucked down behind the Jeep tighter than a turtle's pecker now."

Diana looked horrified at his choice of words, but her disgust was quickly redirected at the sight of two more men rushing out to join Kurz. The Austrian barked orders at them in German and they started to head toward their position up at the side of the compound.

Larsen fired on them, taking one of them out, but then they returned fire and cut down the younger constable in a savage hail of fire. Raking him with bullets that tore into his throat and chest, the junior policeman stumbled back away from the cover of his police car and fell down dead in pile of snow at the side of the drive.

"Larsen's next, Mitch," Golan said.

Riley loaded another round into the chamber and effortlessly killed the other man Kurz had sent up into the hills. "Over my dead body," he said.

"We have to get inside," Decker said flatly. "Now they know we're here there's no telling what they might do to Lena and her Dad."

"Presuming they're still alive," Golan said.

"That's been the presumption all along, Moshe," Riley said. "We don't leave anyone behind if there's a chance they're still alive."

"They're still alive, all right," Decker said. "No way is an asshole like Hagen going to kill them if he thinks they might know something he doesn't know, and Lena and Atticus are going to know that and exploit it. My worry is he'll try and use them as human shields or something."

"So what are we going to do now?" Diana said. "You just saw what happened to those police officers when they tried to get inside, and all they wanted to do was ask a few questions. I don't think Hagen or Kurz will take too

155

kindly to us wanting to come inside to rescue Lena and her father and smash up his little playground."

Decker was already making plans. "We'll get in, all right."

Riley loaded a third round into the chamber of the hunting rifle. "And right now, you have no idea how much I want to bust up that dickhead's little world... wait – Karin's trying to get up to us!"

They watched as the Norwegian sergeant struggled through a hail of fire as she made her way closer to their position on the perimeter.

"She'll never make it!" Diana said.

Golan said, "That bastard Kurz has seen her!"

Riley lifted the rifle once again. "I'll pin him down and give her some cover fire!"

*

Selena looked at her father anxiously. "I don't get it, Dad."

Atticus closed his eyes for a second and shook his head, He just wanted it to all to go away. "The laser we saw in the other room, that killed the man... it's a prototype for a much more powerful weapon, a glorified death-ray – am I right, Tor?"

"Don't be so crude, Atti. A DEW with the degree of power I foresee the Ark enabling it with would be so much more than a common weapon! With such a power we could destroy satellites, inbound nuclear missiles, anything!"

Atticus struggled to comprehend what he was hearing. "And if you get the damned thing airborne you could raze entire cities to the ground."

"Your words, not mine."

156

"And I thought the DNA genome sequencing was insane," Selena said.

"But what I don't understand is, what makes you think the Ark has this power?" Atticus asked.

Hagen looked delighted with the question. "The Bible itself tells us. Any man who touched it was killed on the spot. Some have speculated it had an electrical power, while others have always believed it must have emitted some of kind of radiation. Other descriptions have included metal plates that could be batteries. The list goes on." Hagen's eyed began to glaze over as his mind ran wild with the thought of securing such a power for himself. "Moser has briefed me very well on the Bible."

He turned on Atticus and held the key up in the cold light. "Now, you've had plenty of time to study this. What does it say?"

Atticus looked at Selena and then both looked over at their captor. "It says the Ark was snatched when the Babylonians torched Jerusalem and taken to the Palace of Nebuchadnezzar." He turned away from Hagen and looked at Selena with an apology on his face.

"You mean?"

"Yes, the Ark is part of the Treasure of Babylon."

Bloch entered the room. He looked vaguely rattled but still in control. "Sir, the grounds have been breached. Kurz is involved in a fire fight out the front."

Atticus and Selena shared a look of hope. It must be Decker and the rest of the team coming to rescue them.

Hagen was less thrilled. "Deploy all the men you have and kill the intruders, we're getting out of here!" He turned his head and called out to the man on the balcony. "And now jump, Arvid."

"No!" Selena cried out.

Atticus stumbled out of his chair and lunged for the young man's legs, but it was too late. Arvid had leaped from the balcony and was now tumbling hundreds of meters down toward the rocky mountainside below.

"My God!" Atticus said.

Selena covered her mouth with horror. "He's not even screaming."

"Of course not," Hagen said. "He *wants* to obey."

Atticus ran to the balcony but turned away when the young man's body smashed into the frozen scree a few meters above the surface of the fjord. In a grisly tangle of broken arms and legs it rolled out of sight into a line of spruce trees near the water's edge.

He turned to see Bloch pull a gun from his holster and walk to the door. He waved the barrel of the gun at him. "Come inside, old man. We're going."

Hagen was now talking into the phone on his desk. "The tracker will be on their plane within the hour. Lock these two up in here while we prepare the boat."

23

Decker watched Kurz scramble back through the slush and disappear inside the main entrance of the compound. Karin made the last few meters into the forest and slammed down against the trunk of the spruce beside him and the others. Riley's cover fire had saved her life, and everyone knew it.

"You were right," she said, still breathing hard from the run to the trees. "As soon as we showed them your picture of Professor Moore they pulled guns on us. Jensen went for his gun and they killed him on the spot. I've never seen anything like it before."

Decker frowned. "Have you told your boss, Olsen?"

She shook her head. "Not Olsen, no – he was unavailable. I called a sergeant I know in the IT department, Nina. I called her when I was taking cover behind the police car. I also asked her to send through the schematics for the compound."

"Quick thinking," Riley said. "I like that in a chick."

Diana rolled her eyes.

"Good job." Decker said. "Has Olsen sent them through yet?"

Larsen gave a quick nod as she flicked through her smart phone. "We have all of the schematics here, and reinforcements will be here as fast as possible."

"But it took us nearly two hours to get here!" Diana said.

"Olsen is sending a chopper but it's on a mission fifty kilometers to the north and needs to go back to the station to pick up the armed response team."

"What kind of chopper?" Decker asked.

Larsen closed her eyes to think for a moment. "It's a… Bell Jet Ranger, mostly used as a rescue chopper in the mountains."

"Two hundred and twenty Ks top speed," the American said almost to himself. "Fifty Ks back to the station and then sixty Ks out here means they're not arriving for around a half hour. We can't wait for them."

"Mitch is right," Charlie said. "They know we're here now so we no longer have the element of surprise. Lena and her father are in serious trouble. We have to get in there now."

Decker slipped the monocular in his pocket as Riley shouldered the rifle. "All right," the American said in a calm, businesslike manner. "They could be holding them literally anywhere in the place, but it's my best guess that they're either in Hagen's lab or his private quarters because this is a private residence and not likely to have a brig."

"A brig?" Karin asked.

"He means jail," Charlie said. "He used to be a Marine."

"Sorry," Decker said. "Force of habit, but the point remains they're not going to be locked up in there, so we have that on our side. Can you find those two locations, Karin?"

"Ja, already done it. The laboratory is the building to the north and it looks like it's on two floors with the lower floor underground. Hagen's private quarters are on the top floor on the southern side of the building."

"Dammit," Decker said. "We're going to have split the team. One goes north to the labs and the other goes south to the private area."

Golan loaded the Jericho. "How many armed men do you think he has in there?"

"Difficult to say," Riley said. "There are only a few cars, but that only tells us so much. We know Kurz and his men – minus poor old matey lad in the upstairs window – are in there, plus Moser and Hagen himself. I'm thinking we have the advantage, unless the old bastard's hiding a load of Special Forces under his bed."

Karin took the lead, her service pistol in one hand and the schematics on her phone in the other. In the gathering darkness, they moved in a single file along the snowy forest path until they reached the western perimeter. Silently moving down the path into the compound, they reached an outbuilding and took cover behind its western wall.

"This is where we split," Decker said. "I'll go to the labs with Karin and Moshe. Riley, you take Charlie and Diana to the private quarters. Unless we cross each other's paths inside, we'll meet back at the car."

"Got it, boss," Riley said. He took another look at the schematics and memorized the location of Hagen's living area. After a final weapons check he led his small team south through the dusky Norwegian evening.

"It's this way," Karin said. "If we get into the garage we should be able to take some steps down to the basement level."

The garage block ran along the western edge of the main building. Two large roller doors at the front were both locked, as was a side door, but a small window beside the door offered them a way in.

Golan made short work of the window putting it in with the butt of his pistol and then he reached around and opened the door from the outside. "We got lucky," he said with a surprised smile. "Key's in the door."

"There's no crime around here at all," Karin said. "I'm surprised it was locked in the first place."

Inside the garage, Karin led the way with the light by her phone. A Ferrari California shared the space with a Maybach Cabriolet, each resting on the smooth, polished concrete floor like sleeping tigers. Moving across the space, Moshe Golan admired the cars and gave a low whistle of appreciation. "Not bad."

They crept over to the basement door. Decker opened it with his gun raised into the aim and when Karin shone her phone's flashlight beam into the darkness. It revealed a staircase leading down to the basement and they all shared the relief. They made their way along a corridor lit with ice-blue emergency lighting until they reached another room, and what they found there shocked them to the core.

*

Jens Olsen wasn't very good at poker, and he was even worse at backgammon. Something about the way the probabilities worked just caught him out every time, and yet he was drawn to the gaming tables like a moth to the flame. His debts now totalled more than the combined value of his house in Jåtten and his cabin over at the lakes. His wife Anette knew nothing about it, and that was just how he wanted it.

He had always believed something would fall from the heavens and light his way out of the disaster, and that something was a telephone call from Tor Hagen. The weird old man up at the place they called Valhalla had called and offered him five million Krone.

All he had to do was get past his old friend the harbormaster and attach a GPS tracker to an old float plane down on the water. Simple and easy – and all the debts were gone, just like that.

He was an ethical man, but the gambling had taken a hold of him. As he drove across town from the police station he was surprised at how easily he was able to shrug off his conscience and collect the tracker from one of Hagen's men. It was one of those weird ones with the dead eyes he saw from time to time up at the fjord near Valhalla.

He took the tracker and parked up outside the harbor. Finding the correct aircraft wasn't hard – Hagen had told him to look for a 1940s float plane and there was only one that fit the description. He checked his phone and found a missed call from Karin Larsen and then stepped out into the cold wind.

This would only take a second.

*

Decker and the others were in some kind of storage facility, and they all shared the same disgust and horror when they saw the product of Hagen's scientific research.

Dozens of Formalin specimen jars filled with the results of hideous medical experiments, all signed off by someone of the name Korhonen. They were lined neatly up on a series of shelving units running along the north side of the room. Labels with carefully printed information obscured most of the contents, but there was still enough visible to turn their stomachs with fear.

Karin looked way in disgust, instantly burying her face in Decker's shoulder and hiding her eyes from the horror. "Å min Gud!"

"This is an abomination," Golan muttered under his breath.

Decker didn't know what to say. He felt his heart beating in his chest as Karin squeezed his shoulder for comfort. He'd read about this sort of thing – DNA manipulation, genome sequencing... Nazi eugenics – but he never thought he'd be confronted by it. He felt everything coming together in his mind – the connection between Moser and Hagen, the hideous results of the Norwegian's scientific research and most concerning of all, the Ark of the Covenant.

"We keep going," he said at last. "Lena and Atticus need us to keep going."

Then a noise. Karin collected herself and came back to life, raising her service pistol in the direction of the sound. It was footsteps, and they were coming toward them from the door they hadn't yet reached. The police sergeant listened as two men approached and talked to each other. "They've been ordered to check the garage," she said.

"Everyone up against the back wall," Decker said. "And stay in the shadows. The last thing we need now is a gunfight."

They hid in the shadows and held their breath as the two men opened the door and moved through the storage room toward the other door. Opening it, they made their way along the corridor leading to the garage. Golan closed it silently behind them and turned the key in the lock, and then slid a chunky bolt across. "Whatever they do now," he said proudly. "They're not coming back this way."

"Good work, Moshe," Decker said. He took one last look around the storage room and shuddered. "Let's get the hell out of here."

24

Selena struggled against the handcuffs holding her to the chair. Across the room, her father was suffering the same fate only he was handcuffed to a radiator. "I can't believe you told him, Dad!"

"I know, I know!" he said pathetically. "But it only told him so much – the Treasure of Babylon is not just sitting around in a pile waiting for someone to loot it. And don't forget, now we know Riley and the others are coming to rescue us."

"You do realize he's actually going to kill us, don't you?"

Atticus Moore looked bewildered. "Are you sure? Perhaps he's bluffing."

"He's not bluffing, Dad! He's already killed countless people in an insane quest for the Ark of the Covenant and God *only* knows what the hell he has down in the lower laboratory because it sounded like the gates of hell themselves were down there. Maybe more of those freaks he created..."

"Surely you exaggerate, my dear. I'm certain we'll find a way out of this if only we put our..."

"Put our heads together," she said, finishing his sentence for him. "I know, Dad – that's what you always say."

"That's because it's true."

"God, *Dad*," she muttered. "Sometimes I think you're from another world."

"What was that?"

"I said we're in deep sh—, real trouble here and if we don't get out of these cuffs we probably have less than an hour to live."

"No, no – Tor won't kill us so long as he thinks we can help him locate the Treasure of Babylon."

"And can we?"

"I have a lead, yes."

"We have to get out of here before we can follow a lead." She yanked at the cuffs again but succeeded only in carving a deeper groove into the soft flesh around her wrist. "Dammit!"

The door opened, and she gasped when she saw Stefan Kurz and another man standing behind him. Guns drawn, and fear etched on their face, it looked like things were about to shift up a gear.

Kurz stepped into room, and now Selena saw he was sweating. She also saw the other man was Kai Bloch. "All right, you're coming with us now. The boat's ready."

"What's going on?" she asked. "What were those shots?"

Kurz ignored her and ordered Bloch to unlock them. The moment Bloch had freed her father, the old man swung at him with everything he had. Selena gasped again, almost too scared to look as the younger Austrian effortlessly beat her father down to the ground with the stock of his weapon. The anger she felt when her old man had spilled the beans to Hagen evaporated in an instant when she saw him try and defend her from Kurz and Bloch.

"Get your hands off him!" she cried out. "He's just an old man!"

Bloch moved to pile a boot into Atticus's ribs when Kurz grabbed his arm and stopped him. "Leave him!" he said in English. "And unlock the girl!"

Bloch gave him a scowl and padded across the room to unlock Selena's handcuffs. As he turned the key she felt the pressure and pain of the metal biting into her skin fade away. She rubbed them better as she watched her father stagger to his feet and wipe the blood from his bleeding nose.

Kurz and Bloch marched them down at gunpoint from the bedroom on the upper floor and ordered them to take the stairs down to the laboratory. Selena felt her stomach lurch when she heard the word, and knew at once what it meant.

Had Hagen decided he wanted to kill them after all? She knew that anything to do with the lab meant it wasn't going to be fast and painless, and you could take that to the bank.

They reached the laboratory door and Kurz kicked it open to reveal Tor Hagen and Ursula Moser standing together in quiet conversation up against one of the benches. Several men were standing nervously on the other side of the lab, pistols casually wedged in shoulder holsters. Behind them was a double door with a biohazard warning sign across it. It was bolted in three places.

Kurz approached Hagen and then the Norwegian billionaire turned and gave Selena and Atticus a sickening smile. "I'm so very glad you could join us."

A deep, guttural growl emanated from behind the biohazard doors. Hagen and Moser exchanged a knowing look but said nothing.

"What is this?" Atticus said. "I thought you said we were going in a boat?"

"A change of plan – your friends are too close and you two will only slow us down. You're coming with me, Atti, and you're going to help me find the Treasure of Babylon and the Ark. Sadly, your daughter is going to play out her days here with Dr Korhonen's creations."

The gunshots rang out loud and violent in the corridor, and bullets raked a line in the biohazard door. They all dived for cover, with Hagen and Moser scattering away into the lab. Lechner grabbed Atticus and used him as a human shield as he stumbled toward the lab and followed his leader's escape.

"Dad!" Selena's heart was torn in two – her father had been snatched by Lechner right under her nose, but now Decker and the others were here to rescue them at last. "Mitch…"

"Where did they go?" Mitch asked.

"In there," she said. "They said it was the fastest way to the fjord. They took Dad."

Another pained howl.

"What the hell was that?" Decker asked.

Riley looked disgusted. "Don't look at me! I can't describe it. Sounds almost like a human."

"Almost?"

"We think he's been doing DNA experiments," Selena said. "I heard those screams before when we first got here. There's something hiding deep in the agony of those terrible howls."

"Human-animal hybrids?"

"No, some sort of superhumans. We met one upstairs. They have enhanced DNA, They're faster and stronger, have no conscience to speak of and are totally obedient."

"My God…" Decker's voice drifted away into the gloom of the corridor.

"We have to get after them!" Riley said.

Decker nodded. "Someone's got to stay here and keep Korhonen busy – Charlie?"

"Sure thing, Mitch."

"I'll stay, too," Diana said.

Karin grabbed her radio. "I'll find out how far out the reinforcements are."

"Where did they go?" Riley asked.

"They have a boat on the fjord," Selena said. "It's his escape pod in case of the police raiding the place."

"Don't fjords freeze?" Charlie said

"They're full of water from the ocean," Riley said. "So that means higher salt content and a warmer temperature, so not usually no."

"I had no idea you were so knowledgeable," Diana said.

"Thank Sergeant Farrell and his Arctic warfare training."

"We'll do career history later," Decker said, loading his gun. "Right now, we've got to stop Hagen before they get away."

25

Selena stared out across the water. Hagen's fjord yacht was disappearing into the growing snowfall now swirling all around them. "I see them!" she yelled. "At least I think I do."

"Where?" Decker said.

"There, to the right."

He strained to see through the snow. It was hard to make out, but he thought he could just about see the white-painted stern of the yacht as it vanished into the snowstorm. He could just about hear the sound of what sounded like a five horsepower outboard motor coming from where he had seen the ghost ship. "That's them all right, but we've got to hurry. If we lose them in these conditions we might never find them, or Atticus, again."

"So, what are we going to do?" Riley asked.

Karin said, "Maybe we should wait for the police back-up? They said they're nearly here."

The Australian twisted his lips. "Nah, sorry Karin, but that's not exactly blowing my skirt up, I gotta tell ya."

"Huh?"

"He means he doesn't like it," Decker said. "And I'm with him. I say we jump in this tender and get after them ourselves."

They jumped into the tender and Karin fired up the motor. "Is everyone in safely?"

"Gotta love Norwegians," Riley muttered.

"Sure, we're all in safe," Decker said.

She lowered the midsection into the cold water and when the propeller broke the surface the streamlined tender lurched forward into the water. Selena watched the small jetty become rapidly enveloped in the blizzard and then they were in a world of white. They were totally isolated now, just a few people in a small boat in the middle of a fjord in a snowstorm. She'd had better days.

"Where are they?" Riley said.

Decker pointed off their port side. "They're over there now."

"Eh?"

"Looks like they're turning," Karin said. "He's trying to leave the fjord and head out to the coast."

"Makes sense," Riley said. "It's an ocean-going yacht after all. He knows the only way we could chase him is in this tender, and this thing ain't making it in the Norwegian Sea, you can bet the farm."

"We still have the advantage," Decker said. "I heard the motor and no way is it any more powerful than five horsepower. It's a thirty foot yacht designed to sail so that's not going to do much to get them out of this fjord. We're much smaller so we can make better speed, but we have to find them first."

"And then we have to get on board," Selena said. "He's hardly going to stand around doing nothing while we climb up the ladder and board his floating palace."

"Just leave that to me," Riley said.

"No," Karin said. "Leave it to me. We're still in Norway and I have jurisdiction."

Decker turned to the stern and looked at her. "I'm not convinced he respects Norwegian law, Karin."

"Damn right, he doesn't," Riley said. "He wants to settle things the hard way, so the hard way he gets." He unclipped the magazine from his Glock and counted the remaining rounds. Smacking it back into the grip, he stuffed it into the belt of his jeans and wiped the mist from his face. "Fucker."

Karin sighed. "At least let me try and arrest him… read him his rights."

"Fine," Decker said. "You read him his rights and we'll find Atticus."

The mist was mow turning into a sea fog and it was now almost impossible not only to see Hagen's yacht, but even just a few meters ahead of them. "This is getting very dangerous," Karin said warily. "We could run into anything and capsize. If that happens we don't stand a chance out here in this storm."

"We keep going," Decker said. "I didn't give up a perfectly good cargo business to roll over at the first sign of trouble."

Riley patted him on the back and laughed. "Thanks mate, I needed that."

Decker looked confused. "What did I say?"

"There!" Selena said. "I see them over there on our right."

"Starboard," Decker mumbled.

The sea fog was lifting and they had moved into a patch of clearer visibility. There, on their starboard side less than one hundred meters off their bow they saw the yacht. It was heading out to sea just as Karin had predicted.

Riley turned to the Israeli at the back of the boat. "Are you giving it all she's got, Moshe?"

"Everything."

"It's taking forever!" Riley said. "They'll be out at sea before too long and then we're buggered. We don't have the fuel and we're not big enough to handle the conditions out there."

"Take it easy, Riley," Decker said. "We're getting there – just another few minutes. We're faster, remember."

Drawing closer to the yacht now, Golan gripped the tiller and fought against the wake of the giant boat to keep the tender as steady as he could while the others got ready to board.

Decker shielded his eyes from the sea spray and held onto the rail as the tender struck the side of the yacht and nearly knocked him overboard. "Dammit Moshe!"

"This isn't easy, you know!"

When Golan had brought the tender back under control, Riley saw the first opportunity to board the yacht and reached out for one of the ladders toward the stern, but then they saw men running through the mist.

"Bugger it," Selena said. "They must have heard us hit the side of the boat."

Without hesitation, Riley jumped up into the yacht and fired on the men who were making their way through the sea spray along the port side of the super yacht. He hit the first man in the chest and blasted him over the rail into the fjord, but the second took evasive action and found some cover in a doorway.

Riley fired on the man's location. He knew he couldn't hit him, but he had to keep him pinned down inside the yacht to give the others time to get on board.

Selena scrambled up next and slammed down next to him on the deck and then Decker joined them at the rear. Golan dropped back away from the yacht but stayed in sight. If their plan was going to work the tender was the only way back to shore, but they had to rescue Atticus first.

"Fight first, ask questions later," Riley said with a mischievous smirk. He raised his gun and fired on the men standing above them on the mid-deck. They returned fire and raked the lower deck with rounds but it just charged the Aussie SAS man up more than ever. "Come on! Let's give them hell!"

*

Charlie Valentine raised his gun and pushed open the door of the room marked KORHONEN LAB 1. He and Diana were expecting something from their worst nightmares, but when they got into the room they found only a series of empty cages and the door at the far end of the lab swinging shut.

"What the hell is this place?" Diana said.

Charlie scanned inside the cages. "Looks like Korhonen's little Bed and Breakfast, where he kept his freaks fed and watered while he experimented on them."

Chains that had once held the superhumans in place now hung loosely down from their wall fittings. Beds and tables were upturned, and Charlie noticed a gun cabinet on the wall in what looked like an office. It was empty, and several empty boxes were strewn in the floor.

He stooped to pick one up.

"What are they?" Diana asked.

"Elephant tranquilizers," he said quietly. "Not digging this, I can tell you."

"Me neither. What the hell kind of person needs elephant tranquilizers to subdue them?"

"Whatever the hell was going on in here, and whoever was doing it, it's not happening now. They must have activated some sort of escape protocol."

"Charlie, look!"

"What is it?"

Diana was standing at the office window and pointing outside. "They're down there!"

Charlie looked and saw what had happened. A fire door from the lab led down directly to an inner courtyard, and now a man in a white lab coat was closing up the back of a transport truck and running around to the driver's door.

"Dammit! We're too late."

The man he presumed was Mikko Korhonen had escaped with the subject of his experiments and was now pulling out of the compound and driving down toward the main road. He was already half a mile away, and slowly he vanished into the swirling snowstorm.

*

Selena hit the deck and crawled around the starboard side of the pool as she made her way to Riley. He was taking cover in the aft door to the engine room. Decker bobbed up from behind the fuel store hatch and fired on the men again, giving Selena the cover she needed to make it to the Australian without getting shot.

When she was safely in the cover of the engine room door, Decker broke cover and darted around the side of the pool. Bloch and Kurz fired on him aggressively, their bullets chasing him and drilling into the deck a few inches from his feet until he dived into the cover beneath the overhanging deck and joined the others.

"I think we can get to the bridge this way," Riley said.

"How do you know that?" Selena asked.

"This," he said with a grin, and pointed to a deck plan of the yacht fitted into the back of the engine room door. "According to this, there's a pantry just forward of the engine room, and then there's a spiral staircase leading up to the main cabins. From there it's just a leisurely jog along another corridor to the main lounge and then another staircase until we're at the bridge."

"We have no idea they're holding Atticus on the bridge," Decker said.

"When you storm a ship, mate, you take the bridge first. When we have control of that, we'll find old Atticus."

Getting to the bridge was easier than they thought. "This place is like a ghost ship," Riley said as he looked over the control panel.

Decker frowned. "They're up to something."

Then they heard the sound of a chopper over their heads.

"They have a helicopter?" Selena said. "I never saw that."

"Must have been concealed in the top deck," said Decker.

They sprinted up a flight of steel steps on the port side and reached the top deck where the rotors of a Bell Jet Ranger were now almost at full speed. Lechner was dragging Atticus across the deck toward the chopper, but when Riley opened fire Kurz and Bloch returned fire with a vengeance, forcing them into cover.

Decker fired back, striking Lechner in the shoulder. The pain forced him to release Atticus as he crawled up into the chopper and the old man staggered over to where his daughter and her friends were taking cover.

The mighty machine lifted up into the air above the yacht. Hagen was at the controls, Moser beside him and in the back they caught a glimpse of Marchand as well. Hagen now gave them a mocking salute as he turned the helicopter in the air and flew away into the mist.

Atticus finally reached them, full of apologies.

"Forget about it," Decker said. "At least you're safe."

Riley turned and watched the cliffs as they raced toward the yacht. "Am I imaging it, or are we about to smash into those cliffs?"

"Shit!" Decker said, and they sprinted back down to the bridge as Golan pulled in closer to the yacht.

"Get the wheel!" Riley said.

Selena snatched hold of the enormous wheel and pulled it to the left with all her strength. "Riley! Mitch! Someone please tell me just where the brakes are!"

Despite her best efforts to turn the enormous vessel, the super yacht was still speeding toward the rocky cliffs of the fjord's northern shore. "It's a boat, Lena," Decker called out. "Like a plane, it doesn't have brakes."

"Ah…"

"Just throw the engines into reverse!"

"And where would I find those?" Selena said.

Decker scanned the control panel as fast as he could, locating the throttles to the right of the wheel. He reached out for them and pulled them back into reverse as fast as possible. The engines roared in response, sending a deep, vibrating growl through every fiber of the luxury yacht.

Decker was now at the wheel, holding it hard as the boat grumbled to a stop in the water, which it did with just a few inches to spare. As the tip of the bow gently scraped along the cliff face, they all breathed a sigh of relief.

"Pardon my Castilian," Atticus said, taking a handkerchief from his pocket and mopping his brow. "But that was too fucking close for me, old chap."

"We have to get after that chopper!" Riley said. "Redirect the cops or something!"

"No," Atticus said calmly. "No, we don't. They don't have what they need. All he has is Babylon and the Palace of Nebuchadnezzar, and Marchand. I don't rate his chances."

177

"Babylon?" Decker said.

As he spoke, Golan stepped up into the bridge. "Tender's on the stern. Someone say something about Babylon?"

"Sure," Decker said. "Atticus here was just explaining that the symbols on the key inside the Angel of God give the location of the Ark as Babylon."

"But that's not even fucking there anymore," Golan said. "I don't understand."

Atticus explained. "The symbols say the Ark of the Covenant was stolen by the Babylonians when they raided the Holy Lands."

"The Babylonians? You're sure?"

Atticus nodded. "Yes, they took the Ark back to the heart of their empire and it became just another part of the famous Treasure of Babylon."

"So where does that leave us?" Decker asked. "Correct me if I'm wrong, but like Moshe just said, Babylon doesn't even exist anymore! If the Ark was transported to Babylon after the invasion and as neither Babylon nor the palace exist anymore, is this not what you call a dead end?"

"Yes, if you're Tor Hagen, but no, if you're me."

"I don't get it."

"I've already told you that the Treasure of Babylon was stored in the Palace of Nebuchadnezzar, old boy."

"But you also said that doesn't exist either!"

Selena said, "Exactly."

"Then, still not getting it."

"It's simple," Atticus said. "The Treasure of Babylon was stolen a second time in history, by the invading armies of Alexander the Great, who actually died in the palace. It just so happens that one of his key generals, Antipater was known to keep very good records of all the various spoils of war they accumulated on their conquests."

"Still. Not. Getting. It," Riley said.

Atticus sighed. "Soldiers…a recent excavation in Iran has revealed what we're certain is the residence of Antipater, where he lived after the king's death. The dig itself is still very hush hush, but there is talk of the great general's tomb being nearby. If that's not the best place to look for the Ark, then I don't know where is."

A smile lit up Selena's face. "And without the knowledge about the excavation, Hagen's screwed."

"Right," Atticus said. "There are many competing theories as to where the Ark was taken after it was stolen – Babylon is one of many. The symbols on the key make it clear it was stolen during the Siege of Jerusalem and taken back to the Palace of Nebuchadnezzar. That gives us a distinct advantage over the piece of human garbage that is Tor Hagen."

"But if the dig is so hush hush, then how do you know about it?" Decker asked.

"It was done by an old friend of mine."

"I think we need to see this friend," Decker said. "Don't you?"

Atticus grinned. "You took the words right out of my mouth."

26

Iran

The following day Selena was waking up over the vineyards and rice paddies of Zanjan Province. A few hours in Bucharest had enabled everyone on board to stretch their legs wile Decker refuelled the Avalon and continued never-ending maintenance on the vintage aircraft.

Counting both legs, they had been in the air for nearly twenty-four hours now, and she felt a strange blend of exhaustion on the one hand and a compulsion to reach the tomb before Hagen on the other. She had tried to sleep, but her mind was buzzing with the thought of finding the Ark to such a degree that any rest was impossible, and the only cure was to finish the mission.

Like everyone else, she was pleased they had finally given Hagen the slip and had a solid clue as to the location of the Ark, but the fact he and Moser were still out there worried her. They were the type to hold a serious grudge, plus the sobering news of what Charlie and Diana had described when Korhonon escaped from the lab had also put them all on edge.

Yawning and stretching her arms, she unbuckled her belt and pulled herself out of the old leather seat and made her way to the drinks cabinet. It was a work in progress she had insisted on as part of the deal when Decker joined the LMA. Her head had been turned at the idea of having her own private aircraft, and as soon as the American had signed up she started renovating the old plane.

What had been a battered, dented old cargo plane when she first saw it was now almost up to her standards. More seats and bunks had been fitted into the cavernous cargo area at the rear, and a seating area had been installed up front behind the cockpit.

It was up here where she had fallen asleep, and here too where the portside wall was now complemented by an art deco drinks cabinet of polished walnut. She'd bought it online and had it professionally fitted. Throw in a few scatter cushions on the leather couch and maybe tweak the lighting a little and it could almost be a miniature luxury hotel with wings.

She loved it, but Decker was sceptical. He told her it "smelled wrong" now, whatever the hell that meant. Maybe he preferred it when it was all container chests and leaking oil pipes. *Men.*

She pulled a bottle of mineral water from the chiller cabinet and stepped into the small "business area" behind the cockpit. Riley was up front with Decker, but Diana, Charlie and her bruised father were already awake after the night flight from Romania and chatting about the mission ahead of them.

"Good morning, dear," Atticus said. "Sleep well?"

"Not at all," she said, taking a seat and cracking the water. "I just can't get the thought of the Ark out of my head."

"Not me," Diana said. "I'm still thinking about just what on earth Korhonen was loading into that truck."

"Me too," Charlie said, fiddling nervously with his straw hat. "Gives me the shivers just thinking about it. In fact, I'm starting to think this mission has beaten us."

Atticus smiled wisely. "In order to achieve anything, you must be brave enough to fail."

"Socrates?" Charlie said.

181

The old professor shook his head. "No, Kirk Douglas."

Selena rolled her eyes and drank some water. "Oh, *Dad…*"

"What?"

"Nothing, I'm just glad you're here, that's all. Still alive."

He nodded with a pensive frown. "Call me old-fashioned, but so am I."

Diana started to tie her hair back. "You really think we've lost Hagen?"

"I reckon we have," Charlie said. "And thank fuck for that. We all know what kind of a man he is. The idea of letting him get his hands on the Ark of the Covenant is completely unthinkable."

Riley climbed through the cockpit door, whistling to himself. He pulled up at their table and looked at them with a very serious expression on his face. "All right tossbags, Cap says we land in ten minutes so strap your arses into something safe."

"How did you ever let this gem get away, Lena?" Atticus said, winking at the Australian.

"We talked about this, Dad."

"My mixture was too rich for the lady," Riley said. "That's the sorry truth of it."

She rolled her eyes and stepped into the cockpit.

"Riley says we're hitting the deck in ten?"

Decker smirked.

"What?"

"Nothing."

"What, Mitch?"

"The hitting the deck thing," he said. "Doesn't sound like you."

She fought hard not to look embarrassed. "Just trying to speak in your *vernacular*."

"No problem, and yes – we're hitting the deck in ten."

Without warning, she leaned forward and kissed him. He kissed her back, bringing his hand up to the side of her face, but it was crudely ended by the sound of her father clearing his throat a few feet behind her.

"Not interrupting, am I?" Atticus said.

"Er, well…" Decker turned his gaze to the instrument panel. "Just gotta check all these babies and make sure there aren't any problems with…" his voice trailed off, and Selena climbed back into the first officer's seat.

"Oh, good," Atticus said, glancing from Decker to his daughter. "Because I wouldn't want to think you'd crash us into the Iranian desert because you were too busy kissing my little girl."

"Dad, I'm in my thirties."

He gave a grunt of disapproval, and then looked down at his phone. "Oh, smashing! Hassan's agreed to show us around."

"Who?"

"Dr Hassan Larijani. He's an old friend of mine from Birkbeck. Fantastic archaeologist and a really good laugh. He's flown in from Tehran just to lend us a hand."

"Where's he meeting us?"

"Airport," Atticus said, frowning. "Where else do you think he'd be meeting us?"

Decker smirked as he lined up with the runway and got final landing clearance from the tower. "All right, everyone – back to your seats and buckle up."

*

Riley looked with astonishment as the luxury SUV pulled into view, sparkling in the Iranian sunshine.

"Thought you said this Dr Laryngitis was an archaeologist?"

"I did, and it's Dr Larijani."

"Sure, but that's a Bentley Bentayga, Prof. It's worth nearly half a million dollars! Just how much do they pay archaeologists in Iran?"

"The normal salary I would think, although I might have forgotten to mention that Hassan's father owns one of Iran's biggest business conglomerates."

Riley grinned, not taking his eyes off the metallic gold Bentley SUV for a second. "Now I'm with you. Think he'll let me drive it?"

"Not unless he's insane, pal," Charlie said, clapping him on the shoulder.

Hassan drove them from the airport and east out of District 9 until they were cruising through central Tehran on their way to the National Museum of Iran. He led them past security and into the museum. They followed him as he led them through a labyrinth of corridors, the heels of his Italian leather shoes clicking on the ancient geometry of the Islamic floor tiles. Their host turned a beaming smile on them. "It's just through here."

"It's a beautiful museum, Dr Larijani," Selena said.

"Things are looking up for us, yes. After the sanctions it was very difficult for us to work with other museums, but now both the Louvre and the Hermitage are working closely with us on a number of very exciting exhibitions."

The corridor opened into a large, light-filled space. Statues from Persian antiquity were positioned around an impressive internal courtyard, and high above it all on the far wall was an extensive stained-glass window. Tourists meandered quietly here and there, politely observing the statues and studying the array of colors as the sun streamed through the window.

"This way, please."

Hassan led them down a short flight of steps and they moved into the archaeology department. The tiled floor was now replaced by polished marble and stud lights in the ceiling illuminated a vast collection of artefacts, sculptures and statues from throughout the country's long history.

"Oh, *my*," Selena said, almost gasping as she approached an enormous human head sculpted from gray, mottled marble.

"Now that's something else," Riley said.

"It's a capital," said Selena.

"Looks like an old dude with a crown to me."

"No, I mean it's a column capital – the head of a column. This one's from an excavation in Persepolis – am I right, Dr Larijani?"

"Indeed you are," he said, glancing at it admiringly. He turned to Selena. "And please, it's Hassan."

"Right you are, *Hassan*."

"Here we have precious objects discovered in digs all over Iran, from Persepolis to Qazvin and from Rey to Turang Tappeh. Over here is an impressive winged lion – a stone capital, such as this exhibit here – and even a wonderfully preserved inscription in cuneiform declaring the greatness of Xerxes himself."

"I'll never forget where *I* was when I heard the news," Riley muttered to Diana. She gave him a playful slap on his shoulder and shushed him as Hassan continued his informal tour.

Hassan led them into his office – a neat space with a tiled floor and cool, blue walls. "Please, take a seat, and tell me how I can help you."

Atticus scrunched up his face. "What I'm looking for, specifically, is … We're working on the theory that the ancient Babylonians took the Ark when they raided Jerusalem thousands of years ago, and that it passed down through the generations until finally reaching the palace of Nebuchadnezzar where it stayed for centuries after his death. After that things go a bit sketchy, but we recently found a key covered with inscriptions that lead me to think the Ark was stolen and became part of the Treasure of Babylon."

"Which was of course stolen by Alexander the Greek," Hassan said casually.

"Exactly," Atticus said. "And we know from very well-established archaeological and historical records that this treasure disappeared after the death of Alexander."

"Indeed we do," said Hassan. "And now I see why the discovery of Antipater's tomb has come to mean so much to you, Atticus." He grinned widely. "You are a sly old dog."

"Why, *thank* you, Hassan. Did you speak with relevant authorities as you said you would?"

Hassan nodded. "Yes, and I have good news for you all," he said with a broad smile. "The Minister of the Interior has given us permission to widen the excavation area at the site of Antipater's residence, near the Iraqi border. I think the chances of finding his tomb are good. We can drive out there at once."

27

Diana Silva peered out the modest porthole of the Grumman Albatross and studied the olive groves and sugar cane plantations of Khuzestan. The landscape wasn't a million miles away from some of the dryer regions of her native Portugal, and the unique color of the olive trees took her back to lazy days on her grandparents' farm in the hills of Beja.

Thinking of family brought dark memories of the day Madan Rakesh kidnapped her parents and threatened to kill them during the Shambhala mission. She shut her eyes and wished away the memory of them bound and gagged. She prayed with all her heart that nothing like that would happen this time.

Hers was a quiet life of research spent mostly in the study of ancient symbols and long forgotten languages, not flying around the world in an old crate with treasure hunters and adventurers. But at the same time she was secretly happy that Selena had drawn her into this world of ancient enigmas and mysteries, and as the old plane banked to port and prepared to land, she smiled at the thought of helping her friends find the missing Ark.

The airport at Ahvaz was a single runway and the air was dusty and hot as the plane bounced down on the asphalt. Thanks to a strong crosswind blowing in from Basra and the western desert it wasn't the softest of landings, but anything beat landing on water so she kept her complaints to herself when a smiling Mitch Decker emerged from the cockpit and opened the cabin door.

"Let's get this show on the road people."

Hassan Larijani had hired a substantial Jeep to drive them out to the site. Looking at the map had shown an isolated area a few kilometers from the Shatt al-Arab river where the mighty Euphrates and Tigris rivers converged before running into the Persian Gulf.

There were no natural landmarks at the locations and certainly no man-made structures and when they pulled up there they saw nothing but sand and rock in every direction. Anyone looking at the area without their knowledge would have no idea what was directly beneath their feet.

Decker adjusted his sunglasses as he climbed out the Jeep and shoved his hands in his pockets as he took a good, slow look at the place. The landscape brought back memories of his time in Iraq. As a pilot in the US Marine Corps he had served in several operations during the war, including many not too far from exactly where he was standing now.

If he closed his eyes and listened to the wind as it howled across the sun-scorched drifting sands, he could hear the bitter sounds of war – the artillery fire, the screams, the *whomp whomp whomp* of helicopter rotors. He was a young man at the time, a baby with no understanding of the world.

This place and Afghanistan before it had changed all that.

"Earth to Mitch Decker!"

He turned to see Selena at his elbow. She had gotten out of the Jeep and joined him, leaning up against the side of the hood. He was looking at the excavation site, with tents flapping in the desert wind. The entire site was empty of archaeologists, but its remote location meant there was no need for security. "Sorry, I was miles away."

"Talk about the middle of nowhere."

"Damn right," he said. "You could hide an army out here and no one would ever know, never mind a goddam palace vault."

"Talking of which," Charlie said with a sparkling grin. "Why don't we get on with it? Hassan and Atticus have bet on who can find the tomb first."

The hours passed as they searched the excavation area for any sign of the tomb. Slowly, the hot sun sank ever lower in the west and a desert twilight began to gather when Hassan cried out. "I have it!"

They ran to where he was standing beside a jumble of flat, broken rocks. He dropped to his knees and heaved another rock to the side. "Under here!"

The idea of searching for the tomb in the darkness appealed to no one, and as they made their way down inside the broken, crumbling shaft the sense of relief was palpable, if mixed with a good dash of fear and anticipation.

When they reached the tomb's main chamber, it was obvious the place hosted an enormous amount of wealth. Gold and silver coins were scattered on the floor, and everywhere they looked were piles of priceless relics. In the center of it all was a modest, stone tomb, surrounded by yet more bags containing ancient jewellery propped up around its base.

"Look at this gold!" Riley said.

Selena raised an eyebrow. "We're looking for his memoirs, not gold, Riley."

They burned up another half hour in search of what they were looking for, and it seemed odd to be moving piles of gold out the way to look for something else. Just when they were losing hope, everything changed.

"This is it," Selena said, pulling an old document out of an old chest. "These are Antipater's battle memoirs."

A look of disbelief crossed Atticus Moore's old face. "You mean we really found them?"

She handed him the manuscript and rolled her eyes. "Look for yourself, Dad."

He took the document and fumbled for his glasses in the breast pocket of his crumpled linen jacket. Sliding them on his face, he stared down and started to study the crumbling papyrus. "Good God... you're right. This is just what we need."

His mind flitted about with visions of Alexander the Great seizing the Treasure of Babylon and the Ark when he conquered Persia thousands of years later. "This is incredible! These are indeed the full memoirs of Antipater himself, just as we had hoped. They appear to detail all the battles he and Alexander the Great were engaged in, internal power struggles in the palace... *everything*. They cover his whole life, and then the final parts, the parts detailing Antipater's death are written by a soldier named Bastian."

"But does it tell us what we need to know about the Ark?" Decker said, bringing things back to business. "That's what we flew halfway around the world to find, not a history lecture about Antipater's diplomatic struggles."

Atticus looked at his daughter over the top of his glasses. "Selena, where did you find this heathen?"

"Hey!"

"It says that the Satrap of Persis, who at the time of Alexander's great offensive was a man named Ariobarzanes, took the Ark and tried to flee east with it stop it from falling into the hands of Alexander the Great. It says that when Alexander the Great won the battle, his general Antipater seized it and kept it hidden under the king's orders."

"What happened next?"

Atticus returned to the crumbling text. "Antipater buried it."

Riley sighed. "Please tell me he painted a big red X over the top of where he buried it."

"No, he did better than that," he said. "According to Bastian, here right at the end, when Alexander the Great died, General Antipater buried it with him, in his tomb."

"Alexander the Great's tomb?" Selena said.

"Yes."

Decker turned around in the spot and shook his head. "This is nuts! You mean the tomb half the world's been trying to find for the last few thousand years?"

Selena smiled. "Apparently so."

"Talk about two for the price of one," Charlie said.

Riley frowned. "So just who the hell was this Ariobarzanes?"

Atticus said, "He was a *satrap*, or protector of the land – this land – over two thousand three hundred years ago. He was the top man around here when things started to go pear-shaped for the Persian Empire. It was Ariobarzanes who fought the infamous last stand between the Persian army and Alexander the Great at the Battle of the Persian Gate."

"A terrible battle," Hassan said with a sad shake of his head. "Many of his men died that day and it heralded the Macedonians' victory at Persepolis. It was the end of a great era in the history of my country."

"And the beginning of a new one," Atticus said with a mischievous wink.

Hassan grinned. "You could say that."

"And what about this Bastian bloke?" Riley asked. "Is he straight-up or some kind of joker. He could have written anything just to send the wrong kind of treasure hunter on a wild goose chase."

"Bastian was a warrior who fought with the general during many battles and became a trusted companion. According to what he has written here, he appears to be Antipater's most loyal servant," Atticus said. "And this is pure gold dust. It describes how Ariobarzanes fled with the Treasure of Babylon, including the Chest of Power as he calls it, to stop Alexander the Great from getting his hands on it. He describes it as having a terrible power – a fire that eats men alive. He says it pulsed and made the earth shake beneath their feet, and glowed like the sun."

"Encouraging stuff," Charlie said.

Atticus glanced at him, sensing everyone's nerves. "He goes on to say that this Ariobarzanes fought valiantly that day but lost to the Macedon – that's Alexander the Great, Riley."

"You're *shitting* me?"

"He must mean the Battle of the Persian Gate," Selena said.

Riley clicked his fingers and sighed. "You were a second before me. I was going to say exactly that."

"Shut up, Riley."

"You got it."

"Bastian goes on to say that General Antipater of the conquering forces of the ancient Macedonian army promoted him after the battle and made him his chief advisor, and he remained so until Antipater's death. This is *fascinating*."

They left the tomb and stepped back up to the surface. Outside, the moon was rising over the desert in the east as they walked back across the sand to the car.

"Ark location?" Charlie said.

Atticus was silent for several seconds. "Bastian goes into more detail here. He says that when Alexander the Great died, Antipater had the Ark buried with him in Chogha Zanbil."

Selena was stunned, "Wait, what?"

"The general had the Ark buried with Alexander the Great in a subterranean tomb beneath the southern wall of the Ziggurat at Chogha Zanbil."

"So you mean to say that not only do we know the location of the Ark of the Covenant," Selena said excitedly, "but that we also just found one of the most famous missing tombs of all time?"

Atticus looked up at his daughter, the manuscript shaking in his trembling hands. They both burst out laughing at the same time. "We did it!"

"Where is this Chogha Zanbil place?" Decker asked.

"Maybe a little over one hundred kilometers to the east," Hassan said. "Antipater must have decided to hide the body of his king and the Ark in a location far away from any possibility of them ever being discovered again."

"If what Bastian says about the powers of the Ark are even half true, then I can't blame him," Decker said. "It sounds like he's describing some kind of WMD or something."

Riley nodded. "I don't like the sound of it – strange glowing, pulsating noises – men vanishing from the face of the Earth. Sounds like bad karma to me, Lena."

Selena looked from Riley to her father and gave a shallow nod. "But we have to find it, right? We've come this far, after all."

Atticus gave his daughter a fatherly shoulder-squeeze and smiled. "That's my girl! Never afraid to venture into the unknown."

"Sure," Charlie said, looking anxious. "But there are unknowns and then there are glowing Arks that turn people to dust in a heartbeat."

Riley frowned and rubbed his face, leaving a smear of sandy dirt on his cheek. "Wait, if we know where it is, why are we still here?"

And with that, they were gone, but none of them noticed Kai Bloch lying flat against the ridge of a sand dune with Riley's Spectra Laser Mic in his hands.

28

"Four flat tires?" Charlie said, kicking one of the rear wheels. "Are you kidding me?"

"This is no coincidence," Riley said. "We've been rumbled."

"Impossible," Selena said. "Hagen has no way of knowing we're even in Iran.

"Either way, we need to get going," said Decker. "Looks like we're running on the rims till we get to the next garage."

Hassan gently pressed the accelerator and the SUV pushed away from the isolated site like a cruise ship leaving port. Surrounded by leather-clad luxury, Selena thought about sleep for the first time in a day, but the views of the landscape as they drove across the desert were too great to be missed, plus the sound of the wheel rims scratching along the asphalt were not exactly conducive to good sleep.

They changed the tires at the first garage, and then they raced north, skirting the eastern banks of the River Karkheh as they went, and all the time the bright Iranian moon climbed ever higher into the sky above them. Outside, the heat was lingering. This was the region where eighty-seven degrees had once been recorded, but inside the air-conditioned cocoon of the Jeep they were shielded from the heat outside.

"This is very beautiful country," Hassan said proudly.

Riley scanned the horizon from time to time, taking extra care to check behind them for any sign of Hagen and his forces, but the road was long and desolate, and there was no sign of any trouble.

Decker leaned forward closer to Hassan and Atticus in the front. "Any ETA on Chogha Zanbil?"

"Not long now," Hassan said. "We leave the wildlife reserve soon and then we turn east. After that, we'll be at the ruins in less than half an hour."

Decker checked his watch. "Good. Let's hope there are no nasty surprises when we get there. The four flat tires have put me on edge."

Hassan shook his head and gave a sigh of wonder. "Atticus, do you really believe the tomb of Alexander the Great is located in the Ziggurat?"

"Truthfully, I really couldn't say. My heart wants it to be true, but people have been searching for that tomb for over two thousand years. Every realistic option has been burned out and now people are starting to waste time and money on very unrealistic options. If it's here in Chogha Zanbil then that's as good a place as any, I suppose."

"At least it makes sense historically," Selena said from the back. "We know he died only three hundred miles west from here in Nebuchadnezzar's Palace. It wouldn't have been the toughest job for Antipater to bring his body here and hide it in the Ziggurat. The orthodox theory is that his body was taken much further afield than this, after all."

"Where?"

"It was supposed to go back to Macedon in modern-day Greece but it got seized by Ptolemy and taken back to Memphis instead, so he got around even in death. The next king, Ptolemy II then moved it to Alexandria."

"They took his body to Tennessee to see the king?" Riley said. "That really *is* getting around."

"Stop being a twat, Riley," Selena said. "You know damn well I mean Memphis in Egypt."

Riley raised his hands in an exaggerated act of surrender. "All right, I'm sorry."

"I forgive you."

Riley lowered his voice into an Elvis slur. *"Thank you very much."*

Selena rolled her eyes but turned to the window so the Australian didn't see the smile on her lips.

They arrived at the famous ziggurat to find several Jeeps parked outside. After checking the coast was clear, they clambered out into the night and took stock of the situation.

"If this isn't connected to the flat tires, I'm a monkey's uncle," Decker said.

"Looks like we're definitely too late," Charlie said. He cupped his hands and peered inside the rear window of one of the Jeeps. "I'm going to go out on a limb here and say you're average party of tourists doesn't turn up to a place like this with three black Jeeps."

"It's not out of the realms of possibility," Atticus said, mopping his brow. "It could be load of Chinese business executives, for instance."

"At this time of night?" Diana asked.

"Well..."

"With a Grade A 50 Cal ammo box on the back seat?"

"Ah."

"It's Hagen, all right," Decker said. "But how the *hell* did he know we were Iran?"

Riley scanned the area with Decker's monocular. "He didn't post anyone on sentry duty, at least."

"He's confident," Selena said.

"Too confident," said Diana. "He thinks he can just walk in there and steal the Ark, just like that."

Hassan gave a wise smile and shook his head. "A thief is a king until he is caught," he said. "Old Iranian proverb."

"Well, this son of a bitch is about to taste some of that medicine," said Decker. He pulled his gun from his holster and checked the magazine. "Let's get in there and get the Ark."

29

Hagen clenched and loosened his fists compulsively as Kurz ordered Bloch and his three genetically-modified men to start work on the chamber wall. The GPS tracker Olsen had put on the Avalon had allowed them to track the aircraft to Tehran, and from there it was simply a matter of trailing them from a distance. Bloch's use of the laser mic to pick up the location of Alexander the Great's tomb was the final touch in a well-oiled machine that had brought him closer to his true destiny than ever before.

He watched the superhuman workers as they hefted chunks of rock in the attempt to break through the ancient wall. Korhonen had met them at his private plane, and after ordering the men into the aircraft, he had commanded the Finnish scientist to return to the compound and get busy on the shredders and destroy the labs. He knew the authorities would be onto him now, and it was time to move on to another of his many secluded residences.

He checked his watch and sighed. Even here, standing deep below the surface levels of the world-famous Ziggurat of Chogha Zanbil and closer than anyone had ever been to the tomb of Alexander the Great, he was tense and nervous. The great king's tomb would be enough treasure and glory for most men, but not for Tor Hagen. For him, only the lost Ark of the Covenant would ever be enough.

Kurz and the other men were struggling to break a hole through one of the many subterranean tombs that were built into the foundations of the ancient structure. He sighed heavily and wiped the sweat from his brow as one of the weaponized super-soldiers pushed him aside and lifted the rock effortlessly out the way.

"Now you see why my work is so important, Stefan," Hagen said with a fiendish smirk. "Leif here can do the work of five men, and so can Marius and Oddvar. Just imagine when I have an army of hundreds, or thousands of them. The power in the Ark will allow me to speed up DNA sequencing and manipulation more than ever before and give me the very power of God's creation! Imagine!"

"Yes, just imagine," Kurz muttered under his breath.

Hagen beamed as his three creations cleared a path to the tomb wall, moving the heavy granite blocks as if they were made of balsa wood.

"A simple deletion of the myostatin gene has doubled their muscle mass," Stefan. "That and a number of other more complex procedures have created these majestic servants."

"It's very *impressive*, sir."

Hagen was proud of his work – proud of his manipulation of God's work, as Moser had tried to put it – but it was still as nothing compared to what was hiding behind the ancient baked bricks of the Ziggurat. There, hidden for over two thousand years inside the tomb of Alexander the Great was the greatest prize of all time: the lost Ark of the Covenant, and the powers contained by the Ark would enable him to take the final step he needed to take in order to become a living god.

With the last of Antipater's annoying granite defenses out of the way, he was able to see the tomb's rear wall for the first time. More baked bricks stared back at him, only unlike most of those on the outside, these were carefully glazed and decorated with gypsum and intricate cuneiform inscriptions carved into their smooth surface.

"We're almost there, Ursula. Can you feel the power?"

Moser glanced at him and taking one look at the expression on his face she took a step back without even thinking about it. He hadn't shaved since they left the Valhalla complex and now his silver stubble was catching the lamplight as Kurz and the super-soldiers were preparing to knock a hole through the tomb wall.

"Can't you feel it?" he said again, raising his hands above his head. "It's radiating through the bricks. It *wants* me to take it. The Ark actually *wants* me to control its power!"

Moser and Henri Marchand looked doubtful, and even Kurz was starting to look apprehensive, but when Hagen ordered the wall to be broken down, he obeyed as he knew he must. It was too late to back out now, and even if he did Leif and the other synthetic soldiers would do the work anyway, faster and easier than he could do it and without questioning anything the old man ordered them to do. They were genetically programmed to obey, after all.

After exchanging an anxious look with Ursula Moser, Kurz approached the wall and started to search for an area weak enough to blow out with their explosives. "This is the best place." He was running his hands over the smooth baked bricks just above the sandy floor. "The bricks are weakest here."

"That must be what Antipater used as his exit after hiding the tomb," Hagen said. "He filled it in afterwards but left it weaker than the rest of the section, trusting in the granite blocks as a last line of defense."

Hagen ordered Bloch to place the explosives and then they took cover behind the granite defense blocks. Holding their hands over their ears, Kurz detonated the C4 and the chamber was filled with a thunderous roar and an enormous cloud of brick dust.

With the smoke and dust still in the air, an excited Tor Hagen got to his feet and made for the newly blasted hole. "There!" He pointed at a man-sized aperture in the wall of baked bricks. "I was right! This is how Antipater must have accessed the lower section of the Ziggurat."

He walked to the freshly-formed entrance and after waving the remnants of the smoke and dust away from his face he craned his neck inside the black hole and snapped his fingers impatiently behind his back. "Flashlight, now!"

Bloch fumbled to remove a flashlight from his utility belt and handed it to the boss.

Hagen shone the flashlight inside the entrance and after several generous sweeps of the beam from side to side he smiled and nodded with satisfaction. It extended a few meters to the east, and then turned into a series of crumbling stone steps which receded into total darkness somewhere deep beneath the Ziggurat. "We've found it. I can see boot marks on the floor of the tunnel and even some old tools dumped just inside the entrance. This is without a doubt the access tunnel used by Antipater."

Moser took a step forward. "Are you certain?"

"Bring the equipment," Hagen said, ignoring the Austrian woman's question. "We're going in." Slowly, the old man made his way inside the depths of the Ziggurat.

Leif picked up the diesel generator and headed silently into the tunnel while Marius and Oddvar collected the weapons, ammunition and the rest of the archaeological equipment and followed him inside. Moser, Kurz and Bloch gave each other a look of uncertainty and fear, and then followed up in the rear with Lechner and Marchand trailing behind them.

*

"Looks like they found a way into the lower levels," Riley said.

"So what next?" Diana said. "Do we just follow them inside, or what?"

Decker studied the chamber as he thought about what to do next. He could still smell the C4 in the air, and he noticed several large cracks running out from the hole Hagen's team had blasted in the wall at the far end.

He knew enough about engineering to appreciate the damage the explosives had done to the integrity of the chamber's ceiling and far wall, and he didn't much like the idea of thousands of tons of baked brick above his head that could come crashing down at any moment.

"We have no choice," Riley said. "There's no one else within calling distance and Hagen's minutes away from discovering not only the tomb of Alexander the Great but also the lost Ark of the Covenant. It's up to us to stop him, guys."

"Riley's right," Selena said. "We can't allow a man like Hagen to seize what is easily the most important archaeological and historical discovery in history. He has the ethics of a sewer rat."

Images of the laboratory storage facility back in Valhalla rose in Decker's mind like phantoms. He closed his eyes for a moment to clear his head of the vision of that terrible place. "Let's end this."

*

Hagen led the way down the stone steps with only his flashlight beam for light. The staircase was cold and damp and cobwebs hung from the ceiling, untouched for thousands of years. Behind him, his three super-soldiers grunted as they hauled their heavy loads through the darkness, and further at the back, Moser and her strongmen brought up the rear, their shadows bobbing about in the flashlight beams.

At the bottom of the steps Hagen found himself faced with a heavy wooden door. He tried the handle. It was not locked, and he cautiously pushed it open with the toe of his boot. Shining the beam into the darkness beyond, he was so shocked by what he saw that he gasped and instantly dropped the flashlight.

He fumbled around in the dusty floor and snatched it back up again.

"What is it?" Moser called out.

He heard Leif and the others come to a stop a few paces behind him, but for this moment he was the only man in the world who had seen it. "I found the tomb," he called out. "I found Alexander the Great's tomb."

Moser pushed her way past the super-soldiers and joined Hagen in the tomb. She shone her beam into the darkness and saw what he had seen. There, in the center of an enormous chamber ringed with pillars and darkened archways was an ornate sarcophagus covered in ancient Greek letters and intricate carvings.

"Isn't it magnificent?" Hagen said. He took a step closer and approached the small stone structure. Running his bony fingers along the top of the lid, he shone his flashlight along the carvings in the ancient stone and read the inscription with tears coming to his eyes. "Attic Greek," he said quietly. "It reads, Here Lies the Great King Alexandros." He turned his watery eyes up to the Austrian woman. "I found it."

"You found the tomb," she snapped. "But where is the Ark?" Sweeping her flashlight around the chamber she saw nothing but dust, gravel and more cobwebs. "There's not even any treasure in here."

Hagen had been so consumed with Alexander the Great's tomb, he had failed to notice that the Ark was nowhere in sight. He pulled himself up to full height and scanned the chamber with his flashlight, almost as if it might illuminate something Moser's beam had failed to find. "Hva i helvete?"

"I told you, nothing."

"Leif! Marius, Oddvar! Get the lid off this tomb, now."

Because he had not been given the order to put down the heavy generator, Leif was still holding it. Now he lowered it to the dusty floor and padded impassively over to the tomb. The other two super-soldiers followed his lead, but they were not needed.

What Hagen had speculated must be at least a ten thousand pound stone capstone was lifted up and pushed off the tomb effortlessly by Leif alone. It crashed to the floor with a deafening thump that shook the entire chamber.

Hagen moved through the cloud of dust and shone his beam inside the tomb. "It's a sarcophagus, all right," he muttered. "And it's certainly that of Alexander the Great, but it's just the body. There's no sign of the Ark. Steikje!"

He swung the beam around in a desperate search for any clue that might tell him what happened to the Ark. "It must be here! I know it was here…"

Decker moved into the chamber and raised his gun. "Hold it right there, Hagen!"

30

Hagen moved to raise his hands, but at the last minute shone the powerful Maglite beam in Decker's eyes. The American moved his arm up to shield himself, but that was all the time Kurz and Lechner needed to dive for cover and fire on him.

Decker hit the dirt and rolled into the cover of a tomb as he returned fire. He yelled at the others to stay where they were in the tunnel, but Riley was already at his side. The young man had sprinted through the firefight to give the former marine some much needed backup.

"They're behind the main sarcophagus over there," Decker said. "But no sign of Bloch."

Riley pushed himself up against the stone wall of the tomb and wiped the sweat from his face. "That's not good... holy crap, Mitch! They've got Diana!"

Decker raised his head above the edge of the tomb and saw Kai Bloch gripping Diana and pushing a gun into her neck. "Bastard must have found a way to get around behind them in the tunnel."

"Drop your weapons!" Hagen shouted. "Drop them or I'll give the order to kill her!"

They dropped their weapons, and Hagen had Kurz and Lechner march them up against one of the walls with their arms raised above their heads. It was then he noticed a collection of symbols carved into the wall behind them.

Hagen looked at them with contempt, and then returned his attention to the French archaeologist. "Well, Marchand? What do you make of these new symbols?"

The Frenchman studied them for a moment, passing his hands over the ridges of the carved symbols in the hope this might help him translation. "I'm sorry…"

Hagen gave a weary sigh and he raised a gun and held it at Diana's head. "Will one of the Professor Moores please step forward and translate these. The Ark is supposed to be here, right here, but as we can all see, it is not. Perhaps these will offer some clue."

Selena stepped out of the line, but Atticus pushed her back. "I'll do it."

Atticus passed Marchand, giving him a look of disgust as he approached the wall. He too spent several moments studying them before shrugging his shoulders. "Never seen anything like them before."

"Too bad for you," Hagen said, and cocked his gun. "You have sixty seconds to tell me their meaning or I will kill you."

"Wait!" Diana cried out. "Please, don't kill him! He doesn't know, but I do."

Hagen looked from Atticus to Diana. He pushed the archaeologist into the dirt and then pointed his gun at the Portuguese linguist. "Then this is your time to shine, my dear. You had better get busy telling me what this says. Why is the Ark not here?"

Diana stepped cautiously forward, glancing behind her at her friends for reassurance. Riley gave her a wink and told her it would all be okay.

"This is written in Classical Hebrew," she said, tracing her fingertips over the strange letters carved into the brick wall.

"The language of the Bible?" Charlie asked.

She shook her head. "Yes and no. It was spoken, yes, but it was never referred to as Hebrew back then. They called it Judean, or the tongue of Canaan. In Greek texts the language was called Hebrew."

"And that's what this is?" Hagen said, pushing the pistol into the small of her back. "You're certain?"

She flinched at the feeling of the gun in her back. "More or less, but there are some differences. The consonants are written in a different way, but I can still read it."

Moser stepped closer to the wall. "And what does it say?"

"Yes," Hagen snapped. "What?"

"It says the Ark was taken by descendants of one of the Lost Tribes of Israel."

A bleak silence rose up to meet her words.

"I want more!" Hagen snapped.

Diana looked over her shoulder at him, her dark brown eyes loaded with fear and doubt. "In fact, the carvings on this whole wall were made by the Lost Tribe. They're writing a history of why they came across the desert to find the Ark, and where they took it."

"They say where they took it?" Moser said.

Diana nodded. "They left the location here in case the descendants of other Lost Tribes also found their way here."

Hagen sighed angrily. "And where is this location, Dr Silva?"

"It's given here by a man named Jehu. He was in the Tribe that found the Ark, and he writes here about how he travelled on... I can't understand this section – it's mentioning dates, I think... but here he says that he travelled with the Ark to its new location and then returned to leave this message as a kind of map for others."

"How kind," Hagen said. "Where did he take the Ark?"

"Africa... deep inside a mountain named Namuli. They built an underground city there."

"Namuli?" Moser said. "Where is that?"

"Mount Namuli," Kurz said. "It's in modern-day Mozambique."

Moser looked like she was slipping into a dream. "So *that's* where they went..."

"Where *who* went?" Kurz asked, but Hagen interrupted him.

"The Lemba people!" A look of wonder lit Hagen's wrinkled face.

"Was?" Bloch asked in German, irritated.

"The Lemba people," Hagen repeated. "There have always been legends about how the Ark was taken by the Lemba people down to Zimbabwe. I never believed it, but it held a shred of truth to it – the Lost Tribe took the Ark to Mount Namuli instead!"

"But there's more," Diana said.

Hagen pushed the gun into her temple. "Do tell."

Diana looked at the black muzzle of the gun and swallowed in fear. "It's talking about how the Ark contains both the means to create life and bring death. It's difficult to translate as the words are very general in their meaning, but I guess the power of destruction could be translated more directly as the crystal of death, and I think maybe *prima materia*... first matter, is the closest I can get to describe this creation-substance."

Hagen gasped.

"The crystal of death must be the superconductor you told me about," Moser said.

Hagen's eyes widened. "Ja... and the primitive material from which all matter derives! This is what I

209

always dreamed of! This must be the semiconductor material. The Ark really *does* contain the power of both creation and destruction!"

"A semi-conductor?" Decker asked. "Just what the hell are you up to?"

Hagen gave a grim smile. "The crystals in the Ark are superconductors, superior to anything we have. These are necessary for the creation of my superlaser, yes. If my research is right, the *prima materia* Dr Silva has translated is a new substance, entirely unknown to modern science. Its structure contains free electrons that will assist the flow of electricity like no other substance on Earth, allowing me to create the most powerful semiconductor chip ever built."

"What the hell for?"

"To create the world's most powerful DNA sequencing tool. With this material I will be able to extract chemical information from DNA samples and transfer it into digital information faster than ever before. What I have done so far with Leif and his friends is nothing compared to what this power will allow me to do. With the power in the Ark I will be able to manipulate and alter DNA more and faster than anyone has ever dreamed of."

"My God," Selena said with utter contempt. "You really *are* going to create an army of slaves like Leif."

31

"So you have found out what you wanted to know all along." Hagen looked at her with utter contempt and then broke his stare to order Kurz and his men to speed up in the evacuation of the tomb.

"You think I *wanted* to know this?" Selena said, unable to hide the horror and disgust from her voice. "This is the vilest thing I have ever seen in my life. You intend to use the power of God himself to further your horrific human experimentation! How could you even contemplate doing such a thing?"

"For a man with a mind like mine, contemplating such things is natural. Your mind is too small to comprehend the beauty of such an idea. You are too ignorant to fully appreciate the implications."

"And I thought the Directed Energy Weapon was bad," Atticus said.

"Too ignorant?" Selena said, indignant. "The implications of your *beautiful* idea are the stuff of horror movies. You're talking about creating synthetic human beings in their hundreds of thousands, genetically programmed to do your bidding. This is beyond depraved, Dr Hagen."

He dismissed her with a casual flick of his wrist. He turned his eyes to heaven and started to dream, drunk with the possibility of such unlimited power. "Then there's synthetic human genomes to consider, and what about the possibilities of recreating great men and women from the past? You have not even begun to think about such a thing! The search for newer, better semiconductors to make more efficient sequencing machines goes on.

Imagine being able to extract, sequence and synthesize Julius Caesar's genome, or Einstein's!"

"Or Hitler's, or Stalin's?" Decker said with disgust.

Another dismissal. "The Ark crystals will allow much greater superconductivity than even yttrium barium copper oxide, a ceramic material that is currently the best we have. Previously much of these experiments had to take place at super-cooled temperatures, but recent advances in the Max Planck Institute have shown this work can be done at room temperature. The crystal inside the Ark will be even more powerful than this!"

"Just what the hell *is* a semiconductor, anyway?" Riley asked.

Decker said, "It's a material that conducts electricity at varying temperatures. Most metals conduct electricity always at the same temperature, and other materials, called insulators – glass, stone, plastic – mostly never conduct electricity." He looked around at the others and shrugged. "Science major."

"Yeah, which is why you jam a wooden spoon into the toaster, right?"

Atticus said, "So you're using the semiconductor crystals in the Ark to further your DNA experiments, and the superconductor material – the material of destruction – is for your damned laser?"

"Exactly!" Hagen exclaimed. "Superconductors are materials with no electrical resistance, which means it allows electricity to flow right through it as if it wasn't even there. In a material of normal conductive nature, the electrical current will reduce over time because it will lose energy due to overheating of the conductor. This never happens with a superconductor. Because there is no resistance, the current just flows forever without dissipation."

Riley scratched his head. "Dammit, I was just starting to get the toaster thing."

"I'm really beginning to understand your interest in it, Hagen," Decker said.

"Currently, if you'll excuse the pun," Hagen stopped to chuckle at his own joke, "our superconductor materials are limited, and this is why the Ark has so much power – it contains within it both the power of creation and the power of destruction. Creation in the shape of the most powerful semiconductor known to man, and destruction in the form of the most powerful superconductor known to man. The materials of the Ark were God's most fundamental tools to create and destroy life. That was its power, and soon it will be my power. I will use the creatium to build life and the destructium to annihilate it."

"If you're right about it being in the Ark," Selena said.

Hagen gave a shrug of false modesty. "Three decades of research, Professor Moore... I am more than confident that the Ark contains these materials."

Charlie shook his head with disbelief. "And your first thought of what to do with it is to create the world's most devastating direct energy weapon so you can destroy the world order and then let an army of superhuman monsters go free range."

"You make it sound so crude," Hagen said. "My creations are perfect, and totally obedient to me and only me."

"You can't seriously think we can let you do this," Decker said. "What you're talking about doing would be the greatest crime against humanity in history."

"The way I see it, Mr Decker, you have absolutely no choice in the matter. Bloch! Kurz! Lechner! Kill them!"

The first bullet plowed into Hassan's heart, killing him stone dead. He dropped to the floor like a lead weight and collapsed into the sand.

"No!" Atticus cried out, and everyone scattered for their lives. A skirmish broke out and quickly tumbled into a full-on fistfight. Riley and Decker disarmed Lechner and Marchand but Kurz and Bloch proved tougher and the chamber was rapidly filled with the sound of gunfire. Leif and the other men had to be ordered to take cover and Decker saw that their obedience was also their Achilles heel.

Bloch threw a grenade to clear a path to the tunnel, and in the mayhem. Selena spun around and dived to the floor of the chamber. She buried her face in the sand and grit as the bullets flew over her head and drilled into the walls all around her.

She had never seen anything like it. Bloch was relentless, marching forward, the stock of a Heckler & Koch pushed into his hip to absorb the recoil of the powerful automatic weapon. Full metal jackets flew from the muzzle like birds of death, raking over the surface of the backed bricks and blasting clouds of orange dust into the air.

Selena strained to look up and find her friends in the chaos. Coughing brick dust from her lungs, she clambered up on her elbows and crawled through the mayhem toward the entrance tunnel. A series of rounds ricocheted off the wall above her head and made her gasp with terror. She thought they'd hit her but it was chunks of brick blasted out of the wall by the bullets, striking her back at high speed.

"Lena!"

She looked up and saw Decker. He was on his knees and crouched down behind the right-hand side of the tunnel's exit about ten meters ahead of her. "I'll give you some cover fire – get ready to run!"

"Are you freaking kidding me?"

Riley's dusty face appeared on the other side of the tunnel's exit arch. "It's the only way, babe. Run, now!"

"I can't believe I'm doing this," she muttered.

Up ahead, the figures of Decker and Riley appeared in the low, dusty light at the tunnel's entrance and started firing their weapons. She saw the muzzles of their guns flash in the gloom and the ear-piercing *chak-chak-chak* of the bullets firing at Bloch who was now diving for cover behind the sarcophagus.

"Now, Lena!"

They raised their weapons and started firing much higher now, allowing her to scramble to her feet and make a dash for it. She sprinted with every bit of strength she could muster, the vision of Kai Bloch firing into her back motivating her to run faster than an Olympic champion. Her boots slipped and slid in the loose, dusty gravel on the tunnel floor but she made it, diving for the cover of one of the pillars just before the Austrian commando had reloaded. He poured fire into the dank tunnel but the dust in her wake made it almost impossible for anyone to see through to the other side anymore.

"He's a persistent little bastard," Riley said.

She slammed up against the wall next to Decker, her chest heaving up and down as she fought to get her breath back. "Thanks."

Decker was clicking another magazine into the gun. He paused to wipe the sweat from his face and left a streak of gun oil and grease over his cheek. "Huh?"

"I said thanks. For saving my life."

"Don't mention it," said Decker.

"You're welcome," Riley said sarcastically from the other side of the archway.

"Sorry, I meant you too."

"It's like I don't even exist," he said. "I try to open my heart to people but every time I get hurt."

"I said I meant you too, you idiot."

"I'm just yanking your ding-dong, Lena. Any idea where the others are? They kind of got lost in the chaos."

"I think Hagen still has them," Decker said.

"No he hasn't," said Atticus.

They turned to see the old professor looming out of the dust on the other side of the antechamber. Charlie Valentine was beside him, clutching his arm through a blood-soaked shirt.

"What happened to you?" Decker said.

Charlie winced. "Got nicked trying to save Diana."

"Trying to save Diana?" Selena said, worried. "What's happened to her?"

"Sorry folks, but they've got her."

"Fuck me sideways," Riley said. "We've got to get her, guys. We saw what Hagen does to people he doesn't like back in Norway. It's not nice."

Selena looked around the antechamber and tried to find the exit. The grenade detonations had filled the entire lower floor of the Ziggurat with so much dust and smoke that it was almost impossible to see her hand in front of her face.

"I can't find it," she called out.

"Stay together," Decker said firmly. "If we get split up now they'll pick us of one by one."

"I hear someone coming," Atticus said. "Behind us."

"Where are you Charlie?" Selena said.

"Right here."

"Then it's got to be Bloch."

It was. The Austrian commando emerged from the tunnel, sucking a cloud of smoke and dust into the antechamber in his wake. He charged forward with a total lack of fear as he swept the submachine gun from side to side and blasted everything in sight with nine mil rounds.

"He's brave," Selena said.

Riley shook his head and grinned. "That's not bravery, Lena. He's foolhardy. There's a big difference and it's a lot easier to exploit the latter."

They heard Moser shouting in German and then Bloch turned and slipped back into the smoky tunnel.

"Why order him to retreat?" Atticus said.

"There's only one answer to that," Decker said. "They must have found another way out and they're hoping to get away with Diana and use her to find the final resting place of the Ark."

"Let's get in there, then!" Charlie said, racing to the tunnel.

Riley grabbed his arm. "I wouldn't, mate. Bloch was an Austrian commando. No way he's retreating without leaving booby-traps. You go into that tunnel in all that smoke and dust and I'm guessing you're not going to make it to the other side."

Selena sighed and leaned up against the wall, slowing her breathing. "So, what then?"

"Yeah, what?" said Charlie.

"Hey, just everyone calm down. We know where they're going, right?" Decker said. "So, let's get our asses down to Mozambique."

32

Namuli Mountains, Mozambique

"They're murdering bastards," Atticus said coldly. "They killed Hassan in cold blood, and now they're holding the rest of our team as hostages. They have a hell of head start on us, too."

Decker sighed as he looked out of the small cockpit window. Atticus was right about Hagen having a head start on them, and it was true his old Albatross was slower than modern aircraft, but it had two advantages over newer jet planes. First, there wasn't an airline in the world that would fly them to a place like the Namuli Mountains, and second, it was a float plane.

Terrain like this would never allow a regular landing on the ground, so whatever aircraft Hagen had used to fly to Mozambique would get them only so far and then they'd have to transfer to boats. The Avalon could land anywhere there was a sufficient stretch of water, and if tropical Zambezia had a shortage of anything, it wasn't lakes or rivers.

"Any more word of this Mocumbi character?" Decker asked Riley, referring to an old friend of the Australian's whom he thought might be able to help.

"No phone signal out here, mate. I know what you know."

"There!" Selena said. "I see boats on the river!"

Decker glanced over the starboard side of the cockpit. She was right – three boats were moored on the north

218

bank of an unnamed river. Considering the epic scale of the rainforest landscape stretching to the horizon in every direction, he knew it must have taken Hagen's party a long time to make it this far on those boats.

"Land as near as you can, Mitch," Selena said.

"That's what I'm trying to do." He was still surveying the landscape. "Looks like the mountain in question is a former volcano – looks like the form of a caldera beneath the undergrowth…wait – what do I spy over there?"

Selena and her father peered over the instrument panel. "Oh my gosh!"

"Do my eyes deceive me, or is that a plane wreck?" Atticus asked

"It's a wreck all right," Decker said. "Looks like an old war plane."

"What the hell's it doing out here?"

Decker shrugged. "I'll give you one guess."

Selena looked over at him, disappointment on her face. "Looking for the Ark! So we're not the first."

Decker rubbed his chin. "That plane is World War Two, no doubt, and you can see from the undergrowth all over it that it's been here for decades."

"One of ours?" Atticus asked.

"Not American."

"I meant British, old boy."

Decker gave him a look and turned the Avalon to get a closer look. "Looks German to me."

"Wartime German?" Selena said. "As in Nazis?"

"Yup, pretty much."

"The plot thickens," Atticus said. "We better get this thing down."

Spying a good straight section of a broad, chocolate-colored river a few hundred feet below, Decker banked the old plane to port a few degrees and reduced power to the rotary engines. The lower torque made itself felt through a series of bone-shaking vibrations as Decker lined the plane up over the river. "All right, guys," he said into his headset. "Brace for landing."

As he descended toward the rushing river, memories of his landing in Tibet's Yadong Valley during the Shambhala mission rushed into his mind faster than the tropical rainforest canopy was approaching the bottom of the Avalon. Flying no higher than seventy feet above the river, the tropical tree-tops flashed past the cockpit windows as he fought a powerful crosswind and tried to keep the plane level.

"This is a bit hairy, isn't it?" Atticus said, tightening his seat belt and gripping the back of Selena's seat until he squeezed all the blood out of his knuckles.

"He's done it before," Selena said, giving Decker an admiring glance through the cockpit door.

"Any sign of Mocumbi?" Charlie asked.

Decker shook his head and his voice came through their headsets. "Not yet.

"And who is this man again?" Selena asked.

"Carlos Mocumbi," said Riley.

"And how do you know this guy?"

"I don't, not personally. A mate of mine from the regiment spent some time in Mozambique as part of his international risk management company."

"And what does that involve?" Selena said.

"Mostly maritime security, specialist training and so on."

"You mean mercenary, right?" Decker said.

"Tomato, tomahto," said Riley. "Anyway, he worked with Mocumbi a few years back around Nacala. They were hired to recover a number of ships that had been hijacked by pirates sailing through the Mozambique Channel on their way into the Indian Ocean."

Decker shook his head and lowered his voice to a cynical whisper. "*Risk management...*"

"You want his help or not, buggernuts?" Riley said.

Decker lifted his hands from the yoke. "I'm sorry, Riley. Sure, we could use his help. I'm presuming he's bringing some muscle along with him?"

Riley nodded. "That's what Mick said. Maybe three or four guys, all former Mozambique Defence Armed Forces, army mostly."

"Sounds like we're in with a chance," Atticus said.

Decker put the Avalon down in the river and powered it over to the eastern shore. It didn't take them long to unpack their equipment and move it to the riverbank. Hauling their packs up away from the water they stood silent for a moment, more aware than ever that they were about as close to the middle of nowhere as it was possible to get. Thousands of square kilometers of African rainforest stretched in every direction and the only way in or out was the Avalon, now moored to the riverbank and quietly bobbing up and down on the water.

"Can't be many places as remote as this," Selena said. "I don't like it."

"Hey, we're not remote as long as we got the Avalon." Decker said with a reassuring smile. "It's a private hotel with wings, remember?"

"We have enough fuel to get back to Pemba, right?" Charlie said.

Decker gave him a weary look. "I know how to make fuel calculations, Charlie. I've been flying planes all my life."

"Just checking, boss."

"Hmmm."

Selena flicked her head to the right and pointed into the undergrowth. "What's that over there?"

Decker and Riley drew their guns and aimed them where she had pointed.

Atticus took a step closer to his daughter and lowered his voice to an anxious whisper. "What did you see?"

"I thought I saw something move."

Decker squinted into the dusky tropical gloom and saw some shadows moving in the rainforest. He tightened his grip on the gun and stood in front of the others. "You see that, Riley?"

Riley nodded and then shouted loudly. "Is that you lurking out there, Mocumbi?"

Charlie slapped at a mosquito on his arm and stared into the trees. "Well, is it?" he whispered.

The shadows turned into men dressed in jungle camos and armed to the teeth. There were three of them in total and when they had finally made their way out of the jungle and stepped onto the riverbank, one of them stepped forward and nodded his head. "You are Corporal Carr of the Australian SAS?"

"Guilty as charged," Riley said.

"Maybe you would like to lower your weapons?" the man said.

Decker moved to lower his but Riley told him keep it where it was and then fixed his eyes on the man. "Where's number four?"

"What?"

"Mick Smith told me there were four of you. Where's number four?"

They heard a laugh from behind them and whirled around to see another man moving through the jungle toward the front end of their aircraft. "You're just as suspicious as Mick said you would be, and his surname always used to be Davison. Has he changed it for some reason?"

Riley smiled and lowered his gun. "You must be Mocumbi."

"Guilty as charged," Mocumbi said, and extended his hand. "Nice touch with the last name trick."

"Just checking, the Australian said.

Mocumbi searched through his sweat-soaked camos for a crumpled pack of Grande Turismo cigarettes. He fired one up and offered them around, but they all declined. "Next time you see Mick, you tell him he still owes me five thousand meticals for the bet he lost about the stripper."

Riley slipped his gun back in the holster. "I'll be sure to do that, Carlos."

"Good," Mocumbi said, taking a deep drag on his cigarette. "So we have four Mozambique soldiers and one Australian SAS, but who are the rest?"

"Captain Mitch Decker, retired US Marine Corps," Decker said, shaking hands with Mocumbi. "And this is Charlie Valentine, ex British secret service; Professor Selena Moore and her father Professor Atticus Moore, and our translator Dr Diana Silva from Portugal has been taken hostage by the enemy."

"OK," Mocumbi said with a smile. "You said one of your friends was murdered in Iran?"

"That's right," Riley said. "An archaeologist called Hassan L…"

"Larijani," Atticus said, helping the young Australian out. "Dr Hassan Larijani. He was one of my PhD students in London. Hagen murdered him in cold blood."

"And how many men does this Hagen have?" Mocumbi asked.

"There are at least eight of them," said Decker. "But some of them have been genetically modified."

Mocumbi looked confused. "What?"

Selena said, "Mr Mocumbi, the man we are hunting is a genetic scientist who has been snatching people and conducting experiments on them."

"I don't understand – how exactly?"

"Gene therapy," she said. "It's been possible for some time to replace old genes with newer, stronger ones and change the body in that way, but Hagen has taken things much further and created a number of men with extraordinary strength, speed and agility."

"Super-soldiers, basically," Charlie said with a sigh. "And he'll be able to do a lot worse if he gets his hands on what he's looking for here."

"How many of these super soldiers?"

"Three so far," said Decker. "Or three that we know about, at least."

"Plus he could have hired more men locally," Atticus said.

Mocumbi shook his head. "No, not possible. The boats they arrived in could only carry twelve without equipment, so with their packs and weapons I would say we are looking at the original eight, and there's something else too."

"What?"

"Since we got here, I've had the feeling we're being watched, and not by Hagen."

"So who, then?"

Mocumbi shrugged and gave a toothy grin. "Ghosts of the jungle."

Riley laughed it off, but it was obvious the others were more concerned. He picked up his bag and started heading into the trees. "No ghost's stopping me from getting

Diana back and finding the Ark. Anyone coming with me?"

33

Tor Hagen's destiny was almost within his reach. Soon, he would possess the true treasure of Babylon – the power of God himself would be in his hands and the whole world would come to fear him. Now, he watched as Leif and the other two super-soldiers ripped at the giant spider webs, vines and tropical mistletoe covering the entrance of the ancient temple. Finding the entrance at the base of Mount Namuli had taken over twelve hours even with the LIDAR, or Light Detection and Ranging system.

But now, the search was over. "We have finally arrived, Fräulein Moser! Your God has delivered his power unto us!"

Moser studied Hagen's profile before replying. "Let's hope my God is in a generous mood when we break into the temple."

Kurz and Bloch exchanged the most subtle of glances and then each man readied his weapon. Somewhere in the distance the desperate cry of an Egyptian vulture filled the lush canopy far above their heads.

Leif and Marius continued tearing the thick, tangled undergrowth from the temple's façade while Oddvar started work on removing the boulders that had fallen from the upper parts of the temple and crashed in front of the entrance. This time, Hagen knew he wasn't looking at another defense strategy of Antipater, but the inevitable result of the many earthquakes suffered in this part of the country.

Hagen turned to Diana and fixed his piercing, pale blue eyes on her. "You see now how useful my modified men are, no?"

The Portuguese academic strained and tugged at the torn shirt still binding her numb hands together. When Oddvar had tied her up, he pulled the knot so tight she thought he had snapped both her wrists. "Men?" she said with contempt. "They are no longer men. You took that away when you turned them into mindless automatons."

He raised his hand and stroked her bruised cheek with his finger. "Perhaps when we return to Valhalla I will modify you? Perhaps you will prefer life as a mindless automaton, serving me in total obedience?"

She spat in his face. "I will kill myself before you get a chance to do such a thing!"

He wiped the spit from his face and delivered a hefty back-slap to the right side of her face, nearly knocking her over. "You will pay for your insolence, Dr Silva. I will not allow you to kill yourself, and soon enough you will see me as your god."

"He's almost through!" Bloch called out.

A flinty look of determination jumped into Hagen's eyes. "Our time is nearly here."

"That's presuming it's in there," Moser said. "We thought we'd found it back in Iran, and look what happened then."

"She's right," Kurz said. "For all we know someone beat us to this temple as well and the Ark is long gone. Remember that plane wreck by the river?"

Hagen heard their words but dismissed them from his mind. "Nei! Nei, it's here, all right. I can sense it."

"And I can sense trouble," Kurz said, lighting a cigarette and leaning against the truck of a jackfruit tree. "Big trouble."

Moser glanced at him but gave no reply. She turned back to the main event just in time to see Leif pick up a pick-axe and start piling its head into the ancient stone blocks. Chips of Mozambique granite sprayed out in all directions. Bloch turned his head and cursed as he wiped the tiny splinters out of his face, but Leif just kept piling the head of the axe into the temple's masonry.

Marchand took a break from the front line and wandered over to Kurz and Moser. He sat on one of the giant roots protruding from the base of the jackfruit and took his boots off. He peeled off his wringing-wet socks and squeezed them dry, letting his feet dry in the air but it was a fool's errand in such high humidity.

"This place is beautiful," Moser said, glancing at Marchand's damp feet with disgust.

"You mean this place is cursed," replied the French archaeologist.

Behind them, the roar of one of the many waterfalls continued to fill the air, and the crash of the water on the rocks at the base of the falls was sometimes almost deafening. "When the hell are they going to break through?" Kurz said, anxiously scanning the jungle with his miniature binoculars. "Decker and his team could be anywhere."

"Don't worry about Captain Decker and the Moores," Hagen snapped. "If I know Atticus I would not wager on him making very fast progress through terrain like this, and they know I'm serious about the girl if they try and stop me again."

He turned to Diana, but she looked away in disgust and turned her eyes to the hybrids working in the jungle. The one they called Leif finally broke through, and Hagen after a short celebration he ordered everyone inside the gaping new hole in the mountain ahead of them.

The entrance was two meters wide and not much higher. Cut into the walls on either side were small cavities for ancient wooden staves used as torches to light the darkness. Now, there was nothing but the remnants of greasy ash, sulfur and lime on the bottom of the tiny holes, left over from the ancient fires that burned here thousands of years ago.

Time ticked away as they pushed ever deeper into the depths of the mountain, lighting their way through the labyrinthine tunnels with their puny flashlights. The air temperature had dropped significantly after the humidity of the jungle back on the surface, and they started to wonder if the legends were right after all.

"There!" Moser said. "I see something up ahead – a ravine."

Diana saw it too. A ravine at least twenty feet across lay ahead of them, and when they reached it they saw it stretched into the blackness on either side of them like a black snake. The only way across was the flimsiest rope bridge she had ever seen in her life.

Hagen swept his flashlight beam along the bridge. The bright light fell over the frayed rope and crumbling wooden planks. "This is the way. You first, Dr Silva."

The fear crawled out of her stomach and started to choke her as she stared down at the bridge. It looked like it wasn't strong enough to support a small child, and the blackness spiralling away beneath it terrified her.

"What are you waiting for?" Hagen said. "We haven't got all day."

A loud smashing noise filled the cave. "What was that?" Moser said.

"It was a gunshot," Marchand said.

Bloch laughed. "That was no gunshot."

Kurz looked at him. "If not a gunshot, then what?"

"Maybe a rock fell," Lechner said.

Hagen's eyes betrayed his worst fear. "We're being followed. Bloch, go back and find out who it is, and count their guns. We will go on to this underground city and find the Ark."

"Yes, sir."

"Now, Dr Silva – get on the bridge."

34

"Damn it, Dad!"

Atticus watched the rock he had dislodged as it tumbled down the side of the ravine and crashed into the ground with a deep thumping noise. They had been inside Mount Namuli for less than ten minutes and he'd already nearly given them away. "I'm sorry. Do you think they heard us?"

Mocumbi and his men exchanged a glance.

"Are you kidding?" Riley said. "I'm debating whether my family back in Australia heard us or not."

Atticus's face contorted with regret. "I'm so sorry."

Forget about it," Decker said. "There's nothing we can do about it anyway. We keep going."

Descending further into the darkness, they continued to make progress down the crumbling stone steps leading ever deeper into the mountain. The tunnel roof was a semi-circular arch supported by wooden struts. The centuries had taken their toll on them, and many had collapsed downwards under the massive weight of the earth and rock above. Charlie swept his flashlight beam across them and frowned. "I'm not like the look of that. If this roof falls in we're as flat as pancakes in half a second."

"We can't think about that," Decker said. "Hagen and his goons might have already found the Ark, plus they still have Diana. We have to keep going."

"They are *fascinating* though," Selena said. She approached one of the wooden supports and inspected it closely with her torch. "The workmanship is incredible for the period."

"I'm more worried about us getting crushed to death than the carpentry skills of the Lost Tribe," said Riley.

Atticus moved forward and joined Decker at the front of the line. Shining his light down the steps into the blackness, the American gave him a nod of acknowledgement. "How much further down do you think this thing goes, Professor?"

Atticus sucked his teeth and wobbled his head a little as he searched his vast memory of archaeological facts for an answer. "That I cannot answer, but I can say that the Phrygians created the famous Derinkuyu underground city in modern-day Turkey nearly three thousand years ago and they're around two hundred feet deep."

"Impressive," Decker said. "We can't have gone any further down than maybe a hundred so far."

"But who knows what we'll find?" Atticus said. Excitement and fear fought for supremacy in his voice. "The Derinkuyu complex could shelter over twenty thousand people – it's vast! This could lead to an underground city even bigger and more complex than that."

"Wait," Decker said. "Down there – is that the bottom of the steps?"

Atticus tracked the American's beam with his own and squinted down into the gloom. "By Jove, I think you're right."

"Not quite as deep as that place built by the Frigids, then?" Riley said, joining them at the front.

"Phrygians," Selena said with an eye roll. "And don't speak too soon because I see another decline, only this time it's a tunnel, not more steps."

"Bugger me, she's right," Riley said.

Decker saw it too. At the bottom of the steps they had just descended was a small, cramped landing area he had mistaken for the journey's end, but leading away sharply to the right was a steep tunnel pushing even deeper into the mountain.

Charlie came up from the rear of the line and joined them on the tiny landing. "It goes down even more?"

"Looks that way," said Decker with a sigh. "And we're on the right path – look in the dust."

"Footprints!" Atticus said, again squinting into the distance. "Are they from Hagen's party or perhaps those left by the Lost Tribe?"

"Unless the Lost Tribes had military grip hiking boots," Decker slowly turned to face Atticus with a sarcastic smirk, "I'd say Hagen's party."

"Ah, yes – quite right. I can see that now."

They followed the tunnel to its conclusion and emerged on a narrow path snaking around the outside of an enormous pit. Decker shone his flashlight into it but the beam ran out in the darkness. "Wherever the bottom is, it's further down than four hundred meters because that's the beam length of this flashlight."

Atticus was shocked. "Four hundred meters? Why, that's over thirteen-hundred feet!"

Decker gave him a look. "Scary, huh?"

It stretched as far as they could see in either direction, but dividing the great black snake in two was a flimsy rope bridge.

"Stand back everyone," Riley said, his voice deadly serious for once. "Anyone goes over there they're going to have at least seven seconds to think about what it feels like to smash into rocks at terminal velocity."

"Quick math," Decker said. "Impressive."

"SAS, mate. I've jumped out of more aircraft than you've had hot dinners. Now, let's get across this bridge!"

*

"I went back as you ordered," Bloch said. "And you're right – Decker's here."

"Decker?" Hagen said, almost incredulous. They had spent the time since Bloch's recce staring up at a series of inscriptions above an arch which marked a fork in the path. Now, Hagen turned to Kurz, his face red with rage. "I thought I told you to kill them!"

Kurz was at a loss. "I thought they were dead, sir. No one could have survived the gunfire in the Ziggurat."

"Obviously you were wrong," the Norwegian said with contempt. He contemplated shooting the Austrian for his incompetence, but a quick calculation told him that with Decker in the underground city he would need every man he had. "Where were they, Bloch?"

"They had followed the same route we took, except they went north after the main entrance gates when we went south. Now they're at the bridge."

"They must have seen our footprints in the sand," Hagen mused, and a stony frown set on his face. "Old Atticus thinks he's found a faster way to the Ark than you." He turned to Diana. "What do you think of that?"

She said nothing.

"Luckily, I have more faith in you than Atticus and Selena have," he purred, brushing the back of his hand against her cheek.

She recoiled in disgust, but kept her mouth shut.

"I want that Ark, Dr Silva, and I want it before your friends find it. Can you find it before the professors?"

"Why should I?"

"Simple rivalry, perhaps?"

"Drop dead, Hagen."

He pulled the pistol from his holster, clicked the hammer back with a steady thumb and pushed the muzzle into the center of her forehead. "How about, if you don't find it before the old man, I'll put a bullet in your brain?"

Diana felt the cold steel of the gun's muzzle pushing into her skin and swallowed her pride. "If you insist, Mr Hagen."

He grinned and lowered the weapon. "Then hurry up."

"We need to go this way," she said, taking another look at the inscription above the archway.

*

Decker said a prayer before every single step he took on the swaying rope bridge. The planks of wood crumbled and cracked beneath his feet as he made his way across, and the frayed guide ropes felt like they were going to snap at any moment. He had told the others to stay behind and let him test it, but not even halfway across and he was starting to wish they'd searched further along and searched for a better way across.

After a few heart-stopping moments he finally reached the other side and cautiously declared the bridge safe for use, but only one at a time and with the greatest of care. Whether or not it would take the strain of them all coming back again was another matter, but for now it was all they had.

When they were all gathered safely on the other side, the former US Marine took a second to focus his thoughts and then began sweeping his flashlight beam around in the hope of finding a way forward.

"Wait!" Atticus said. "Did you see that?"

"What?"

"Over there – your torch shone on an archway!"

Everyone raised their flashlights in the direction indicated by the old professor and saw what he was talking about. A few meters to the west of their position beside the rope bridge was an archway carved into the side of the cavern, and above it a lengthy inscription.

"My God," Atticus said. "It looks like a variant of Old Egyptian!"

"It is," Selena whispered, already transfixed by the symbols. "The language of Moses."

"So we were right," Riley said. "One of the Lost Tribes really did find the Ark in Babylon and bring it south into Africa. Fuck me."

"Over to you, Lena," Decker said, casting a disapproving eye over the Australian.

Selena went to work, immediately studying the ancient carved symbols and slowly deciphering them. "I need Diana really, but from what I can tell, these really are very much like Old Egyptian, perhaps closer to Archaic Egyptian. It's this language that evolved into Demotic and then Coptic, but here it's been perfectly preserved inside this mountain."

Decker cut to the chase. "What does it say?"

"It's hard to translate literally, but it's basically saying that this way leads to the Ark of the Testimony."

Riley looked confused for a second. "That's what we're looking for, right?"

"Yes, dear," Selena said. "That's what we're looking for."

They followed the tunnel once again, and even Mitch Decker was starting to think they'd taken a wrong turn. Made a mistake. Gone wrong, down here in the darkest pit any of them had ever seen. It was hard to believe a place like this had been protecting the greatest historical relic of all time, and it was that thought that drove him on.

236

And they saw it.

Emerging from an archway at the end of the tunnel, they stepped out onto a ledge and saw it all, stretching away from them like an ocean, as far as their flashlight beams would light.

The Underground City.

35

"God *damn* it." Decker scanned the labyrinthine streets of the underground city from the elevated position of the ledge. "It goes on forever. It must have taken centuries to build something like this."

"But do you see any kind of shrine, or somewhere the Ark would be stored?" Atticus said.

"I'm not sure."

"I see nothing," Mocumbi said.

"Just admit it, old man," Riley said as he took the binoculars from Decker. "You have literally no fuckin' idea what you're looking for."

"He's right," Decker said with a sigh.

Riley passed the binoculars to Atticus. "We might get a bit further if you have a look."

Atticus Moore took the field glasses and surveyed the winding streets and alleys from on high, stopping here and there to admire some architecture he liked. "I think our best bet is to head over there by the fountain. It looks like the heart of the city and a good place to search for a shrine, or some kind of religious space."

They cautiously made their way down the steps and finally reached the same level as the city. Entering the ghostly tunnels, lit only by their own flashlights, Decker found it hard to believe that any population could survive in such a place, or even want to live like this.

They reached what looked like some kind of meeting place, in the center of which an ornately carved fountain, now as dry as dust. What had once been a polished marble pathway led from the fountain over to a chamber in the far wall. Now it was covered in dust, spider webs and rubble like everything else, and Decker tried to clear the way with his boots as he led the way toward the chamber. Inside, they saw a small waterfall. The water tumbled out of a slit in the rock near the roof of the cave and crashed down into a churning lake.

"This has to be the way to the Ark!" Atticus said. "Absolutely without any doubt at all, this is the resting place of the lost Ark of…" His words ran out as he started to choke up. "It *has* to be."

"How right you are, old friend."

Decker felt the hairs on the nape of his neck go up. The animal part of his brain knew at once what had happened, and the rest of him caught up less than a second later when the gaunt, wicked face of Tor Hagen emerged from the gloom of the shrine chamber. Before anyone had a chance to react, the Norwegian dragged Diana out of the darkness and they all saw he had a gun pushed into the small of her back.

"Drop your weapons, now."

There was no hesitation. Everyone could see that one false move and Hagen would blast a bullet through their friend's back. Even with professional paramedics it would be touch and go, but in a place like this it meant certain death, and the look on Diana's terrified face struck fear into all of them.

"Good," he croaked. "Very good."

"Let her go, Tor!" Atticus said. "You don't need her now. We're unarmed. You've got all of us."

"It's not as simple as that." His voice was cold but steady. "It turns out Dr Silva is sharper than you are, old friend. She got us here before you, but only by a few seconds. I have not had time to admire my discovery yet. I have not had time to admire the Treasure of Babylon. I think for now, I will keep my hostage a little longer if that's all the same to you." Hagen moved closer to the chamber, dragging Diana behind him as he went. "Is there any sign of the entrance?"

"There, where the river flows from the tunnel!" Kurz shouted. "It looks like some sort of concealed entrance."

"Is he right, Marchand?" Hagen snapped excitedly. "Is there a concealed entrance?"

"I'm not sure…"

Hagen pushed the French archaeologist hard between the shoulder blades and sent him stumbling forward to the river. "Go and see, man!"

Marchand moved forward and after a few moments stumbling about in the waterfall, he returned, soaked to the skin. He raised his right hand and gave the team a thumbs-up.

They followed him through the waterfall and emerged into a large cavern with white-painted walls. The moving water sparkled on the white paint, and there, on a small island in the center of the lake was what they had been searching for.

They had found the Ark.

Hagen staggered forward, barely able to control himself. "We are looking at the substance that created the universe itself!" He stared at the strange, glowing yellow metal with obsessed, glazed eyes that saw nothing but his own destiny finally coming to fruition. "God himself used this to create our world, and now it's mine! Jericho will be as nothing compared with what I will use this power for."

"Jericho?" Charlie asked.

"The Battle of Jericho," Hagen snapped. "The Israelites marched on Jericho with the Ark. Once a day for seven days, seven priests walked around the city walls with the Ark, and on the seventh day they did it seven times. It was a ritual, in effect... the word of God. The priests then blew their horns and the walls of Jericho fell." Hagen paused, and turned to point at their discovery. "It was the Ark's power that destroyed the walls of that city and won the Battle of Jericho."

"Still just looks like a big treasure chest to me, mate."

"It's no matter what you think," Hagen said dismissively. "You will be dead within the hour."

Drawing ever closer to the Ark, it started to glow. As he neared the island upon which it had sat for so many millennia, bolts of blue and orange electricity start to crackle and jump in the air. He came to his senses and stopped. Turning on his heel, he spun around and pointed a trembling finger at the French archaeologist. "Monsieur Marchand, it's time for you to open the Ark."

Marchand was conflicted. His round, sweating face showed he was excited but also very anxious. His eyes danced over the wood and gold chest but he was wringing his hands with uncertainty. "Of course... I have dreamed of this my entire life, *mais...*"

Hagen raised his pistol. "There is no *but*, Felix. Open the Ark."

Marchand pulled a filthy handkerchief from the pocket of his khaki jacket and mopped his brow. He took a wobbling breath and looked from Hagen's pistol to the Ark. He looked for a moment like he might be re-evaluating his whole life and reaching a terrible conclusion. When his eyes resettled on the gun pointed at him, he gave a brief, business-like nod and accepted defeat. "Oui, bien sûr... I go to the Ark."

Hagen nodded with grim approval. "Now, Felix."

Marchand stuffed the handkerchief back in his pocket and wiped his hands on the sides of his jacket. He took a deep breath and began the short walk over to the strange glowing Ark on the small island. The low hum they had all heard grew in strength until it was a pulsating rumble they all felt beneath their feet.

The Frenchman waded through the cool, blue water and stopped. It was obvious he was gripped by fear, but he tried to make it look like he was simply reporting his findings. "It's getting warmer," he called back. "As I get closer to it, the temperature is rising."

"Move along, Felix," Hagen called out. "You're being paid to discover the Ark, so discover it."

Leif, Marius and Oddvar stood behind Hagen, their dead eyes staring impassively at the final few moments of Marchand's life. "Oui," the archaeologist said absent-mindedly. "I am happy to discover the Ark of the Covenant."

"He doesn't sound too convinced," Charlie said.

Atticus and Selena craned their necks forward as far as they could to see how the Ark was reacting to Marchand's presence. "It's almost like it's sentient," Atticus said in a whisper.

Kurz turned his submachine gun and belted the old professor in between his shoulder blades with the stock. "Silence!"

"Dad!"

Atticus fell forward on his knees into the dirt, and Selena and Decker scrambled to help him back to his feet.

When Kurz was once again transfixed by Marchand's plight, Decker turned to Selena and whispered to her. "Your dad's right, though – the Ark is definitely responding to Marchand as he gets closer. Look at the Angels on the top."

Selena had already seen the four angels. There was one on each corner of the lid, craned in toward the center with their wings folded back behind them. It looked like they were made of gold, but as Marchand made the island's shore they had started to glow a bright white. Now, as the Frenchman made his final approach to the ancient wonder, they were almost too bright to look at.

"And the pulsing," Diana said quietly. "It's starting to make me feel sick."

Riley chewed his lip. "You think that sucker's giving off radiation, Mitch?"

The American gave a shrug. "Maybe – it's hard to say. I'm standing in an underground city in Mozambique watching a corrupt French archaeologist trying to open the lost Ark of the Covenant. At this point in my life, I'd be happy to believe anything."

"I hear you, mate."

"What about you?" Charlie said to Selena. "You think it's radiation?"

But Selena Moore didn't hear a word any of them had said. Watching Felix Marchand had torn her in two. On the one hand, she was almost certain something very nasty was about to happen the Frenchman and that made her glad Hagen had forced him onto the Ark's island instead of her.

On the other hand, she had spent most of her life in the hunt for the Ark. Now, it was right in front of her and yet someone else was going to get the glory of opening it for the first time in millennia.

She sighed. "I can't believe Felix Marchand is going down in history as the discoverer of the Ark, Mitch."

Decker held her around the waist and gave her a reassuring squeeze. "I think Felix Marchand is just going down, period."

"Going up, more like," Riley said, "in flames – check that baby out!"

Marchand was no more than a meter from the Ark now, and starting to reach out with his arms, but the ancient relic was emitting so much light and power that they were barely able to see more than his silhouette.

Like the others, Selena raised her hand to shield her eyes from the pulsating brightness. "This is incredible, Dad."

Atticus looked at her with a father's love in his eyes, but said nothing, choosing to reserve judgement until the Ark had been opened.

Marchand turned and yelled over his shoulder, raising his voice to overcome the deep pulsating rumble now filling every corner of the city. "I see the lid! I'm opening it!"

Hagen took a step back, but kept the weapon trained on the Frenchman. Moser was standing behind him with the other men and a distracted Stefan Kurz was watching the action in the Ark's chamber. He made sure to keep his submachine gun trained on Decker and the rest of the Avalon crew at the same time.

Squinting into the light, Selena struggled to watch Marchand as he lifted the heavy lid of the Ark and leaned forward to peer inside it. "It's like looking into the sun!" she said.

"Well?" Hagen snapped. "What do you see, Felix?"

The Frenchman was still now. The only movement he made was the gentle shaking of his head as he stared deep into the Ark.

"Felix!" Hagen yelled.

Marchand turned to face them. "Oh, my God…" were his only words, and then he burst into flames and was instantly consumed by fire. Selena never thought she would have to watch a man burn to death right in front of her, but she was spared that fate. They all were. Marchand simply vanished in an explosive cloud of light and dust, and then the chamber fell dark and silent in an instant.

The Ark's lid fell back down into place with a loud and heavy metallic clunk.

With the sound of the lid falling into place still echoing around the city, Charlie Valentine blew out a deep breath. "He just vanished!"

Hagen took a cautious step closer to the shore. When he spoke, there was an obvious tremor in his voice. "Min Gud... what happened?"

"It's like he just evaporated," Moser said.

"And the way that horrible pulsating just stopped," Diana whispered. "And the light... I'm scared."

Atticus looked at his old friend with disgust. "You're toying with a power you can't begin to understand, Tor. You have already killed countless men and women in your pursuit of this, and now you can add Felix Marchand to the list. When will you accept that some things are beyond our reach? You are not a god, Tor!"

Tor Hagen appeared to be contemplating his old mentor's words for a few moments. He nodded his head to some internal argument and then raised the gun in the direction of Selena. "Your turn, Professor Moore. Open the Ark and report back to me what you see."

36

Decker moved in between Selena and the loaded gun, shielding her from the weapon with the only thing he had – his own body. "Like hell she will."

Hagen was ready for the heroics. His response was calm and in control. "Don't make me shoot you, Captain Decker. It wouldn't be the first time a bullet has torn through one person and gone straight into another – and then you both will die and old Atticus here can finally contribute something useful to archaeology and open the Ark's lid. What advantage is there to that?"

Mitch Decker knew when he'd been dealt a bad hand, and this was one of those times. He was unarmed and with at least half a dozen guns trained on him. More than that, he knew Hagen wasn't bluffing about shooting them both dead and forcing another member of his crew to open the Ark. To say he was out of options was an understatement. His bluff had failed.

"It's okay, Mitch," Selena said, sensing his predicament. "I'll go."

"You don't have to do this," Decker said.

"I'll open the bastard," Riley said.

"Nei! You will stay where you are!" Hagen said. "I need an archaeologist to report back to me. Marchand first, Professor Moore *junior* second and if necessary old Atticus here third. If none of you can get it right I'll find someone else to do it."

Kurz and the rest of his men exchanged nervous glances.

Decker felt Selena's hand on his shoulder as she stepped out from behind him and straightened herself up to her full height. "I'm not afraid. Marchand had evil in his soul. I can do this."

The English archaeologist moved away from the Avalon crew and started on her short journey to the Ark of the Covenant. The island began to glow once more, and the pulsating noise also started again – low and almost imperceptible at first but getting louder and deeper with each step as she waded tout toward it.

She wanted to stop. The way the light and noise was responding to her movement frightened her, and every part of her instinct told her to turn around. She made a half turn only to see Kurz pushing the muzzle of his submachine gun into her father's stomach. She knew what would happen if she gave up now.

"Keep going, Professor Moore!" Hagen yelled. "I want you to tell me what is inside the Ark before you die."

"You son of a bitch, Hagen!" Decker lunged at him, but one of Kurz's men stepped in and knocked him to the ground with a hefty smack between his shoulder blades.

The American went down like a bag of concrete and his face slammed into the dirt before he had a chance to respond. The blow he had sustained from the gun's stock had almost broken his shoulder blade but he didn't want to give Kurz and his crew the satisfaction of beating him, so he clenched his jaw in agony and grunted the pain down deep inside him as he struggled back to his feet.

Standing now, he saw that Selena had gotten much closer to the Ark. The light was almost as powerful as before, and he felt the deep rumbling pulse through the soles of his boots once again. "For God's sake, this is madness!" he yelled at Hagen.

The Norwegian ignored him and stared unblinking at the vision of Selena as she stepped onto the island inside the glowing cavern and made the final approach to the Ark.

It was momentous. It was terrifying.

It was a cold, hard voice of iron, barking from behind them.

"Stay where you are!"

The command was so loud the words echoes around the underground city. Selena spun around and saw a dozen people standing above them on the city's perimeter wall. They were wearing a combination of what looked like old, ragged Nazi uniforms and khaki jackets and each was holding a gun.

"What the hell?" Decker said.

"Oh My God!" said Golan.

Selena noticed Hagen raise his gun and take a step back. Whoever they were, they were nothing to do with him or his insane plans.

A man in his forties made his way down a flight of stone steps carved into the wall and approached them, raising an old rifle as he drew closer. "Lower your guns!"

"That's a Karabiner 98k," Decker said, studying the weapon. "Issued by the Reich back during the war to the Wehrmacht."

"And the Luftwaffe," the man said. "And you will taste Nazi lead if you don't follow my orders and lower your guns. We outnumber you and we outgun you."

"I don't understand," Hagen said. "Who are you people?"

"We are the guardians of the Ark," the man said.

In the tense stand-off, Ursula Moser stepped out of the darkness and spoke to the leader of the strange group. "Ich glaube, Sie sind mein Großvater!"

Hagen turned his shocked face to stare at Ursula Moser. He locked disbelieving eyes on her as he began to consider the level of deception she had inflicted on him over the last few years. "What?"

The old man with the beard looked just as surprised. "You think I am your grandfather?"

Moser nodded. "My grandmother was Monika Fischer. She died ten years ago."

The bearded man's mouth opened but no words came out. He lowered his rifle for a moment and locked eyes on Moser. "It's true you share a passing resemblance, but..."

"Here," she said, and pulled a photograph from her jacket. "This is me as a younger woman with her."

"Throw it over."

She followed his instruction and flicked the picture over to him.

Wolfgang Richter was curious enough to stoop down and pick it up, but suspicious enough to keep the rifle trained on her at all times. He stared into the small, grainy photograph in silence for a few seconds and then began to mumble as tears came to his eyes. "Mein Gott, this really is Monika, and..."

"And I have these, too." She pulled out a small stack of letters tied with a red ribbon and threw them over to him. "You'll recognize them at once, I think – they're yours, after all."

Richter picked the tiny bundle, pulled open the ribbon and began to leaf through the letters. "These *are* mine," he muttered. "I sent them to Moni as we followed the trail of the Ark... Bucharest, Ankara, Jerusalem..."

Looking up at Moser he realized she was telling the truth. He walked over to her and they hugged as the old man broke down in tears. They spoke in German for a moment and exchanged a few personal details. When he gathered himself, his face was even colder than before, and now he had one more person in his army because he pulled a Luger from his belt and handed it to Moser.

"What the hell is going on?" Charlie said.

Moser stood beside her grandfather and raised the Luger in the direction of Hagen. "In 1943, Himmler sent a contingent of SS soldiers to the Middle East with the specific intention of locating the lost Ark of the Covenant. Hitler was obsessed by the idea of finding it and he told Himmler it was to be his priority."

"Am I dreaming?" Riley said.

"No," Atticus said quietly. "This is a nightmare, not a dream."

"You can say that again," said Charlie.

"Silence!" Richter cried out, and then turned loving eyes on Moser. "Everything you have said so far is correct, and I would like to hear the rest of the story from the lips of my beloved granddaughter."

"With pleasure," she said icily. "The unit flew out of Berlin in the summer of '43 and never returned. My grandmother followed their progress for a while thanks to those letters there, but the last one was from Yemen in the autumn of 1943. After that the trail went cold and she never heard from them again – no one did. They all thought you were dead, that you crashed somewhere in the jungle and died."

"And all this time you told me you wanted the Ark for religious reasons," Hagen said. "You deceitful bitch…"

"The Church was a façade, a fake operation set up to get the funds we needed to search for my grandfather. I am not a religious person, and neither are any of my staff."

Decker glanced wearily at Stefan Kurz. "Imagine my surprise."

"But how are you even alive?" Mocumbi said. "The war was so long ago."

"The Ark keeps us alive," Richter said coldly. "But if you open it, it eats you alive."

"My God!" Lechner said, taking a step back.

"What happened next, Grandfather?" Moser said.

"We crashed when we tried to land," Richter said sadly. "We hired a man from Leipzig in German East Africa who claimed to be a treasure hunter. When we told him where we thought the Ark was he told us there were clearings in the jungle there. It was my fault. I should have known better and hired boats, but we were under great pressure from the Führer and he was very convincing. He was also a cheat, a liar and a drunk and when we arrived here the pilot found no clearings so he tried to put the plane down in the river. The starboard wing clipped some of the jungle canopy overhanging the water and the plane spun like a top. No doubt you saw the devastation from the air when you landed here."

"We did," Decker said. "I'm surprised anyone survived."

"Many didn't," Richter said. "Among others, the pilots all died, as did my Commanding Officer and Schulz, the drunk from Dar es Salaam who got us into this disaster. But between the original party from the Fatherland and the men and women we picked up in German East Africa to help in the jungle, there were enough of us to make a small community. Many of our women and children died in childbirth, but still we grew into what you see now."

"And you've been living here ever since?" Moser said with tears in her eyes. "Amazing."

"Doesn't seem possible," said Selena.

"We were trained SS soldiers," Richter snapped. "We treated the wounded and set up a camp. The very next day we resumed the search for the Ark, but it took us six more months to find it, and when we did we found this magical city. The jungle gives us all the food and water we need but it's impossible to leave. The Ark has the power to keep us alive, but those who have enjoyed its sustenance die as soon as they try and leave its light."

Decker looked at the old Nazi. "That's touching but just what do you intend to do with us?"

"We have protected the Ark for decades. You're not the first to come looking for it – a team of Jewish archaeologists from Jerusalem came here fifty years ago. We captured them and that was when we found out about who had won the war. It was the saddest day of my life. Their graves are to the north of here, and yours will soon be joining them."

"Listen, we can talk about this, mate," Riley said.

"I think not." Richter raised his arm in the air. "Fire!"

37

Chaos exploded inside the Ark's inner sanctum. Decker and his crew scrambled for cover behind the razor-sharp stalagmites that ran around the shore, but Lechner wasn't so lucky. The Nazis' bullets ripped through his chest and blasted out his back, sending him crashing down into the smooth surface of the lake.

"Leif!" Hagen screamed. "Take cover!"

Leif obeyed and sprinted for the cover of the nearest rock, but Marius and Oddvar simply stood where they were. Not addressed directly, they remained in the spot as the Nazi bullets ripped them to shreds.

Bloch and Kurz were sharper, moving to cover at a lightning pace and opening fire on the tribe with a vengeance as Hagen desperately tucked himself down behind a boulder for cover. Richter and a handful of his men used their knowledge of the temple to fight their way around to the Norwegian's hiding place and fired on him from a second front.

With nowhere to go, Hagen desperately waded out to the Ark in the hope of escaping the Nazis' fire in the island, but Moser saw him and fired, cutting him down where he stood. He smashed down into the cool water not five meters from Lechner's corpse, but he still had a shred of life left in him.

"Leif! Kill Moser!" he croaked.

Leif spun around and powered over toward the Austrian woman, but she fired her Luger at him and buried three rounds in his stomach. He crashed into the ground like a wounded elephant and bled out on the sand.

"No!" Hagen yelled. With tears in his eyes, he clambered up out of the shallow water and crawled to the far shore, scrambling through the dirt as fast as his wound would allow. Leaving a trail of bloody sand in his wake, he tried desperately to get to the Ark.

Richter saw Hagen's progress toward the Ark and threw a stick grenade at the Norwegian. It exploded beside him and blasted him through the air.

Back on the other shore, Moshe Golan threw caution to the wind, snatching up Lechner's gun and charging at the enemy. The Ark of the Covenant was a stone's throw from him, and if that wouldn't protect him from this evil then nothing would.

Decker looked on with amazement and awe at the Israeli's bravery as Bloch and Kurz fired on him, but in the chaos and darkness their bullets went high and buried themselves in the cavern roof. Chunks of plaster exploded out over his head, but he never flinched. Reaching the enemy's trench, he vaulted over one of the stalagmites and aimed his gun at the first man he saw.

Bloch was pinned down behind the stalagmite but ready for the assault. Sitting in the dirt with his legs pulled up in front of him, he swivelled around and lifted the muzzle of his submachine gun at Golan, but the Israeli was faster and fired on him. The Austrian's skull blasted out, spraying blood and shattered bone and brain matter over the stalagmite behind him, but Golan was already turning to fire on Kurz.

He spun around but there was no sign of him. Instead, he was surprised by the sudden attack of Richter himself who was now charging toward him from the other direction with a knife in his hand. The German lunged at Golan, slashing the blade in the air and missing his throat by millimeters.

The Israeli sidestepped and brought a heavy ball of a fist smashing into the Nazi's ribcage. They both heard one of the rib's crack. Richter grunted with pain and staggered back as he clutched at the fractured bone but Golan whirled around and delivered a brutal riot boot in the man's face, breaking his jaw and powering him back over the wall.

Decker saw Kurz, racing not to Hagen and the island but to the exit. Clearly, the man from Salzburg had decided that he wanted to be anywhere but here. Decker raised his gun and prepared to fire when he watched a spear tear into his stomach and poke out through his back. Then another, and another, making a swishing noise as they flew through the air.

"Holy shit," Riley said. "He looks like an echidna!"

Decker concurred and winced as Kurz fell back into the dirt and rammed several of the spears even further though himself. Blood bubbled from his mouth, and his arms waved pathetically as he went into his death throes, never seeing the hidden tribe who had thrown the savage weapons at him.

"Couldn't have happened to a nicer guy," Charlie said.

Mocumbi came sprinting through the chaos and skidded to a halt beside Decker. "My men are dead," he said. "They killed Richter in a skirmish but then other Nazis got them in a surprise attack over in the city."

Before he could reply, Decker heard a series of detonations rumbling through the enormous cavern above the underground city. The explosions were going off all around them inside the upper rim of the caldera where the vines and jungle roots twisted and snaked around each other to hide the city from the air but still allow light into the streets below.

"They've got the entire place wired!" he yelled.

"He's right," Riley said. "The whole city's booby-trapped."

The detonations continued blasting all around them, high up in the cave walls and inside the root system of the jungle plants directly overhead.

Riley looked up as another explosion ripped into the rim of the caldera. "Fuck me, they're going to bring the whole jungle crashing down on us!"

"We've got to get out of here or we're dead," Charlie said.

Diana looked up at the crumbling roof. "You can say that again."

A second detonation was too close for comfort, and propelled Selena through the air like a rag doll. The force of the blast slammed her into the archway entrance of the Ark island and she fell into the dirt face first and unconscious. Roots and branches began to rain down, and among the detritus falling from the jungle sky were enraged bush vipers, blasted out of their nests and now falling to the bottom of the caldera ready to attack anything that moved.

"Lena!" Decker said, and sprinted over to her.

"Get back!"

Just inches away from Selena, Decker was confronted with the burned, scarred figure of Tor Hagen. Richter's Wehrmacht stick grenade might have been three quarters of a century old but it had proved its savage power in the most terrible way on the Norwegian. He was barely recognizable thanks to a horrific third-degree burn that had rendered the left side of his face into a landscape of melted skin and exposed blackened teeth. His hair was also gone, singed to a grotesque, waxy black stubble peppered on his terrible scarred and burned head.

Decker almost gasped but stopped himself. Hagen was still a man, a human being, and now he had finally gotten the fate he deserved. The former US Marine was too much of a man to mock him, or show horror at what he had become. "She needs my help, Hagen!"

"I said get back!" He waved the Luger at Decker and pulled back the hammer. "Don't make me kill you."

"It's over, Hagen. Just drop the gun."

The Norwegian gripped the Ark and started hauling it through the sand. "It's not over until I say it's over! Now, you're going to help me take the Ark outside to that plane of yours and you're going to fly me out of here."

Decker watched the Norwegian desperately trying to drag the Ark through the sand. "Help me! Help me damn it!"

The American saw it first – a faint glow around the Ark. It looked like someone had highlighted it. It was a gentle glow at first but began to radiate until it was a much brighter light.

Hagen released the Ark and cried out, pushing his hands into the water to cool the burns he had just sustained. His eyes swivelled up to Decker and back to the Ark again. "You have to help me! We can create new life! We can…"

What Decker would later describe as mini-electrical storm exploded around the Ark and wrapped itself around the dying Norwegian. The bright blue and orange lightning rods curled around his body and face and pushed themselves inside his mouth and eyes, growing in intensity until he was almost glowing from within.

"It's healing me!" Hagen cried out, raising his arms into the air. "The power of God is healing me!"

Decker winced. "I don't think so… get down!"

The rest of his crew crouched down behind the stalagmites a few seconds before Hagen exploded in a fiery cloud of sparks and smoke, and then everything went black and silence fell over the temple.

"Good God," Riley said.

Charlie patted him on the back. "Exactly."

"What happened?" Decker asked.

"He never used the key," Atticus said. "The symbols on the key are a prayer, a prayer you have to say before you open the Ark."

There was no time to celebrate. The tribe were still on the loose, and now a section of the jungle high above broke off and fell down into the caldera, striking the central section of the underground city and smashing into a tower. The structure gave way under the incredible weight of the trees and vines and crumbled it to pieces. Broken bricks and earthen plaster spilled down into the street around it and a cloud of dust billowed up into the air.

Decker stared up into the collapsing jungle. "The rim of the caldera's starting to crumble away now. We haven't got long before the whole damned thing comes down on our heads. We'll either be crushed to death or trapped in here until the air runs out."

Mocumbi gave him a doubtful look. "And I'm not sure we're all that welcome, my friend."

"Don't know about you guys," Riley said. "But I'm getting my arse out of here!"

38

Mitch Decker led the way through the ruins deep inside the dead volcano. It was a desperate and hard race for their lives as the entire structure of the place fell down around them in massive car-sized boulders. Staggering out into the light of the rainforest at the base of the caldera, they heaved the breath back into their bodies, each one of them overjoyed simply to have escaped with their lives.

"What about the Ark?" Atticus said.

Riley looked at him like he was mad. "Are you fuckin' *kidding* me?"

"I'm not going back in there!" Mocumbi said.

"Me neither," said Golan.

Atticus was aghast. "But it's the most precious relic in the world!"

Charlie gestured to the entrance they had just burst out of with a generous sweep of his arm. Smoke was pouring out of it in a great, thick column and drifting up through the jungle canopy and into the blue sky high above. "Be my guest, professor."

Atticus frowned and stuffed his hands into his pockets. For a moment, he looked like a petulant child but then a smile broke on his face. "It was bloody amazing to see it though, wasn't it?"

Selena brushed some dirt off his jacket and gave him a peck on the cheek. "It really was, Dad. We found it at last."

"I hate to break up the congrats and all," Decker said. "But we still have a tribe of insane Nazis after us. There's no way they would have set those charges if they didn't know how to escape safely, and something tells me they're going to want revenge on the people who made them blow up their little kingdom."

"Mitch is right," Charlie said. "Let's get back to the Avalon."

Diana sighed. "Supposing they haven't already found it and destroyed it!"

Decker gave her a look. "Thanks for that, Diana. I hadn't thought that far ahead."

After a long and humid march through the jungle, they were all relieved to see the Avalon was still bobbing up and down in the river.

"It's just where we left it!" Charlie said.

"*Her*," Decker corrected. "*She's* just where we left *her*."

Charlie laughed and punched his shoulder. "Anything you say, Captain! I'm just bloody grateful that we can get out of here."

They climbed aboard and got to their seats, and moments later Decker had steered the float plane out into the center of the river and hit the throttles. The vintage Albatross flying boat roared up out of the water and quickly ascended high above the jungle landscape.

A buzz of excitement filled the cabin, but Atticus looked longingly out the little porthole at the smoking caldera above the treetops. "We really must come back and save the Ark one day, though."

"I don't think it wants to be saved, Dad," Selena said. "I think we need to leave it where it is. We're going back to London now."

"Wrong," a steady voice said from rear of the aircraft.

Selena whirled to see Ursula Moser standing just behind the small door leading to the bunks. Her face was smeared with the blood of the grandfather she had known for only a few moments, and hatred burned in her eyes. In her hand she held Richter's Luger.

"What the hell?"

Charlie went to get up.

"Stay where you are." Moser kept the gun trained on them as she moved forward to the cockpit.

"Woah," Decker said, turning in his seat. "Be careful with that thing in here! You could bring the whole plane down and kill us all!"

"I am ready for that fate," she said coolly. "Are you?"

"Hell yes!" Mocumbi said.

"Fuck no!" Riley said. "I'm not even halfway through my bucket list!"

Golan looked at her with disgust. "Your fate waits for you in hell!"

Moser ignored him and stayed cool. "We're flying to Argentina, Captain Decker. Turn the plane."

A long silence was broken by Charlie Valentine. "Well, *this* is awkward."

"We'll never make it across the South Atlantic," Decker said.

"Not in one flight, but there is a refuelling station on the way."

Decker looked confused. "I know of no such place."

"Neither did I until my grandfather told me. Just before you murdered him, he told me I could seek sanctuary in Argentina and that we could stop in New Swabia en route. From there we fly northwest to Argentina. If this aircraft can make the flight from Iran to Mozambique then it can make both those legs as well."

She turned and fired the gun at Atticus, plowing a round into his stomach. The old man collapsed to the aircraft's riveted floor and Selena screamed. "Dad!"

Moser smiled. "I have lost my grandfather, and now you have your father. I will kill another of your team every minute until you turn this aircraft around!"

Decker was horrified as the sight of Atticus Moore crawling on the floor in a puddle of his own blood, and his daughter crying as she cradled his head in her arms. As shocked as he was, his officer training kicked in and he focussed on containing the threat. "New Swabia? You can't possibly be talking about that ridiculous conspiracy theory about Nazis populating part of Antarctica during the war?"

"It's not a conspiracy theory," she said. "He assured me there is a base there."

"Fuck me sideways," Riley said, glancing at the gun in her hand. "Your grandfather hadn't seen a flushing toilet since 1943. How could he possibly know if there was still a U-Boat refuelling station on Antarctica or not?"

"We'll die if we try!" Diana said.

"Diana's right," Decker said flatly. "I'm not flying the Avalon south to Antarctica. We'll be flat out of fuel by the time we reach the coast, we'll have nowhere to land and even if we can find a bay to make a water landing on, we'll freeze to death in days. It's a suicide mission."

Moser clicked back the Luger's hammer with her thumb and pointed it at the back of his head. "You have no choice, Captain."

"We need to get my father to the hospital in Quelimane," Selena said from the seating area where she had dragged her father. He was now slumped down on one of the long sofas. "He took a bullet to the stomach! He needs a surgeon as soon as possible."

Riley charged Moser. She fired again but missed and the bullet tore through the Avalon's port wall and blasted a hole in it. The unpressurized aircraft made no response, but Charlie had flung open the door behind Moser. She spun around and grabbed hold of the back of a seat to secure herself from the gaping void that had opened up behind her, but the wounded Atticus hooked her feet out from under her and she fell back. She had not been expecting the shot man to fight back, and it had cost her life.

"Not bad for just an old man, eh?" Atticus said weakly, pretending to polish his knuckles on his lapel. He went to say something else, but then he passed out from blood loss.

Scrabbling on the floor, Moser fired wildly, and the bullet tore through Riley's shirt, but he turned and punched her out of the door. She flew out the aircraft, screaming as she plummeted all the way down to the jungle hundreds of feet below.

Selena dusted her hands off and slammed the door shut. "We are not going to bloody Argentina!"

Decker turned and looked back down the cabin. "Has she gone?"

"Gone the way of the dodo, mate!"

"And good riddance," said Golan.

Decker looked at Riley and saw the flesh wound on his upper arm. "You got shot?"

"It's nothing," he said. "I've had worse injuries from my Nan's cat."

"We need a hospital right now, Mitch!" Selena said.

Decker turned in his seat and saw Atticus, his face the color of putty. He didn't like what he saw but he kept his thoughts to himself. "Hold on, everyone!" Turning the yoke to the right, he pulled a sharp starboard turn and powered the old Albatross north to Quelimane.

263

EPILOGUE

Quelimane

Selena stepped out of the provincial hospital and into the blazing Mozambique sunshine. Shielding her eyes with her hand as she scanned the grounds for her friends, she soon saw them sitting in the shade of some raffia palms – everyone except Mitch Decker. They were gathered in a small circle on the freshly cut buffalo grass and laughing at something Riley had just told them.

Charlie had been lying down, but now he hooked himself on his elbows and gave Riley a sly look. "Sorry, *what* was that punchline?"

The Australian went to repeat the joke when Selena cleared her throat and he stopped in his tracks. She gave him a look and shook her head. "You're incorrigible."

He raised his hands in a surrender gesture. "I was fine before I joined the army, I swear it."

"I find that very hard to believe."

"Me too," Golan muttered.

Mocumbi smiled and jumped to his feet. "I must go my friends."

"Anything good?" Riley asked.

The old soldier shook his head. "I had a date, but after what happened in the mountain, I want to be alone. I have a cabin outside of Maputo with a bottle of whisky in the kitchen. There, I will get drunk and say goodbye to my friends."

They watched him fade into the crowd, and Selena wondered if she would ever see him again. She felt she was able to relax for the first time since London. Hagen, Moser and their thugs had all met their maker in the jungles of Zambezia. More than that, she had just heard on the news that Karin Larsen had shut down Hagen's research laboratory in the mountains above Stavanger and the local authorities were conducting a full investigation into the activities of both Hagen and Jens Olsen, the corrupt police officer. As for Marchand, he was a disgrace to his profession and he had gotten what he deserved.

She sighed with relief and fell down on the springy grass beside her friends.

"How's your Dad?" Diana asked.

"They say he's going to be all right," she said. "He even spoke to me."

"What did he say?" asked Riley.

"I believe his exact words were that I really need to stop hanging around with Riley Bloody Carr."

"Ha bloody ha," the Aussie said.

"He kind of has a point though," Charlie said with a wink. "You are one dangerous bastard."

Riley laughed and punched Charlie in the shoulder. "Get lost, wanker."

Selena sighed. "They say he'll be ready to travel in a week or two."

"That's a good sign," Charlie said.

"I'm pleased to hear it," said Golan.

Selena gave a nod, and Diana smiled.

"What?"

"A good sign," the Portuguese woman said. "The river here is the Cuacua, but it flows into the Rio dos Bons Sinais. That's Portuguese for the River of Good Signs."

"Spooky," Riley said.

"I think we can rest now," Diana said, stretching back into the grass.

Charlie slipped his phone in his pocket. "We sure can," he said. "That was one of my old friends back at Five. The Austrian Government just pulled the plug on Moser's fake church."

"Thank heavens," Diana said.

Riley laughed. "You can say that again."

Charlie was leaning up against the trunk of a palm, and now he lowered his battered straw hat over his face, stubbed his cigarette out and crossed his arms over his chest. "Think I'll catch a few zees."

"You should quit smoking," Diana said. "They're bad for you."

"How can they be?" Charlie said with a grin. "Didn't you know – more doctors smoke Camels than any other cigarette!"

"Get lost, Charlie."

"I intend to – in a deep snooze. Anyone else?"

Golan shook his head and closed his eyes, folding his arms behind his head as he stretched out on the bull grass.

"Not me, mate," Riley said. "I'm going to raise some hell in downtown Quelimane. Anyone want to join me?"

"I will," Diana said. "I really need a cold beer, and I don't trust you on your own. You need a Portuguese speaker to keep you out of trouble."

"Aww," Charlie said from behind his hat. "She loves you."

Riley kicked his boots. "Piss off, Valentine."

"What about you, Lena?" Diana asked.

"No thanks," she said quietly. "I'll just stay here."

"Yeah right," Riley said.

"What do you mean?"

"If you want to go find Mitch then just say so, Lena."

"All right, maybe I do. Can I borrow your hat, Charlie?"

His response was a low, gently snoring. She took the hat anyway, perched it on her head and walked down the Avenue Julius Nyerere. Catching a glimpse of herself in a shop window she thought it rather suited her, and it gave her an extra spring in her step as she crossed the Avenue Marginal and walked down to the north bank of the Cuacua.

Mitch Decker was leaning on the top rung of a metal fence dividing the grass verge from the river.

"Hey."

"Hey," Decker said. "Suits you."

"I'm sorry?"

"The hat," he said. "I'm guessing Charlie's getting some sunburn right now?"

She laughed. "No, he's in the shade of a palm tree."

She felt Decker's right arm wrap around her shoulder and pull her into him as he kissed her. She felt his coarse, silver stubble scratch her face and raised her hands to the sides of his head.

"So what next?" he asked. "For us, I mean?"

"Dad was talking about something seriously strange down Mexico way."

"Mexico, huh?"

She nodded, and reached out for his hands. "What do you think?"

"It's funny," he said, looking deep into her eyes. "I was just saying to myself, I could really use a few days on vacation. Mexico sounds perfect."

Selena frowned. "Is it still a vacation if Riley's with us?"

Decker laughed, and they kissed again. Behind them, a fat, red sun was setting over the Mozambique jungle, and the bright call of a cape cormorant filled the warm twilight sky.

THE END

AUTHOR'S NOTE

I hope you enjoyed the second instalment of the Avalon crew's adventures, and I'm pleased to tell you that their third expedition is already planned and ready to start writing, but probably not for a few months. At the moment, I am already well into writing Hawke 10 and I'm aiming for an April release date on that one. Things are really hotting up for the ECHO team and this promises to be an unparalleled year of excitement and tragedy for them all, so stay tuned!

If you follow me on Facebook, you may (or may not) already know that the next novel I'm publishing is a surprise release featuring Hawke's former lover and one-woman Special Forces unit Scarlet Sloane, aka Cairo. This novel, *Plagues of the Seven Angels* will be the first in a new series featuring her, and the first three are focused on her taking bloody revenge on the men who killed her parents when she was a child. This is an important part of her history which has been hinted at several times in the Hawke books but deserve their own place to be told. In terms of a release date for *Seven Angels*, I'm aiming for some time in April.

If you enjoy reading my novels, please don't forget to share them and write reviews about them on Amazon or Goodreads. The more reviews a novel has, the longer it stays visible in the Amazon rank and the better it does. If you want more of what you like, please write a review –

one word will do, it only takes a second and it makes a massive difference! Reviews are the single most important thing to the success of an indie writer.

As ever, dear Mystery Reader,
Rob

Printed in Great Britain
by Amazon